THE HEALING STREAM

Further Titles by Connie Monk

SEASON OF CHANGE
FORTUNE'S DAUGHTER
JESSICA
HANNAH'S WHARF
RACHEL'S WAY
REACH FOR THE DREAM
TOMORROW'S MEMORIES
A FIELD OF BRIGHT LAUGHTER
FLAME OF COURAGE
THE APPLE ORCHARDS
BEYOND DOWNING WOOD
THE RUNNING TIDE
FAMILY REUNIONS
ON THE WINGS OF THE STORM
WATER'S EDGE
DIFFERENT LIVES
THE SANDS OF TIME
SOMETHING OLD, SOMETHING NEW
FROM THIS DAY FORWARD
ECHO OF TRUTH
MISTRESS OF MANNINGTOR
FAST FLOWS THE STREAM
THE LONG ROAD HOME
TO LIGHT A CANDLE
A SECOND SPRING
HUNTERS' LODGE *
A PROMISE FULFILLED *
BEYOND THE SHORE *
WHEN THE BOUGH BREAKS *
THE HEALING STREAM *

* *available from Severn House*

THE HEALING STREAM

STREAM

Connie Monk

Severn House Large Print
London & New York

This first large print edition published 2016
in Great Britain and the USA by
SEVERN HOUSE PUBLISHERS LTD of
19 Cedar Road, Sutton, Surrey, England, SM2 5DA.
First world regular print edition published 2012 by
Severn House Publishers Ltd., London and New York.

British Library Cataloguing in Publication Data

Monk, Connie author.
　　The healing stream.
　　1. Large type books.
　　I. Title
　　823.9'2-dc23

　　ISBN-13: 9780727894052

Severn House Publishers support the Forest Stewardship Council™
[FSC™], the leading international forest certification organisation. All
our titles that are printed on FSC certified paper carry the FSC logo.

Typeset by Palimpsest Book Production Ltd.,
Falkirk, Stirlingshire, Scotland.
Printed and bound in Great Britain by
T J International, Padstow, Cornwall.

One

Amelia Pilbeam had once said that when the time came for her funeral most of the pews would be empty. 'At my age there are precious few friends still waiting their turn, and any there are can't be up to an unexpected journey across to the island.' Her granddaughter, Tessa, seemed to hear the familiar voice as she walked up the aisle to take her place in the front pew. Of one thing she was certain: all those she had telephoned to tell of Gran's sudden death would be as close in spirit as were any from the village who, despite Amelia's expectations, had donned black and made their way to the parish church. Did Gran know? Tessa felt that she did; she could almost hear the old lady's mirthful chuckle and see her still-pretty face as they shared the knowledge – not as something sombre but as a secret joke.

All eyes were on Tessa as, looking straight ahead of her, she took her seat on the otherwise empty pew. Was it just her imagination or was the silence broken by a hiss of whispering? Well, let them think what they liked, she told herself silently. Gran would have hated me to wear black. 'A lot of poppycock.' That had been her view. 'What's the use of believing in a hereafter

1

and then weeping and gnashing your teeth because someone's got their ticket to go there? When my time comes, Tessa, you put on the prettiest you have. Rejoice! That's what folk should do. Unless their grief is for themselves because they are frightened to look ahead without the one who had meant so much. Oh, but how I grieved when your darling mother was killed.'

The organ started to play, there were movements by the church door, then footsteps. Tessa clenched her fists, making sure that she still looked straight ahead and not letting herself turn to see the men carrying the coffin into the building. But these hurrying footsteps weren't those of pall-bearers; it must be a latecomer.

'Couldn't get here sooner – just in time.'

She turned at the whispered words as a man took his seat at her side, then dropped to his knees for such a brief time he could have done no more than send up a quick apology for his late arrival.

'I thought you couldn't spare the time to come,' she whispered back, her voice holding no welcome. 'I thought the cows were more important.'

'Naomi said she could manage until tomorrow. Didn't like leaving her – but there are things I must attend to here. Hush – they're coming in.'

Through the days following Amelia's stroke Tessa's anger towards her Uncle Richard had grown by the hour. What work could be more important than the knowledge that his mother was helpless, unable to speak, almost unable to move? In the moment of her collapse their futures had been changed – her own and Tessa's too. And yet he had said his animals needed his constant attention! If he could be here now, when it was too late, why couldn't he have come sooner? How must Gran have felt when she realized that he didn't care enough to want to be with her? As the rector preceded the cortège up the aisle, the sound of his solemn voice breaking the silence, Tessa hung on to her resentment towards the man at her side; it helped her to bear the moment she had been dreading. Despite herself, her glance moved to the coffin less than six feet from where she sat. Gran was lying in there; Gran who had been her entire family almost as far back as she could remember. Don't think about the future . . . don't imagine coming home each evening to an empty house, no easy companionship that paid no heed to the generation gap . . . no one to share the excitement of watching their latest acquisition, a television set that brought distant happenings of the world so much closer . . . no one to share her interest in changing fashions, for Gran had never let herself become 'old', and yet neither had she tried to appear younger than she was, and she always delighted in seeing Tessa in up-to-the-moment styles now that clothes coupons were just a memory. It had been important to Amelia Pilbeam to look her best and surely there couldn't be a woman in the village who hadn't admired her; always smart, a weekly visit to the hairdresser making sure her standard didn't fall, her face made up and yet never looking painted. Gran,

I'm not going to cry; if I did it would just be that I'm sorry for myself. Rejoice, that's what you said. That's why I told Mr Brent these were the hymns we wanted him to play, all full of glory and triumph. Can you hear everyone singing? Uncle Richard got here in the end, but what's the point of coming now? It's just *show.* He should have been here when you needed him. You love him, I know you do, so I must try and be polite. But you and I, we both know it will only be surface politeness. She seemed to hear the familiar chuckle. 'Things to attend to,' that's what he said. What's it got to do with *him*? I know he's your son, but he's never made an effort to come and see you. I told you, I'll not be horrid to him because you wouldn't want me to, but I feel sort of screwed up with anger at him. I know when I was away at school you used to go at least once each term to stay with him but since then he hasn't made the effort even *once.* And I bet he's so wrapped up in his own narrow little world that he hasn't even realized how seldom he's seen you.

So her thoughts rambled on with her bitter resentment towards the still good-looking man at her side helping her through the ordeal of the service. The pall-bearers were shouldering the coffin, and she felt Richard Pilbeam take hold of her elbow to guide her to walk with him and follow it as the choir started to sing the *Nunc Dimittis.* 'Lord, now lettest thou thy servant depart in peace according to thy word . . .'

First the coffin, then the rector, then Richard and Tessa, followed at a respectful distance by

4

people who had known, liked and admired Amelia.

'You should have realized you only had to ask me.' Richard spoke softly to Tessa, careful that neither the rector in front nor anyone following would overhear what he said. 'I would have sent you a cheque to buy something suitable to wear. Surely that suit wasn't the most sombre thing in your wardrobe?'

'Oh, no.' She heard the defiance in her tone and rejoiced in it. 'I usually wear a dark grey one to work in the hotel. But Gran hates all that nonsense. Anyway, she and I went to Bournemouth for the day when the January sales were on and it was she who spied this. She said it suited me better than anything I had so I knew it was what she would want me to wear today.'

Richard grunted, the sound doing nothing to endear him to her. In truth he would hardly have been human if he hadn't realized how attractive this niece of his had become. Recalling the skinny six-year-old he had seen at the memorial service for her parents who had been killed in a raid on London in December 1942, it was hard to believe she had turned into such a beauty. For that's what she was. If she'd been six when his mother had become her guardian, according to his arithmetic that would mean she must be nineteen. In less than two years she would come of age. How different it might have been if he and Naomi had been made her guardians right from the beginning. She would have been the daughter they'd never had. One thing was certain: brought up at Chagleigh Farm she

5

wouldn't have kitted herself out like she had today. Not that she didn't look attractive – damned pretty, in fact – with those clear eyes just the same dark brown as her hair. But it wasn't right to come to her grandmother's funeral in a red suit even if it flattered her, and as for those matching shoes, he'd never seen heels so high. And too much rubbish on her face, too; even her eyes were made up. No, if she'd been brought up at the farm she wouldn't have filled her head with such nonsense. His mind jumped to Naomi, his precious, unchanging Naomi. Whatever she did, she did with all her abundant energy. Was there ever a woman like her? Running their home, working in the dairy, tending the chickens, helping clean the pigsties, tackling any task that came her way, his never failing constant companion and friend . . . friend? Friend and lover, too.

While his thoughts had been back at the farm with his wife, the coffin had been lowered into the ground. Mother dead . . . just a memory. Well, that she certainly would always be: a very dear memory. Never once had she suggested he neglected her when he couldn't spare the time to visit her.

Not many people had come to the graveside, just the rector's wife (who, although to look at her no one would have guessed it, was thinking who she might inveigle into buying and arranging the church flowers on the fourth Sunday of each month now that Amelia was gone), and Thomas Sedgley, Amelia's solicitor ever since she had moved to the Isle of Wight some twenty-five years ago. Both of them were on the other side of the grave facing across the lowered coffin to where Richard stood with Tessa.

Tessa smiled in recognition at the ageing solicitor, remembering how kind he had been when she had gone to him with the news of her grandmother's death. Unsure what she had to do she had called at his office for guidance and he hadn't failed her.

Then it was over. Before moving off, the rector's wife shook hands with Richard and kissed Tessa; the rector shook hands with both of them then hurried to join her. Only the solicitor waited.

'Thomas Sedgley.' He introduced himself, holding out his hand to Richard. 'You must be Mrs Pilbeam's son. I'm glad you were able to get here.' Then, with what Tessa saw as extra warmth in the smile, he turned on her. 'Hello, my dear. I see you managed all the arrangements very well. So many people there to say goodbye to a dear friend.'

'Do you have a car with you or can I give you a lift to the house?' Richard asked.

'If you would be so kind. My office is only just along the road, so I walked.'

'To the house?' The invitation had cut through Tessa's armour of reserve. 'You mean people will be coming back to Gran's – for tea or something? I hadn't thought . . .'

'No, my dear, my visit is something different.' Thomas laid a restraining hand on her arm as he told Richard. 'As I arranged with you, I have the papers with me.'

'Then we'll all drive back together. I'm glad we can go over the will today; I want to catch the mid-morning ferry tomorrow. I can't be away any longer.'

Ignoring what he'd said, Tessa told him, 'You follow behind then; I've got Gran's car.' And with that she left them and, with her head consciously high, crossed the road to Middle Lane where she had parked. She had never been gladder of her ability to handle the car.

'God knows how she walks in those ridiculous shoes, let alone drives in them,' Richard muttered more to himself than to Thomas Sedgley.

'A remarkable young lady. She and your mother were very close, I believe.'

'You don't know whether she had been made aware of the arrangements Mother wished for her? I haven't had an opportunity yet to talk to her myself.' Then, with a sudden and unexpected smile, 'She's got it in for me right enough. Can't you just feel the way she bristles?'

'Not on account of the future arrangements, I fear, for until I give her the letter that Mrs Pilbeam left in my keeping some years ago I am sure she is in ignorance of any such idea.'

'I wish Mother had told her. Face-to-face it might have been easier for her. Most of Mother's visits to the farm were during term time while the child was away at school and, since then, she always came on her own while Tessa holidayed with old school friends. I dare say you know the girl much better than I do. Despite being nineteen years old, and despite the way she has dealt with the arrangements for today, she strikes me as being unworldly – like a child dressed in grown-up clothes. Damn it, girls a year or more younger than she is were in uniform and serving their country not so long ago.'

'Her life has been sheltered, Mr Pilbeam. It used to worry your mother that having spent so many years in boarding school on the mainland the child had no friends of her own age on the island. I understand she has friends from her school days but no one for day-to-day companionship. I have a granddaughter a few years her junior, living here on the Isle of Wight. She and her friends have their heads filled with adolescent rubbish, film stars, tap dancing, and beastly noisy records for their gramophones, unimaginable nonsense. I know it worried Amelia that Tessa missed out on all that sort of fun once she came home from school.'

Richard opened the passenger door for the solicitor, who apparently had been on closer terms with his mother than he had realized. Just at that moment Tessa drove past them without a glance.

Putting on his half-moon glasses Thomas took the parchment will from its envelope and spread it on the table before him, cleared his throat and started to read.

'This is the last will and testament . . .'

A sum of two hundred pounds was to go to Violet Dinsdale, a local woman who had worked in the house daily as long as Amelia had lived there. Everything was to be disposed of, debts settled and an amount of four pounds for each month until Tessa reached the age of twenty-one to be paid to Richard, who was Amelia's executor. The residual estate was to be equally divided between Richard and Tessa.

Taking Tessa by surprise, she was suddenly filled with a feeling of hope, of promise. Life was suddenly there for her to grasp. Things would be new and different. She could see no real shape but, despite that, she could make her own decisions, choose her own path. And all because Gran was making it possible. With the rush of excitement came another emotion: guilt that she could look to the future with hope when darling Gran was gone. But of all people *she* would be the one to understand, for she had had such joy in living. The thought of having the extra four pounds Richard would send her a month as well as what she earned working at the hotel made her imagine herself wealthy. She knew nothing of legal affairs but it seemed unnecessarily complicated that her four pounds should be paid to her uncle instead of straight to her, but that must be because he was the executor. Gran might have imagined that if she had it a year at a time she would go on a spending spree – spending sprees had always been such fun for the two of them together. Pulling her thoughts back into line she saw that Mr Sedgley was passing her an envelope with her name on it written in handwriting she knew so well.

'Gran wrote it for me?' Eagerly she took it, feeling the elderly lady's presence very close. As she tore open the envelope she didn't even notice that the two men were both watching for her reaction.

'My darling Tessa,' she read, 'I hope this letter will never be given to you. I hope I will be there to celebrate your twenty-first birthday. But we none of us know when the call will come and if I get mine and leave you before then, I am handing care of you to Richard and Naomi. Oh dear, I can just picture your face when you read this but if it's on the cards that I come to the end of the track while you're underage at least I shall hit the buffers in peace knowing that you will be in good and loving hands. You hardly know them, and that's been my fault: I ought to have seen to it that we visited the farm together, but when we had a chance to have a jaunt somehow we always found such "fun things" to do. So read this – no, don't frown, just trust me, dear Tessa – and make yourself accept with a smile. That way, life is so much easier. Richard and Naomi have a home full of love; it will be impossible for you not to be happy living with them in Devon. Although we are all so far apart I honestly love them deeply, as I am sure you will too once your ruffled feathers are smoothed down. It's what I truly want for you. Make yourself smile and accept even if you are angry and fearful – and that way, even though your life will be very different from the one we have here, you will find happiness and give happiness to them, too, just as you always have to me.

'I'm pretty fit, but I have to face the fact that whilst you are fourteen' – and glancing back to the start of the letter Tessa saw it had been written five years previously – 'I have just had

11

my eightieth birthday, so it's time I put my house in order. Richard and Naomi are aware that I am writing this to you and are happy with the arrangement.

'It's a strange feeling to know that should you ever be given this to read it will mean that I've gone from the world. But Tessa, you mustn't grieve. Rejoice for the gift of life, rejoice for all the fun and love we have shared through the years, and be sure that even if I'm done with living I shall always be there for you, wanting to know you are happy. Take life by the horns, love with all the faith and strength that's in you, for that's the way to have a full life. Always your loving Gran.'

Tessa felt trapped. Emotion was tearing her in all directions: fear, anger, grief such as she'd never believed possible, those were uppermost, crushing the hope and excitement for the freedom she'd briefly believed would be hers.

'Did you know about this?' She tried to sound strong, self-assured so that Richard would see that she was mature enough to live by herself. But where? The house was to be sold . . . the furniture would go to the auction rooms . . . the car would go . . . there would be nothing left of the things that had been home to Gran and her. If she were that fourteen-year-old her grandmother had written the letter for, then she could have cried and no one would have been surprised. But she was grown up. Gran had known how she would feel if the time ever came that she was given the letter. Tessa was resolved not to fail her grandmother, but equally to let it be firmly understood that nineteen was a far cry from fourteen.

'I was just a child when Gran wrote this; she wouldn't expect you and Aunt Naomi to be tied to things that were said all those years ago.'

'We talked about it in May when Mother was at the farm and you were holidaying with a friend in the Lake District. It was almost as though she had a premonition.' Richard spoke gently, his manner making it even harder for Tessa to hang on to her composure. 'Naomi has your room ready for you. You must have heard me telling Mr Sedgley that I mean us to be on the mid-morning ferry tomorrow.'

'*Us?* I can't do that!' Tessa could feel her face twitching despite the effort she was making to hold back her tears. But her voice refused to be controlled; she heard it break, rise to a high pitch far different from what she had intended. 'I'm not a piece of baggage to be parcelled up and put in your case. I'm *me*. I live *here*. I have a job; Mr and Mrs Briggs at the hotel have been kind and let me have time to do the things I had to this last week, but tomorrow I shall go back to work. I *will*! Even if you make me live with you, I can't come yet. I have a job. I can't just walk away as if it's not important.' She shouted defiantly but her final thread of composure was lost; she was sobbing uncontrollably. In her misery she didn't care that her face was contorted and her mascara leaving black streaks on her cheeks.

'Listen, Tessa.' Richard reached across the table where they were sitting and took both her hands

13

in his. 'Mother knew how upset you would be – Naomi and I both expected you to feel as you do. If you hate living in the country—'

'I won't come. I told you – I'm *not coming*. I'll ask Mr Briggs if they'll put me up at the hotel until I find somewhere of my own. I could work extra hours to make up for it,' she managed between hiccoughing sobs.

'Your work there is finished. I found the number of the hotel from Directory Enquiries and talked with him last night. I explained the situation and he completely understood. I suggested sending him a cheque for four weeks' salary or however long notice was expected, but he wouldn't hear of it.'

'You had no right to interfere! Do you think that's the sort of thing Gran would have wanted? You're not my gaoler, even if you think you are.'

Richard was at a loss. Even allowing for grief and fright, surely hysterical behaviour like this wasn't normal. He thought of the peaceful, busy routine at the farm; he imagined Naomi shouldering his work as well as her own. If only she could have been here perhaps she would have been able to take away some of Tessa's fear – because surely it was fear and pent-up grief that was behind her outburst. He looked helplessly at Thomas Sedgley.

'Now then, my dear' – the elderly man took the cue – 'you take this and wipe away your tears.' He passed her a snow-white folded handkerchief and sent up a silent thank you when, without a word, she took it and started to mop up. 'Now, I

14

know I'm an outsider but I was very fond of your grandmother and she used to talk freely to me. I knew what was in the letter because she told me; and she told me, too, that it worried her that you wouldn't want to go to live at this farm. I remember her words: "Even if Saint Peter lets me through the pearly gates, how can I be happy if I know Tessa is fighting what I've arranged for her? Make her understand, Tom, make her see that I want to know she's there with the others. The three of them are all the family I have left and I shall rest easy if I know they are caring for each other". I've thought of those words many a time over the years. She was a very special lady; we were all blessed to have had her.'

What a sorry sight Tessa was as she gave her face a final rub and returned his handkerchief, by this time smudged with mascara, eyeshadow and lipstick, generously diluted with tears.

'Rejoice,' she said with a hiccough, 'that's what she wants me to do. Can't fail her, can I?' For a second or two she was silent, but when she spoke again her voice was quiet. It was as if all the fight in her had been washed away with her tears. 'I've got to do as she says. Just can't picture what it's going to be like. Sorry I made a scene. Didn't mean to start crying – I started and couldn't stop. It's all so different. I ought to have realized. Just pictured living here, working at the hotel, everything the same except I'd be on my own. Was silly of me.'

'If that were possible, my dear, then Amelia – your grandmother – would have no peace in her soul.'

Tessa nodded. Already the future was beginning to have a structure. She would pack all her things in her school trunk before she went to bed. And she'd take the photograph album, and that picture of Gran and her that the street photographer had taken by the pier in Bournemouth when they went for the day during the July sales. The house wouldn't be theirs any longer; someone else would cut the roses next summer, but no one and nothing could take away memories. Chagleigh Farm was only a few miles from the coast; she'd find a job in a seaside hotel. Before she knew it she'd be twenty-one.

The greatest advantage of youth is its ability to hear the beckoning call of Life.

Her hysterical outburst had left her drained of emotion. How else could she have dragged her trunk from the roof space adjoining her bedroom and packed, clearing drawers and wardrobe? Habit made her fold each item carefully, training from years at boarding school. In normal circumstances packing a case always held excitement. But on that evening it held nothing: no anticipation, no aching misery. She felt as lifeless as a robot as she stripped her room. With drawers, wardrobe and bookshelf empty, furniture that had been part of her life as long as she could remember meant nothing. She felt no pain; she felt no hope.

In the same numb state, next morning she helped Richard carry her trunk out to the car. They were both making a conscious effort to be

16

polite. He hoped that it might make a base to build on and was prepared to put the previous day's scene out of his mind. She didn't ask herself why it was she behaved with forced friendliness – perhaps she subconsciously knew that if she asked the question the answer would have melted the ice that protected her. She was doing it for her grandmother; deep in her heart she knew that was the truth, but her hurt was too new to probe.

Youth came to her rescue as they boarded the ferry that took them on the first stage of their journey, from Yarmouth to Lymington. Once on the mainland they set out westward.

'Keep your eyes open for a pub or even a roadside café where we can get a bite to eat a bit later on,' Richard said as they left the New Forest behind. 'We mustn't waste too long on a meal but we shall need something.'

'Yes, all right,' Tessa answered automatically, craning her neck to take a last glimpse of a group of ponies standing together just off the road. 'Gran and I used to come this way when we went to Bournemouth. It was longer, but the forest is so special.' Then, remembering her resolve to try to behave as her grandmother would have wanted, 'What time do you think we shall get to your farm?'

'Home? Later than I'd like, I expect. I wanted to be back in time to see to the late-afternoon milking. You'll understand when you've been at the farm for a while just how impossible it was for us to get away. With a shop you can put a sign on the door and lock up, but a herd of cows live to a strict timetable, Christmas Day, Good Friday, hell or high water.'

'Yes, Gran always said that's why you could never get to see us. It was a shame – but she understood. And she used to come to the farm quite often when I was at school, didn't she? She used to talk to me about it.'

And so the drive to Chagleigh Farm progressed. It was a few miles from Dorchester when they saw an inn with a car park sufficiently full to hint that meals were being prepared.

'What about there?' she suggested, aware that despite all her inner misery she was hungry and eating out was a treat.

'Looks promising,' he agreed, turning in to park alongside the cars already there. And promising it certainly was. They found a table and turned their concentration to the menu chalked on a board.

'I'll have steak pie. What about you? And what to drink?'

'I'd like the same, please – and cider.' Consciously she kept a pleasant tone in her voice, frightened that if she let the facade of friendliness slip her control would be lost.

The order given, Richard came back from the bar with her cider and his beer.

'I hope they're not going to be long,' he said, as much to himself as to her.

'I expect you're fed up having to waste your time on me like this. You needn't have, you know. I'm not stupid.' Careful, she told herself, wishing she hadn't spoken her thoughts, but it was too late. 'When Gran wrote all that, I was

18

only a school kid. I'm grown up now and quite capable of making my own living. She said she'd talked about it to you and Aunt Naomi, but that was ages ago. Even now you could dump me off. With that four pounds a month I could get a room and still have enough until I found a job. You live in the sticks, so how am I going to get work there? Much better you drop me off in town somewhere. I haven't even got a car to drive now Gran's has gone so I'll be stuck.'

Putting down his tankard he looked at her very directly, somehow making it impossible for her to avoid his gaze.

'Tessa, Mother and I talked about this when she was last with us at the farm – you remember, she visited while you were holidaying with a friend. Even if Naomi and I had ever looked on the idea as an inconvenience we should have agreed. But, believe me, we don't see it that way. We don't know you; you don't know us. But surely we can all give each other the benefit of the doubt and try and believe we shall get along.' Then, with a sudden smile that transformed his stern face, 'I promise you, I have never considered myself to be your gaoler.'

'That was rude and horrid of me. Gran would have been ashamed. But you *must* see, I don't need to be taken care of. Gran and I looked after each other; we were sort of equals. She was the boss, of course, but I was fitter, quicker – well, of course I was – and between the two of us we were a good team.'

He could see her eyes were looking threateningly

pink and reached across the small table to take her hand. 'We have one thing in common, all three of us: we all loved Mother. Two things in common, in fact: she loved each of us.'

Tessa nodded. 'I know.'

Then the man from behind the bar shouted, 'Number sixteen, ready,' and Richard got up to collect their food.

'Do you reckon she can see us here?' said Tessa.

'Perhaps. One thing is certain, whether or not she knows it, she is pretty close.' Then, embarrassed by what he'd said, he hurried to the bar to collect their tray.

The food looked good and he attacked it without further ado. If his words hung between them, they pretended not to be aware.

'Do you want pudding?' he asked as she put her knife and fork together on her empty plate.

'No, thanks. We'd better get on the road, I expect.'

'Good girl. I shall be glad to get home. There's too much there for one person.'

So they continued their journey. Whether they'd come closer to knowing each other neither was sure, but the tension between them eased. Tessa had never known a moment's shyness and in her effort to be agreeable she made herself sound genuinely interested as she questioned him about the farm. But, after a moment's silence he surprised her by saying, 'You'll be no good at Chagleigh in those stilts you seem able to walk on. Why girls do it I can't think. By the time you're sixty your feet

20

will be fit for nothing. Naomi says she thinks it's a reaction from wartime; years of sensible, long-lasting brogues.' Then he surprised her with a sudden laugh. 'My poor love – not even a pair of sensible walking shoes for her unless it's when she goes off sometimes for eight o'clock church on a Sunday morning. No, from the moment she steps outside the door each day till she comes in to start cooking the main meal around teatime, she's in wellies the same as I am – and you will be too, young Tessa, if you're to be one of the team.'

Such an idea had never entered Tessa's head. 'What? Work on the farm, you mean? I've never even visited one until today. I'd be useless. I've been working for two years and you won't find I'm long getting a job. I've learnt a lot about hotel work. And you know I can drive. Gran taught me; I didn't have a single lesson from anyone else. You know, I never thought of her as being old. There's more to age than years, don't you think? She was bright as a shining button. But I was telling you about what experience of work I've had. The day I left school, Gran picked me up and drove us down to Bournemouth for a few days. It was our first jaunt – with me grown up and not on school holiday, I mean. We had such a gorgeous time, she enjoyed it as much as I did, buying me proper smart grown-up clothes. After we got back to the island we put our heads together about what sort of work I might do. I was pretty average, not stupid but not the sort to stay on at school with the idea of going to university or training for a proper career. Then, in stepped Fate. It usually does, don't you think? In the local paper was an advertisement for a trainee manager at a small hotel about a mile from the house. I wrote and applied, not thinking I had a chance because I'd never had a job before and it sounded very grand. But, there you go! Fate again. Of course it wasn't as highfalutin as it sounded in the advertisement and I expect no one with experience could have applied. The hotel was small, only fifteen bedrooms and run by the owner and his wife – with daily staff to help, of course. To start with I was just a general run-about; but like Gran said, if you don't get a good firm foothold on the first rung of the ladder you can't climb. Anyway, I got taught things. For the last year I looked after the wages, got the cheques all ready to be signed to pay the bills, took bookings, did the typing – self-taught, but I go really fast using four fingers. Even then, though, I still had to turn my hand to anything else that needed to be done whether it was clearing up in the kitchen, arranging flowers, rushing out for anything that had been forgotten. I did all sorts of odd jobs.'

'I ought to have let you speak to the owner yourself. I suppose the truth is that I suspected you would be against doing what Mother wanted and thought it better to make your resignation a *fait accompli.*'

'I shall write to Mr and Mrs Briggs, the owners. But Uncle Richard, I expect you did what you thought was best. And, I feel ashamed about yesterday. I know I was rude and . . . and . . .

obnoxious. I felt sort of trapped. But like Gran always said: if things aren't plain sailing that's because life is giving you a challenge.'

Turning to look at her, Richard thought how pretty she was and how delightfully honest. Give her a few weeks at Chagleigh and she'll be a real asset, he decided. Time Naomi had a break. His expression softened as he imagined her. By this time she would be well on with the milking, sitting there on the stool with the side of her face pressed against the animal's warm flank, probably singing softly under her breath or talking coaxingly, while her strong, gentle hands encircled the animal's teat as she worked with firm pressure so that the milk spurted into the pail with a steady rhythm.

'It seems warm to me,' he commented. 'I'll pull in and we'll fold the roof back. Not too windy for you if we have the top down? I know what women can be like about their hair.'

'Yes, let's. Gran's didn't have an open top and we often said we wished it had. She never worried about her hair; it always looked lovely but she never fussed over it. We used to walk on the cliffs when we could hardly stand up in the wind.'

He drew to a halt and together they opened the hood.

'That's better!' she said as she settled back in her seat. 'Uncle Richard, it must have been a bit of a blow for you and Aunt Naomi when you were told Gran wanted you to be lumbered with a niece you'd hardly ever seen. I wouldn't want you to think I don't appreciate that it's as bad for you as for me. But I promise I'll soon get work. And even if it's in town somewhere, once you get to know me you'll see I'm quite capable of taking care of myself.'

'My dear child, of course you will make your home with us. And as for looking for a job, you'll be kept so busy you won't have time to think about it. Naomi and I keep very fit, but she has far too much to do. She's one in a million, always busy, never complains that she's tired, but it'll be a relief to me to know you're helping. She'll teach you the dairy work. Then there are the chickens, the geese, a flock of rare-breed sheep, cattle – and the pigs. We have no arable land, but animals make a damn sight more work than wheat. But, bless her, she's always been the same, no job too much for her. By the time we get home she'll be putting the afternoon's milk through the cooler and getting it in the churns. They have to be taken to the gate on the lane so that when the lorry comes this evening they're ready for collection. Too heavy for her – but if I'm not back she'll grit her teeth and get them on to the trailer and take them to the gate herself. She won't let anything beat her.'

Without warning Tessa's hard-fought-for acceptance was stripped from her. It took every ounce of courage to keep her face from giving away the misery that filled her. A fortnight ago there had been nothing to suggest the changes in store. Staring straight ahead it wasn't the distant open country that held her mind but the moment when she'd found her grandmother lying where she'd fallen, the teapot in fragments on the tiled floor, the spreading puddle already cold. She must have been lying there helplessly for hours. Amelia had been the one stable factor in Tessa's life. But, more than that, they had been kindred spirits, sharing the same sense of fun, the same outlook on life.

'Nearly home.' Richard's voice cut through her thoughts. 'The gate's just along the lane we're coming to here on the left. There! What did I say? She's managed to get the churns down to the gate on her own.' Tessa heard pride in his tone, pride that his wife was such a workhorse. She had a vague memory of her Aunt Naomi, but it didn't fit with the image he was portraying. 'Here we are, then. Your new home. And there's your aunt waiting to greet you.' Did she imagine his over-cheerful words were forced? She wished she were anywhere but here. Why had Gran written in her will that she entrusted 'my dear son Richard to take my granddaughter Tessa into his home in the event of my death before she reaches the age of twenty-one'? Twenty-one was nearly two years away . . . two years to be spent in the middle of nowhere surrounded by mud, smelly cattle, pigs, chickens – probably rats and spiders. She wished she could get out of the car and run, just run as fast as she could to find freedom anywhere, anywhere but here. And they couldn't possibly want her; she was here because they'd been asked to give her a home. Could that woman coming to meet them be Aunt Naomi? Tessa only had a vague memory of meeting her, but she had pictured her as being smart, not a mixture between gypsy and tramp. If I stay here they'll expect me to get like that, she thought. Well, I won't! I'm *me*, and I'm going to stay *me*.

'Tessa, welcome to Chagleigh.' Naomi Pilbeam greeted her, opening the passenger door as the car stopped. 'Come away in. You'll want to get out of your tidy things, Richard. Food will be ready by the time you've changed and Tessa has got acquainted with her room.'

As she talked she led the way through an outer lobby hung with an array of old coats and mackintoshes, with wellington boots in a neat row beneath, then, opening the latch door, ushered Tessa into the kitchen.

'This is nice.' Expecting the room to be in keeping with her aunt's appearance Tessa spoke without thinking, letting her surprise be heard.

Naomi laughed. 'What did you expect?'

'To be truthful, I don't know. I've never been to a farm before.'

Naomi led the way upstairs, followed by Richard and Tessa carrying the trunk. As they turned into the spare room Richard dragged it to the foot of the bed, then went to change into his working clothes and hang away his charcoal-grey suit. Looking around the room that was to be her sanctuary Tessa caught a glimpse of herself in the wardrobe mirror with Naomi, who seemed utterly content in the isolation of the farm and the barns, cowsheds, chicken houses – and mud, everywhere there was mud. To be fair that was mainly due to the night of thunderstorms but, as Tessa had heard nothing of them in the Isle of

Wight, she assumed that mud was a normal part of existence at Chagleigh. The contrast of Naomi's reflection and her own couldn't have been more pronounced. Naomi's glance met hers in the mirror.

'Just look at us.' The older woman laughed, in no way nonplussed by her appearance. 'Talk about chalk and cheese.'

'When you came to that service for my parents you were really smart. That's the only thing I remembered about you. In fact, I don't remember a lot about any of it.'

'I don't expect you do; it must have all been frightening for a little one like you were. And what a blessing it was for Mother that you were there; without having you to care for she would have gone to pieces when she lost your mother. I always felt having you gave Mother her youth all over again.'

'Gran never got old,' came the defensive answer.

'You miss her, of course you do. But Tessa, if ever a woman had determination it was Mother and she would want you to take what life has thrown at you and make it work for you.'

Tessa nodded, turning her head away so that her aunt wouldn't see the tears that were burning her dark eyes.

'It won't be easy for you, love, I know it won't. But Richard and I are here to help you. And I've always believed there is nothing like hard manual work for pushing everything else out of your thoughts.'

'I don't want to push any of it out of my

27

thoughts; I want to remember it all.' Did Naomi guess that the aggressive tone was defence against the misery threatening to break loose? 'All I know about cows and pigs is that they smell and make filthy, disgusting messes.'

Naomi's laugh was spontaneous as she put her arm around Tessa's shoulder and gave her a quick hug. 'And that's about all either of *us* knew when we took on this place. As soon as Richard was demobbed in nineteen nineteen we were married. We spent our honeymoon in Deremouth, the nearest town from here. That's when we found Chagleigh. It was in a dreadful state, no indoor toilet, no drainage, no electricity. But we were both young – and everything was so different in those days. Where does the time go? Now look at me!' With her arm still around Tessa's shoulder, she sat on the edge of the bed pulling the young girl down to her side. 'If you're happy the years fly. And, I suppose, if you're miserable it works the other way. My parents were appalled that we meant to set up home here. They'd said we could live with them until we found somewhere but we wanted more than anything to be in a place of our own. We would have set up home in one of those cowsheds just to have somewhere of our own,' she said, and from her voice Tessa knew she was little more than thinking aloud as her mind took her back down the years.

'We met before either of us had even left school but we felt we were grown up. First love hits with such intensity. Then came the war and Richard immediately volunteered and before we knew it he was in France. Nothing changed for us though and, like I said, we married and came here as soon as he was demobbed.' For a few seconds she seemed lost in her own private thoughts. Then, perhaps no more than speaking them aloud, 'Such a dreadful war, so many young lives wasted. Both my brothers were killed – and my cousin, Dennis. But thank God Richard came home safely.' She seemed to become aware of what she was saying. 'Hark at me, and you wanting to do your unpacking. And all because I told you we knew no more about farms when we came here than you do. Tessa, I'm not good at saying things, but I want you to understand that although Mother left the request that you should come to Richard, we really *do* want you here. We've never had a family. Not that we wouldn't have been pleased to have babies; I mean, we tried. Now, though, you've come to us and it sort of completes the family. Don't be frightened by such different surroundings. If you look on it all as a bit primitive, remember what I told you about how it was when we came here. And yet, right from the beginning, we loved it, every stick and stone of it.'

'That was different. It was a future you wanted to make together.' Tessa was in no mood to look on the bright side. 'Anyway, when the war was first over everyone must just have been thankful to have people they loved come home.'

'I'm thankful for all of it, then and now, too. Now I'm going to leave you to hang your things away. The bathroom is the door just across the landing and you'll find the water is warm; even. in the summer I keep the range burning because it heats the back boiler, so there's always plenty of hot water.' Then, with a wide smile that deepened the prematurely well-etched lines on her face, 'You must admit that's an improvement from an earth closet across the yard and water pumped up from the well.'

Tessa found the smile infectious and replied to it like for like. 'Sorry I sounded such a grump, Aunt Naomi. I really am grateful to you and Uncle Richard.'

'We'll all get along fine, just see if we don't.' And with that she left Tessa to undo her trunk and set to work.

Five minutes later, her outer clothes hung in the wardrobe and a pile of her favourite books on the dressing table, Tessa decided to leave the rest of her unpacking until later. She crossed the landing to the bathroom. From the room next to hers came the sound of voices. Naomi had gone to talk to Richard while he changed into his work clothes. Their words weren't clear, but there was something in their soft tones, a sort of intimacy that made Tessa aware that she was an outsider. She'd start looking for a job straight away. They couldn't be more than about fifteen miles from the coast and there must be a lot of hotels there. Her optimistic nature was coming to the fore. Back in the bedroom she brushed her easy-to-care-for wavy hair. While she was touching up her make-up she heard Richard and Naomi going down the stairs then, a minute later, she heard the lobby door slam and saw him slushing through the mud –'and worse' she thought with distaste – towards the cowshed. He looked older, rougher; in fact, she had seen plenty of scarecrows as well dressed.

Turning from the window she ran down the stairs then, her high heels clip-clopping on the stone-flagged floor of the hall, went to the kitchen to find Naomi, resolved that her stay would be only temporary and she'd start straight away to look for a 'proper job' – and freedom.

Two

By morning the mud in the yard had dried, the world smelt fresh and new. Perhaps it wouldn't be so bad after all just for a short while.

Surprisingly quickly some sort of routine evolved. Tessa didn't want Richard and Naomi to think she wasn't doing her share. Soon it became routine for her to clear away the breakfast things, make the beds, see the rooms were tidy and the windows open, tidy the bathroom and clean the bath and basin. Her years in the hotel had taught her to be quick and efficient. Then on with the hated wellingtons and off she'd go to offer her services in the dairy. Naomi had welcomed the idea of having help churning butter (a tedious job which took too much of her time) and scalding the cream, but soon she looked forward to having Tessa's company for its own sake. Originally the idea of a young girl working with her had brought home to her just how the years had changed her without her even thinking about it. When she and Richard had taken the farm both of them had been inexperienced, filled with enthusiasm, love and thankfulness. Thinking back, she was honest enough to know that in those days she had been as pretty as he'd been handsome. He had matured (not aged, to her he never aged) but it suited him. But she? She'd always been slender, but now she'd become scrawny and her weather-beaten face was etched with lines ahead of her years. Only her bust had remained the same, perhaps the advantage of having no children.

Letting her thoughts fly free, she stood quite still, the pan of cream forgotten. No young girl could find companionship with a work-worn woman more than old enough to be her mother; and yet her heart was still that of the pretty bride who had come here all those years ago. No! No, it wasn't. Now was different. Then we were 'in love', each day was an adventure and each night we found paradise. But I wouldn't change *now* for *then*. What we have now is deeper, broader.

Hearing footsteps she pulled herself back from her reverie just as Richard looked into the dairy.

'All alone? How's it going?'

'Too fast, Richard.' Then, seeing his quizzical expression, 'The years are slipping away. I was just thinking about *us*. We've been here thirty-five years. We're on the downward slope. Will things change for us? Will time change us?'

'As we turn into Derby and Joan, you mean?' he teased, looking at her with affection. Then, giving serious thought to what she'd said, 'I suppose if we look back to the pair of youngsters we used to be, we must have been gradually changing with time. But we'll never change in the way you mean. It was wonderful when we were starry-eyed and wet behind the ears – but, Naomi –' his teasing note gone as he held his hand under her chin and raised her face to his – 'what we have now is . . . complete. Nothing can ever take that away from us.' Then, his momentary seriousness over, 'I dare say youngsters like Tessa would see us as ancient, and think that love is the prerogative of the young. I bet we thought that when we first came here. But we were wrong. What we had then pales by comparison with what we have gained with the years. God, hark at me!' He spoke quietly, scarcely moving his lips while his eyes carried their own message. 'Half past ten in the morning and I want to carry you to bed and ravage you. Must have had the sun on the back of my neck again,' he ended, trying to make a joke of his sudden upsurge of desire.

She wound her strong, thin arms around his neck.

'The young know *nothing*,' he whispered. 'They're still learning.' Then, giving her a quick hug, 'But us? We're fully qualified.'

She laughed softly, buffeting her head against his shoulder and suddenly filled with happiness.

'Boasting again? Hark, I can hear Tessa coming.' She pulled away from him and started to turn the handle of the butter-maker.

'Hello, Tessa,' he greeted the intruder as she joined them, wearing an apron of Naomi's over her summer skirt and blouse. 'I was just about to say to Naomi, how about you doing the village run today? The eggs for Mr Louch are all racked up ready. Do you fancy a drive?'

'Yes, rather. Can I have five minutes to get

34

ready? Anything else we want in the village, Auntie?'

'There's the making of a list on the dresser. Thanks, love. Take my purse out of my handbag.'

In the letter Amelia had left for Tessa she had written of Richard and Naomi's home as a house full of love. Frightened and miserable as she had been, Tessa hadn't even considered there might be truth in what she read. Yet without her being aware of it, as the weeks went by the atmosphere in the farmhouse was casting its spell, and her relation-ship with her aunt and uncle was blossoming as a result. Everyone had worked hard in the hotel but it was nothing compared with what went on at Chagleigh Farm and soon she became as involved as the others. She enjoyed her trips to the village with the deliveries, or for any other errand, but although it was her nature to interest herself in the work she did, in the dairy she gave the animals a wide berth and still detested the 'mud and worse' that was so often a hazard of the yard.

There were two things that remained unchanged from the day of her arrival: one was her desire to find work of her own choosing and the second was that nothing altered the pride she took in her appearance. Although they were delighted to have Tessa's help around farm and would have liked things to stay as they were, Richard and Naomi had made it clear that they wouldn't stand in her way if she were to find a suitable job, and each morning when she came downstairs she was groomed and made-up just as she had been when her days had been spent at the hotel.

* * *

35

Chagleigh Farm was situated about two empty miles from Marlhampton, the nearest village. On the course of those two miles there was only one house, Fiddlers' Green, standing in grounds of about three acres. Approached through wrought-iron gates the house wasn't visible from the road because of the curve of the drive. To Tessa there seemed something mysterious about it, until she learnt that it had stood empty since just after the war. That accounted for the weeds that pushed their way through the gravel of the drive and the neglected and overgrown rhododendron hedge that bordered it on either side. Beyond Fiddlers' Green was agricultural land until just before the start of High Street where there was a terrace of six council houses. On Tessa's delivery or shopping trips she never saw any sign of life from any of them.

Each week she scanned the vacancies column in the *Western Weekly News* but she found nothing to fit the image she had in her mind. With the holiday season well on, did it mean she would have to wait right through a cold, muddy winter before she could pick up the threads of her own life? She hated the thought and, even more, hated herself for having such an overriding need to be free of the home where she had been given affection. The truth was that she had become fond of Richard and Naomi. She honestly wished this could have been what she wanted for her life. Each time she drove the deliveries to Marlhampton she checked the seldom-changing notice board outside the newspaper shop and each day she was disappointed.

Once a month Naomi was responsible for the flowers in St Stephen's Church in the High Street, so on those Saturday mornings Tessa stayed at home to clean out the hen houses and prepare lunch, which at Chagleigh Farm was always a hurried meal. On that day Naomi returned just as it was ready: grilled ham topped with poached eggs, everything home produced except for the still-warm crusty bread she brought with her from the village bakehouse.

'Vera Hopkins was polishing the brass in the church, so I've come home with all the local gossip,' Naomi said as she took her place at the table. 'Most of it wasn't very interesting, but guess what? Fiddlers' Green has been sold.'

'That's good. It must be looking a bit sad after being empty so long. I wouldn't like the bill for putting it in good nick again,' Richard said. 'Let's hope the newcomers have plenty of money to spend on it.'

'You know Vera! How she winkles out all the gossip I can't imagine but she seemed very certain. She said the owner – I forget his name, but that doesn't matter – she said he's an industrialist, a manufacturer of some sort from the Midlands and made his fortune making parts for tanks during the war. Apparently, although he's still chairman of the company, he's more or less retired. There's no wife, just the man, a crippled youngster and a housekeeper. So he'll be looking for domestic staff, I suppose.'

'A crippled child? That's rotten.' Then, his thoughts moving on, 'I can't hang around, I've got Vickers the vet coming this afternoon.'

37

'What for?'

'One of my old ladies seemed to be limping when I drove them in for milking yesterday afternoon. This morning she's worse, so I've left her in the shed and asked Vickers to take a look at her.'

So talk of the newcomers were overtaken by routine events. Tessa took no part in the conversation but she was aware of the companionable atmosphere. She offered to clear away the lunch so that Naomi could go with Richard to await the vet and so the hours of Saturday moved gently on just as every other day of the week.

On her trips to the village Tessa heard the locals talking about the work going on at Fiddlers' Green, but she wasn't terribly interested. One day she noticed men were trimming the overgrown rhododendrons, and a few days later workmen were replacing the long, curved gravel drive with crazy paving. Remembering what Richard had said about the work that would be needed to put the place in order, she decided that the new owner must indeed be a man of wealth. But her interest was so slight that she even forgot to tell Richard and Naomi what she had seen.

Once again it was Vera who brought Naomi up to date on the progress there, polishing the church brass with extra vigour as her excitement increased.

'They've moved in, the new folk at Fiddlers' Green. I thought, well there's no one living near them, no one to welcome them among us so to speak. I must be their closest neighbour, me

38

being at the end of the terrace.' Vera lived in the first of the six council houses. 'So I put on my best and went calling. The housekeeper opened the door to my knock; a frosty-faced woman if ever there was, and when I told her who I was and why I'd come calling, wouldn't you think she would have had the manners to shake me by the hand and introduce herself? Oh, no, Madam High and Mighty just told me to step inside and she'd see if Mr Masters – that's his name you remember, Julian Masters is how he introduced himself to me – was free. Seems he was and, give him his due, he wasn't as stuck up as the housekeeper, Miss Sherwin. "Thank you, Miss Sherwin, that'll be all," he told her when she took me through to him. I could see from the way she hovered that she meant to hang around, so I gave an inward chuckle when he gave her her marching orders. Well, anyway, to get back to what I was telling you. He was very polite – even thanked me for taking the trouble to call and welcome him, but underneath his correct sort of manner I got the feeling that he didn't intend to get himself involved with us locals. Not exactly too big for his boots – no, like I say he was quite cordial, but there was something in his manner that sort of put a barrier up and you knew he'd go so far and no further. I didn't get a glimpse of the crippled daughter. Remember I told your aunt it was a man and his child. But maybe she's not just a kid. If she is, he must have been getting on when he sired her. He's not old, mind you, I'd say about the age of you and me, or maybe nearer the sixty mark.

Now then, how does that look?' She carried the cross back to its stand and stood a few paces away to admire her handiwork.

'She may be quite grown up. If she were a child you'd think he would have a nanny to look after her,' Naomi said, her mind more on where to find a place to put the final rose without throwing out the balance of the arrangement.

'Well, I dare say we shall find out sooner or later. Anyway, like I said, I only saw the man. Don't know if he's a widower or if his wife went walkabouts as they say. Good looking, very distinguished more than handsome, nicely cut iron-grey hair and a moustache that bit whiter. Oh, well, if he doesn't want to hobnob with the likes of us, that's his loss.'

And just as she had a few weeks previously, Naomi laughingly reported Vera's welcome attempt when she got home to the farm.

'You've got to give Vera a point for trying,' Richard said, smiling as he imagined kind-hearted, harmless and gossipy Vera returning home to hang away 'her best'.

'There was an advertisement in the *Western Weekly News* this morning. It's for various positions at Fiddlers' Green,' Tessa told them. 'They want an under-gardener and a general household assistant I think they called it. And, listen to this –' she opened the paper at the right page, thanks to her having dog-eared the corner – 'someone to act as a carer/companion to a partially handicapped girl. Must have sense of humour and be able to drive. Marlhampton Three Seven Two.' She looked expectantly at the others.

'I thought I'd ring and try to get an interview. They may not like me—'

'More to the point, you may not like them,' Richard corrected. 'I can't see you settling to spend your days working for someone cold and courteous.' With eyebrows raised he looked at the niece who had become very dear to Naomi and him in the few months she had been with them. It wasn't likely she would accept the job if her opinion of this man Masters was the same as Vera's. 'Presumably it's not a living-in position – it doesn't actually say.'

'I'd come home each evening and, Aunt Naomi, I'd help you here, honestly. I haven't got the job yet anyway, but if I should get it I promise it wouldn't mean that I didn't do my share here.'

'Never mind doing your share.' Naomi realized how empty the place would be now without Tessa. 'It's your company we shall miss. But if you think you might enjoy the job – and a lot depends on what the girl is like – then fingers crossed that you get it.'

'And they'll be lucky to have you,' Richard added.

With Richard's opinion echoing in her mind Tessa made her phone call that afternoon, answered by someone she had no doubt was the unwelcoming housekeeper.

'The carer, you say? You've wasted no time; the papers have scarcely had time to be delivered. Hold the line while I enquire when you can be seen.' Then, after what must have been the briefest of words, 'Mr Masters will see you at

41

four o'clock. Give me your name. He's a busy man so just see you're here sharp.'

'I'm not in the habit of being late for appointments,' Tessa answered in her most frigid tone. 'My name is Richards, Miss Richards.'

At one minute to four she rang the bell to be greeted by a woman whose appearance in no way matched her manner. A small, thin person, with grey hair knotted to the top of her head. But when she spoke there was no doubt who she was. 'You'll be the appointment. This way.' Then, hardly giving Tessa time to get through the door, she led the way down the corridor to where Julian Masters was waiting. 'The four o'clock appointment, sir.'

'Thank you, Miss Sherwin.' The man at the desk nodded his head, dismissing her, then, standing up, turned to Tessa holding out his hand. 'Miss Richards, I believe.'

'That's right. Tessa Richards.' Tessa answered with a friendly smile. 'How do you do, Mr Masters. Is this your daughter? I imagined it would be a child.' She had never known what it was to be shy and now she turned to the girl who sat in a wheelchair by the side of the desk. 'You must be about the same age as me.'

Her friendly introduction was met with a frown. 'Don't know how old you are. I'm eighteen.'

'I can give you a year then. I shall be twenty in April.'

Appearance had always been important to Tessa and she sensed that in part the disabled girl's scowl was based on envy that she could breeze into their lives, well dressed and with her face

42

made up to flatter and not leave her looking like a painted doll.

'I hoped someone around Deirdre's age would apply. I shall leave you two for a few minutes to give you a chance to get to know one another. Then perhaps, Miss Richards, you will wait outside while Deirdre tells me whether from her point of view you are the answer. After that we'll discuss remuneration, hours – and, of course, whether you are willing to take the post.' With a slight nod of his head he left them.

'That was a good idea,' Tessa said. 'We have a chance to talk and see if we would get on. Who goes first, you or me?'

'Me. It's me who has to choose.' Not a promising start.

'Up to a point it's both of us. We both have to think we can be friends or the whole thing would be a waste of time.'

'Well, you're the one who needs a job.'

'You're half right. I do want a job; I want to stand on my own feet. But I don't *need* a job. I live with my aunt and uncle at Chagleigh Farm and I help in the dairy and in the house so that my aunt is free to be outside. They'd like me to let things stay as they are but before I came to Marlhampton I was assistant manager in a hotel on the Isle of Wight –' how grand that sounded! – 'and when I was brought here to live I made my mind up that I would find work for myself.'

'I suppose you got the sack at the hotel.' From her tone it was evident that Deirdre felt she had scored a point.

'No. Since I was small and lost my parents my grandmother had been my guardian. She died a few months ago and Uncle Richard brought me down here. I can't do as I choose until I'm twenty-one, but we all get on very well and they'd be happy for things to stay as they are.'

'Did you get on with your grandmother?'

'I loved her. Age didn't come into it. Gran and I were such *friends*. She died very suddenly.'

Biting her over-lipsticked bottom lip, Deirdre weighed up her words.

'That must have been rotten for you – her dying like that.'

It was the first breakthrough and Tessa seized it before it faded. 'It was awful. I'm a coward; I don't like even thinking about how awful. But one thing Gran taught me – well, one of lots of things if I'm truthful – is that whatever life chucks at you, you have to accept the challenge and make something of it.'

'Are you saying that to me because of how I am? Anyway, what would you know about it? Life has never chucked anything at you like it did at me.'

Until then Tessa had been standing, looking down at the seated girl. Now she pulled a chair forward so that they were eye to eye.

'You're right and, honestly, I'm grateful for all the good things. I'm fit, I have an aunt and uncle who have welcomed me into their home, I have wonderful memories – and I'm determined to make something of my life. Now tell me about you. You can't just sit in a chair doing nothing

44

all day long. Do you read? Do you paint – or write perhaps? There was a man on the island who had lost both legs in the war and he made the most beautiful wooden carvings.'

'I s'pose you're telling me I don't make an effort. Well, what's the point anyway? I used to ride. That was how I had the accident. I was out hunting on Jasper. We flew over the hedge, then when he landed something happened. I got thrown, that's all I remember. I didn't break an arm or leg or anything, but they say Jasper fell on me. Anyway, my spinal cord got broken. So here I sit. Can't do anything. I expect you think I'm wicked to be wasting my life. Some life!' And from the glower that accompanied her words, her situation might have been Tessa's fault.

Tessa asked herself if she would behave any differently herself if she were in Deirdre's place.

'I'm thinking no such thing. I just don't like to see you miserable. There's far more to life than walking. Think of the things you have going for you: you're pretty –' or you would be if you didn't put your make-up on as if you were a circus clown, she added silently to herself – 'you live in a comfortable home, you have a father who cares about you—'

'Oh, shut up preaching at me. I'm just a horrid person, that's what you're trying to tell me.'

'If I thought that, I would have been out of the house ages ago. You know what I think? I think if we set our minds to it we could get on well and have some fun.'

Deirdre didn't answer, but from her expression it seemed she didn't share Tessa's optimism.

At that point Julian Masters came back into the room, holding open the door for Tessa to wait in the hall while he heard Deirdre's reaction. She had hardly sat down when he called her back into the room.

'It seems you have hit the spot with Deirdre. Take a seat, Miss Richards—'

'Her name's Tessa, she told you so.' Despite having given her approval for Tessa's appointment, Deirdre's tone was as disagreeable as before. 'I didn't say I liked her, I just said that she'd do.'

'That's quite enough! Just remember your manners or Miss Richards will refuse the position,' her father answered. 'You may leave us now to discuss the details.'

Deirdre skilfully turned the wheels of her chair and made towards the door, but not before Tessa had seen how she bit hard on the corners of her mouth in an attempt to hold back the tears.

'Deirdre's right, Mr Masters. It would be nice if you called me Tessa, don't you think? I'm not much older than she is and "Miss" really doesn't suit me. I can start whenever you like and I'm sure she and I will get on like a house on fire.'

So the engagement was finalized. She was to be paid thirty pounds a month and would work from ten in the morning until six, Mondays to Fridays with two weeks holiday a year.

'A funny sort of job if you ask me,' was Richard's opinion, 'and nothing to show for it.'

'I hope there will be plenty to show for it. Deirdre really is a grouch, there's no better way of describing her, but what a lonely, unnatural existence. I doubt if she has any friends of her own age – and certainly not here where they are now. It's as if she's full of resentment and needs to take her feelings out on everybody else.'

'You might say something the same about you.'

'Me?' Tessa was shocked by the remark. 'I know that's how I must have seemed when you came to the island, but I suppose I was frightened and miserable—'

'I didn't mean you were like her in being a – what was it you called her – a grouch? No, I meant that Mother was more than seventy when you lost your parents. Your salvation must have been boarding school. I know it used to worry her that you were always an outsider to girls of your own age on the island. So what companionship did you have after you left school?'

'Gran and I were real friends. If she'd lived to be a hundred, she would never have been old. And I could walk and run and swim and drive, I could get a job and feel I was part of things that matter. Poor Deirdre is so restricted and all her father's money doesn't make a scrap of difference. You know what I want? I want to make her forget to pout and to let her face learn to show she is pleased with life. But it's a tall order.'

Despite her confidence, there were days during the first few weeks when she despaired of bringing

47

a change in Deirdre's attitude. *You don't know what it's like . . . it's easy for you . . . at six o'clock you'll hop on your bike and pedal away into the real living world.*

'Why don't you bring her to see us here at Chagleigh? There is something very healing about a farm,' Naomi suggested, then added with a mischievous twinkle, 'apart from the mud and worse she might encounter in the yard.'

And the very next morning, that's what Tessa did, despite Deirdre's mood of despondency. 'I've got a plan,' she greeted her sulky-looking charge. 'I want to drive us along to the farm where I live. Come on, put a smile on your face. You look about as glum as I felt when I got taken to live there; but, honestly, you'll love it.'

'It's a miserable, dull morning. What's the point of going anywhere on a day like this?'

'I want you to see where I live. It's so one-sided that I know Fiddlers' Green and your father while you haven't been to the farm or got to know my uncle and aunt.'

'They won't want me there. I'd just be in the way in my chair.'

'You sound much like I did when I knew I had to come and live with them. But there's a sort of magic about the place. I can't put it into words, it's not that it's elegant or beautiful, and they both work like Trojans all day long, but no one can feel miserable there. Just wait till you meet them.'

'It was different for you. You told me you worked and could help them. And they'll be too

48

busy to want to welcome a visitor. Did you ask them if you could bring me?'

Tessa chuckled imagining the sort of reception Deirdre seemed to imagine a visit from a stranger merited.

'It was Aunt Naomi who suggested it. Not for any particular day. They don't know we're coming this morning.'

Her answer did nothing to boost Deirdre's confidence. 'They'll be busy right enough, you just wait and see.'

Deirdre gave up the battle and, without putting up an argument even though her expression didn't look any more promising, let herself be wheeled up the ramp into the back of the car. It had originally been designed as a car the same as any other, except that before it left the factory Julian had made sure that it had been adapted to her needs. The front remained unaltered, but the roof of the rear had been raised and it opened with a wide door at the back. A ramp could be pulled out from beneath the chassis; a ramp sufficiently long that the incline was gradual and Tessa had quickly learnt to get the loaded wheelchair aboard and safely secured. Already in the short time she had worked at Fiddlers' Green, the girls had had many outings. An irritable and sulky Deirdre would be wheeled aboard, but a smiling and laughing one brought home. Julian had watched from a distance, sending up a heartfelt thank you that Fate had brought Tessa to cross their path.

On that morning as they approached the farm Richard was in the yard and realized this must be 'the hybrid', as Tessa called the vehicle she drove. By the time they reached the gate he had it wide open for them to drive straight in.

'Hello, girls,' he greeted them as, the gate safely latched, he came to join them in the fortunately dry yard. 'So you must be Deirdre. Tessa has kept us waiting all these weeks to meet you. Naomi!' he called, 'come and see who's here.' While he talked he had brought the chair down the slope, leaving the ramp out ready for reloading. Then Naomi came from the dairy, her thin face beaming a welcome that even Deirdre couldn't ignore.

'Come in the dairy and see where the work's done,' Naomi said as the commotion of their unexpected arrival died down. Did she imagine it (wishful thinking, perhaps) or was there a slight lift in Deirdre's expression? 'I expect Tessa has told you something about it, has she?'

'Might have done. Can't remember.' Oh dear, oh dear, does Tessa have this sort of behaviour to contend with every day?

'Well, once you've seen for yourself you won't forget too easily. I guess lots of people would say the days are monotonous, the same routine almost to the minute. Maybe I'm a sucker, but you know I never find it boring; each day there is such a sense of achievement when the butter gets packaged, the cream put in its tubs, everything ready for delivery to the village shop.' Once inside the dairy she returned to turning the handle of the butter-maker as she talked. 'This and the ducks and chickens – and the mushroom shed – are my responsibility. The real bread and butter of the place is Richard's side of it with the animals he rears. I keep out of that.' Then, with a grin that etched deep lines into her thin face, 'That's man's work. Oh, talk of the devil . . .' as Richard put his head round the door of the dairy.

'Tessa, can you give me a hand for a couple of minutes? I don't want to hinder Naomi; she likes to get the delivery to the village in good time.' Then as a rider, 'As if you don't know! Shan't keep her long, Deirdre.'

Not until they were away from the dairy did he turn to Tessa with a conspiratorial wink. 'I thought it might be a good idea to leave her with Naomi for a bit. I don't really need a hand, I'm only tinkering with the electric fence in the high field.'

'Anyway, I'll walk up there with you. It's a good idea leaving them together. What is there about being with Aunt Naomi that makes it so hard to be miserable? Bet you that when we get back we shall find a very different Deirdre.'

But even they weren't prepared for what they found: Deirdre had her chair pulled close to a side table where the morning's egg collection had been waiting in a large basket. Absorbed in what she was doing, she was packing them into cardboard egg-trays, two dozen in each, then stacking them one on another.

'What a woman!' Richard laughed. 'She didn't waste much time getting you working, Deirdre.'

'I'll be ready to go to the village in no time at this rate,' Naomi said. 'You girls must look in more often.'

'May we?' Deirdre asked hopefully. 'You know what? This is the best morning I've had for ages, even better than when we went to Deremouth to choose my new make-up, Tessa. You never told me there were things like this to do. When you said it was a farm, I expected fields of corn or whatever it is farmers grow – and animals, of course.'

'If you want to see the rest Tessa can take the car as far as the high field. We only have animals, cattle, Cotswold sheep, pigs, poultry – but clearly you know we have poultry.'

'Horses?' Deirdre wanted to know. 'I loved riding. I had my first pony when I was four. I had Jasper for my sixteenth birthday. The accident happened when we were jumping a hedge and he landed with one foreleg in a hole in the ground. I suppose it was a rabbit hole. Anyway, that's how I got thrown. Poor Jasper broke his leg and fell on me. Daddy had him put down, he said he had done internal damage as well as his leg. I thought he was jolly lucky being got rid of like that.' Until those last few words she had been chattering in a friendly, relaxed way, as if she had known them all for ages. Instantly her manner changed.

'I bet you did, too,' Naomi answered, just as if she hadn't noticed the girl's change of mood. 'So would any of us if we were faced with a shock like you had to face. But life has its own way of turning things around. Your life will never be the same as it was before, but you know what they say: "When the Lord shuts the door, he opens a window." I remember thinking

52

the same sort of thing during the war – not this last one – the one before. Oh, not about myself. I was safe at home. But I had two brothers; both of them were killed. And I remember thinking they were lucky compared with my cousin Bertie. He was in the Flying Corps. His plane was shot at and caught fire when it crashed. He was most dreadfully burned, it was awful to look at him. For ages after he came home he wouldn't meet anyone or even go out. Then he started to paint. He didn't paint models, or copy photographs; he painted what he saw in his mind. Dreadful things. But it was as if in putting the images on to canvas he was freeing his spirit. Gosh! Hark at me. Why doesn't somebody shut me up?'

'Go on, Mrs Pilbeam. What happened to your cousin?' Deirdre encouraged.

'He found a sort of peace. You could see the difference in his pictures. Then he met a girl, a sweet girl, shy, talked with a stammer. But not with him. That was what was so . . . so . . . miraculous. When she was with Bertie she could talk the same as you or me.' Then, with another smile at her young visitor who sat holding an egg in her hand as she listened, 'And like in all good romances, they married. He made a modest living from his paintings, she made delicious cakes and opened a tea room in their cottage. Not much money coming in, but I bet there was no happier couple.'

'Bar one,' Richard put in. 'Now then, lady, I'll start stacking the van, shall I? Butter and eggs, that's the lot for a Monday.' Then, to Deirdre,

53

'No one wants cream and mushrooms after the weekend, just bare essentials.'

Deirdre was at a loss to understand why Monday's shopping requirements should be different from any other, but instinct made her just nod in agreement with his remarks. It was suddenly important to her that this kindly, middle-aged couple liked her.

That was the first visit of many to Chagleigh. Soon she found herself working as hard as Naomi and Tessa. Skimming off the scalded cream to fill the cartons or transferring eggs from the wicker basket to the trays, first making sure none were cracked, she worked as fast as the others – and found satisfaction even greater than theirs in what she did.

At other times the two girls 'attacked the shops', something most of their contemporaries might take for granted. Of course there was no quick cure for Deirdre's moods of self-pity and depression, but her scowl appeared less frequently and usually she accepted the wheelchair as nothing more than an inconvenience when shop doorways were too narrow. She learnt to laugh – or perhaps more truthfully she forgot her misery and the smile she had given the world before her accident surfaced from where it had been buried deep in her resentment.

Except at lunchtime Tessa saw nothing of Julian Masters. His manner was always courteous but distant. Lunchtimes were very different at Fiddlers' Green from the chatty half hours spent around the table in Chagleigh Farm's kitchen. Although in the evening Deirdre and her father

54

dined alone, Miss Sherwin – and now Tessa, too – joined them for their midday meal and lively conversation was never on the menu.

'I was in Deremouth this morning,' he said as the maid disappeared, leaving Miss Sherwin to ladle the soup from the tureen, 'in Houghton and Parkes. You know the shop I expect, Tessa?'

'Yes, I do. But I've not lived here very much longer than you have, and until Deirdre and I started exploring I hadn't really known the town. It's a long way to cycle unless there's some special reason.'

'Ah, yes. It seemed to me a very good shop. An outfitting department for ladies on the first floor and a good-sized lift. Deirdre, my dear, it's quite time you took over the choosing of your own clothes. Let Tessa be your guide and find yourself some pretty things to wear, humph?'

If he'd made such a suggestion a month or so previously, it would have been met with a sulky glare and shrug of her shoulders. Now, though, Deirdre turned to him, her eyes shining with pleasure.

'Gosh, Daddy, thank you! How much am I allowed to spend?'

'Just find things you like and spend whatever is necessary. I have opened an account and arranged that you may use it. So you have a free hand.'

'Gosh! Let's go this afternoon Tessa. Gosh!'

That afternoon proved a milestone. With various items to try, Tessa wheeled the chair into a cubicle and even though Deirdre had to be content with fitting what she could while she was sitting, they had a lot of fun. By the time she wheeled the chair up the ramp and secured it, the passenger front seat was piled with parcels.

It was when they returned to Fiddlers' Green that Tessa saw a car following them up the drive. 'It seems you have a visitor,' Tessa said, looking in the driving mirror. 'A green sports car.'

'That'll be Giles. He must be back from London. Giles Lampton – he writes books.'

'*The* Giles Lampton?' If Deirdre had said the visitor was St Peter himself Tessa wouldn't have been more impressed. 'Have you read his books? You know what? I got one out of the library when I came home from school – came home for good, I mean, when I left school. It wasn't a just-published book; it was the first of the series about Burghton village and the people there. I felt as if I knew each one of them. After that I bought all nine of the series. Have you read them?'

'I don't read much. Daddy was always going on at me that I ought to spend my time reading. I suppose he meant because I couldn't do proper things like other people. That's what put me off.'

'That's a pity. I love to lose myself in a book, even if the only time there is has to be in bed at night. Is he a friend of your father's?'

By this time they had parked the car and Tessa was getting out ready to fix the ramp.

'I suppose he must be. He sort of comes

56

casually as if he belongs to the family; he always has. Shh! He's coming over. Don't let's be talking about him.'

Living with her grandmother, Tessa's had never considered her life to be different from other girls' of her age. For many of them, trips to the cinema were responsible for the first stirrings of adolescent dreams; pictures carefully cut from movie magazines were pinned to bedroom walls. But not for Tessa. Working in the hotel meant she wasn't free in the evenings so what more natural than she should look for friendship in books? And of all the books she had read, none had become part of her life as those about the people of Burghton. And now she was about to meet their creator!

'Let me do that for you.' She heard his voice as she was opening the back doors of the hybrid, a beautiful voice just as she'd known it would be. She was almost frightened to look at him for fear that the picture she had built in her mind would be shattered. 'I'm quite adept at it, aren't I, Deirdre? I'll get you out and then you can introduce me to your friend.'

'She's Tessa.'

'Ah.' With the chair wheeled down the ramp to the ground, he turned and held out his hand. 'How do you do, Tessa. I'm Giles.'

'Yes, I know. You're Giles Lampton.' She found herself gazing at him in awe. 'Deirdre told me. You're like I expected.' And she believed she spoke the truth as she gazed at the creator of Burghton, the place she knew so well. He was tallish, slim and yet he gave the impression of strength, his brown hair was neither straight nor curly. But it was his eyes that seemed to hypnotize her, light blue and fringed with dark lashes, she felt they saw right through her.

Giles laughed. 'What did she tell you then?'

'I mean, I didn't know what you would look like. I'd never thought about it. But because I know the characters in your books: Chilvers from the bakery, Reverend Maidment and the family at the rectory, Percy the milkman and his wife Margot, all of them, because I know them as if they're family really, it's as if I know *you*, too.'

All the time she'd been speaking he had still held on to her hand.

'That's the nicest thing you can say to any writer.' What a delightful creature she was, he thought, aware that he was the object of her adolescent hero worship and enjoying the situation. He came in for plenty of flattery from the opposite sex and accepted it for what it was worth. But this girl was different. Despite her confident manner, she still had the innocence of childhood about her. And those luminous dark eyes refused to keep the secret of her innermost thoughts.

'Daddy is at the dentist's,' Deirdre was saying. 'But you can come in and have tea with Tessa and me if you like.'

And 'like' he most certainly did, meaning to milk Tessa for all the adulation she was willing to shower on him.

Much later, driving back to his cottage on the edge of Downing Wood he felt less certain. Yes, the adulation had been there, there was no doubt of that; what he hadn't been prepared for was a strange and unfamiliar feeling. Tenderness? Yes, but not the sort of tolerant tenderness, probably tinged with humour at the situation, that might be felt for a hero-worshipping youngster. And that's what she is, he reminded himself. I'm old enough to be her father. Remember the natural way she walked on those ridiculously high heels: straight-backed, seemingly unaware that she'd been bestowed with such natural grace. Smartly dressed in a suit with a tight-fitting straight skirt that had made him conscious of the slight movement of her bottom with each step. Fortunately for Giles there was almost no traffic on the country road, for his thoughts refused to be kept in check. Slender legs, legs right up to that provocatively moving bottom. His journey nearly over, he crossed the main Exeter-to-Torquay road and took the lane on the western side of the Dere estuary leading to Otterton St Giles, but before he reached the village he turned up a track to the right and there on the edge of Downing Wood was Hideaway Cottage, his isolated retreat.

Next morning he went back to Fiddlers' Green.

'Have you two any plans for this promising-looking day? I thought I might take you to a pub I know on Dartmoor. Is your father in? Do I need his permission to run off with you both for the day?'

'He went early this morning to the works and won't be back until the end of the week; I'll just have to tell Miss Sherwin. Sounds nice, Giles. I'll go and tell her now.' As Deirdre spoke she was turning her chair to propel herself back indoors.

Face-to-face with Tessa, Giles lost some of his usual confidence; the memory of the way she had haunted his evening seemed to hang between them.

'You said you wanted to take us. But Mr Lampton—'

'We established yesterday that my name is Giles. I realize what you're going to say: her chair won't go in my car. And you're right. It means the converted job that you drive.' Then with a teasing smile, 'I'm not used to being driven. You'll take care of me, wont you?'

She nodded. 'I'll do my best. You could drive except that I don't think the insurance would cover us if you did. It used to be just for Mr Masters until I came and then he added me as a named driver. That's really why he engaged me, because he found he wanted Deirdre to go out more often. In the advert he said he wanted a carer-oblique-friend. Funny sort of job description, don't you think?'

'I'll bear it in mind for the time I'm tired of my own company.'

'But you never need to have just your own company. You have friends galore in Burghton.'

'I'll tell you a secret. They seemed all to shut their doors on me last evening. I went home intending to work, but it was your fault I couldn't. I kept hearing your voice telling me you knew each one of them as if they were part of your family. Does it sound crazy when I say I felt it was I who was the outsider?'

'Oh but that's silly. If it weren't for *you* they wouldn't be there at all. You make them live and breathe. *They are you.* That's really what I meant yesterday when I said I felt I knew you already.'

'Believe me, Tessa, the life I live is a far cry from the good folk of Burghton. Ah, here comes Deirdre all ready for our day of adventure.'

For some reason Tessa hadn't tried to fathom, she hadn't told Richard and Naomi about her meeting with Giles Lampton the previous day. She had wanted to hug it to herself, to relive each second. By the next evening, after their trip to Dartmoor she made herself talk about the outing, explaining that Giles was a family friend and it had been through him that Mr Masters had heard about Fiddlers' Green.

So without her actually saying so, the impression was given that Julian Masters and Giles were friends and contemporaries. That ought to steer them away from guessing her innermost thoughts.

The Deirdre of earlier days might have given more thought to the frequent visits of Giles Lampton to Fiddlers' Green. Not that she was particularly interested in him; she had known him all her life. Why he was a family friend she had no idea, for certainly he and her father didn't appear to have much in common. Perhaps it had been her mother who had brought him to the house in the first place; and at the thought Deirdre's expression showed her contempt. For, keen to shake off the ties of marriage and motherhood, Julian's wife had deserted him for a younger and wealthier man leaving him with a toddler. Deirdre had never been interested enough to wonder where Giles fitted into the picture any more than she wondered why, as winter took hold, his car was so often parked in the drive.

Then, towards the end of the January, she glanced out of her bedroom window and there he and Tessa stood talking. What was so strange about that? If she and Tessa were around when he visited, he always came to talk to them. Watching them now, she turned the wheels of her chair so that she was close enough to the casement window to open it and then move out of their vision in case they turned her way. So from where she was shielded by the curtain she strained her ears to hear what was being said.

'It's on the edge of Downing Wood, west side of the estuary. I want you to see it, Tessa. Please let me take you there.'

'We'd have to arrange a time so that you'd be in. I mean, there's no point in your coming to fetch us when I'd have to bring Deirdre in the hybrid.'

Deirdre willed him to speak loudly enough for her to hear. Why did he want to take them to this Downing Wood place? Then she wished she hadn't listened.

'It's *you* I want to see the cottage. What time do you finish here?'

'At six o'clock. I'll have to go home with my bike. Don't call for me – I'll meet you at the end of the lane at, say, half past six.' Tessa's spontaneous reaction was to say nothing to Richard and Naomi; the evening ahead was too wonderful to be idly enquired about.

But Giles misjudged the reason for the secrecy and laughed, putting his hand on her shoulder then moving it to the back of her neck and gently ruffling her short hair.

'Funny girl. Are you frightened your family wouldn't approve of your visiting a lonely bachelor's cottage? You'll be quite safe. We shall eat dinner together.'

It was the teasing note in his voice that made her embarrassed and prevented her finding a quick retort. She felt gauche and was uncomfortably conscious of the difference between his life and her own, and sure that he must be able to see into her mind. If only she were older, more worldly – more like the women he was probably used to entertaining in his flat in London.

Her only defence was to answer him coolly. 'If you'd like to meet my aunt and uncle of course you can call for me at the farm. But it's a rough, narrow lane; I thought it would be easier for you to meet me on the proper road.' Even though she heard it as a lame excuse, she forced herself to speak calmly, sounding as if the whole incident were of no importance. He listened with his eyebrows slightly raised.

'Not this evening. Next time, perhaps. Tonight we'll have a secret assignation. I'll pick you up at the corner of the lane at half past six. That should give you time to get home and give them some plausible reason for going out.'

Tessa clutched at the words 'next time', her

hard-fought-for coolness lost and her eyes telling him more than any words.

Listening, Deirdre scowled. Her former jaundiced view of life must have been waiting just below the surface. The idea of going to the cottage hadn't held much appeal, but hearing what Giles had said was a reminder, as if she needed one, of how different she was from other girls. She moved away from her listening post just as Miss Sherwin came into the room.

'You still in here, child? I thought you and Tessa were going to take a ride out. If you don't get a move on the daylight will be fading.'

'She's busy hanging around Giles Lampton. Haven't you seen the way she looks at him?'

'Then she's sillier than I gave her credit for. She'll bite off more than she can chew with that one. He's a regular Casanova – and Tessa's nought but a child.'

'She's nearly twenty.'

'It's not the number of years that count; it's whether or not you hang on to the trust and innocence you had as a child. It's my guess young Tessa has never been pushed into the rough and tumble. Well, let's hope Giles Lampton soon loses interest in the Devon countryside and takes himself off back to London. I'm not stupid and I've watched that young man for years enough – well, he was no more than a lad when first I knew him when you were a babe in arms. And I tell you, I'd not mind a five-pound note for every woman he's kept dancing attendance on him. Keen as mustard some of them; silly creatures. Give a man a bit of success – and he's had more than his share of that – and they're all over him. Now then Deirdre, before I help you into your coat I'll just take you along to the bathroom. By then I dare say Tessa will have brought the car round to the door.'

Promptly at half past six Tessa hurried up the lane to the road where she could see his car waiting.

'They let you out?' he greeted her in that same teasing note.

'How do you mean, let me out? I told them you asked me out to dinner,' she answered in a voice aimed at showing she was mistress of her own destiny. Then, that established, she settled in the passenger seat prepared for what she thought of as a magic evening. In her mind's eye she saw a country cottage, tastefully and elegantly furnished, a log fire burning in the open grate, a faithful retainer bringing a tray of food to the table. She imagined Giles taking her to his study and perhaps even showing her the work he was doing on this latest book about the people of Burghton. In her wildest and very private dreams she imagined him falling in love with her – but such were the dreams of many an adolescent whose head was filled with thoughts of some hero of screen or literature. Tessa allowed herself to dream, but even when at the end of the day she was in her own warm bed and cut off from the world, as she let her thoughts carry her where they would, she had no illusions. Dreams and reality were poles apart and she knew that was how they would remain. But on that evening reality was carrying her across the border; in a few minutes she would be warming herself by that great open fire, letting the atmosphere and elegance of his country retreat paint a lasting picture on her mind.

The evening was a milestone and there would be no turning back.

Three

Reaching the main road, they turned to the left then, instead of continuing over the long bridge that crossed the Dere Estuary, Giles took a turning to the right towards Otterton St Giles. Before they reached the village he again turned right into a narrow lane, the dark night made even darker by the trees of Downing Wood.

'There's only just enough width for the car. Are there any passing places?' Tessa asked in a voice she hoped sounded politely curious enough to hide her wild excitement for the evening ahead.

'The track turns into a footpath, hardly that even once we get to Hideaway Cottage. Hideous name for it, even though it's very appropriate. The postman leaves my mail at the village post office; I have no telephone. When I want to work undisturbed, this is where I come. No visitors, and not even a wireless. A week here is worth a month in London. Sometimes with so much going on, it's hard to stay immersed in the atmosphere one is creating. So if it's only to be for a few weeks I come to Devon. In Spain I have a finca – a house in agricultural ground – but it's not worth driving all that way for just a few weeks.'

But it wasn't the seldom-visited house in Spain that interested her, it was what he'd said about the cottage: no visitors, no wireless. And yet he was bringing *her* there. Did he see her as different from an ordinary visitor?

'That's a contradiction in terms,' she laughed. 'What am I if not a visitor?'

'You? I am bringing you to my hideaway because I have imagined you there when I've been alone in the evenings. This evening we have to fend for ourselves, no silver service. Just a gas cooker. Are you still glad you've come?' There was a teasing note in his voice, almost as though she were still a child.

'I like cooking. When I lived on the island with Gran I always did the cooking on the days I wasn't working at the hotel.' A reminder to him that she had lived an adult life before she became carer-oblique-friend to Deirdre. 'Look! I can see a light through the trees.'

'I left the lamp on in the porch. We leave the car on this patch of scrub – there's no room for it in the garden. Nearer the truth, there's no garden; the woods are my garden. Out you hop.' Leaning across her he unlatched the door and pushed it open for her to get out. 'Wait there while I park, then I'll guide you around the puddles.' Once the lights from the car were out nothing pierced the darkness but the dull light from the porch. 'Now then,' Giles said as he walked unerringly to her side, 'there's a puddle just here, I'll steer you round it.' He had his arm around her shoulder; she wanted the moment to last forever.

Grow up, she told herself, what's the matter with you? You'll soon be twenty. At your age most girls have probably been out with men lots of times. But I never have, this is the very first time and he isn't like ordinary people, he isn't just *anybody*, he's Giles Lampton. Even now, in the light from the porch, he's still keeping his arm around me. Does that mean he feels like I do, so churned up with – with – with what? Love? But he can't be, not with *me*.

'You're miles away,' he said softly. 'What is it, sweet Tessa? Are you frightened that I've brought you here, just the two of us in the middle of the dark wood? Are you remembering all the wise warnings about being alone with strange men?'

'Of course I'm not frightened. And you're not a strange man. If you were I wouldn't be here with you. I'm really interested to see your cottage.'

He cupped her chin in his hand and raised her face. 'My cottage is merely an excuse to get you to myself for the evening,' he said in a voice that made it impossible for her to meet his gaze. Surely he must know how hard her heart was beating. But apparently he didn't, for when he spoke again those last wonderful words might have been a dream. 'Don't expect too much of it. It's a bit of a tip, really.' Then releasing his hold of her and taking a large key from under an empty upside-down plant pot, 'Although I did my best to tidy it before I came to meet you.'

'You needn't have done that. Honestly, I wouldn't have minded. Silly, isn't it, but if I went into a house belonging to another woman and found it a muddle I would mind. But it seems different for a man.'

He laughed as he ushered her inside and flicking his cigarette lighter held the flame so that he could see the box of matches left in readiness to light the oil lamps. 'A very proper sentiment,' he said with mock seriousness.

'I didn't mean that men have to be fussed over and waited on. I don't believe that at all. It's just that I expect they have different priorities. Actually Uncle Richard is very tidy, always puts his wellingtons properly side by side in the lobby, folds the newspaper, opens his envelopes with a blade, things like that. But I don't expect all men are like that. Are you?'

'I've never thought about it. Tell you what: I'll watch myself and let you know.'

She chuckled as she said, 'Silly!' That moment of self-awareness in the porch might never have happened. 'What a dear little house. And lamp-light is so much nicer than electricity, don't you think? So warm, sort of full of comfort.'

Watching her, Giles thought what a delightful child she was. Child? As unworldly as a child, certainly, yet there was something wise about her for all her naivety. A delightful child, he repeated silently, that's what she is and that's how I must think of her. In the glow of the hurricane lamp swinging from the hook in the porch he had felt he had seen into her secret soul. Don't be an ass, he told himself; you know damn well she has some sort of adolescent crush on you. What he hadn't expected was an emotion within himself, an unknown sensation. Right from the day he had first met her, often he'd found it hard to put the thought of her out of his head. It had come between him and his work, it had haunted him as he lay in bed unable to sleep, it had followed him into his dreams. There had been plenty of women in his life, women of his own sort, enjoying their sexuality. So why couldn't he put Tessa from his thoughts? What he felt for her was lust, unadulterated lust, he told himself repeatedly. If he were completely honest he had even let himself imagine how this evening might have turned imagination into reality. But he mustn't let that happen. Somewhere in the world there must be a young lad who would one day be her husband, who would awaken her dormant passion; for beneath her rather old-fashioned manner he instinctively knew there was passion, like a silent volcano waiting to erupt.

It took no more than seconds for these thoughts to chase across Giles' mind.

'There's no heating in the kitchen so you may prefer to keep your coat on while we organize supper. Steak, mushrooms, crusty bread. Not much of a feast to invite you to share – especially to share the cooking of it.'

'It sounds delicious and sharing getting it ready will be fun. I don't need my coat: the grill will keep me warm.' Then, watching him light the oil lamp that hung from a beam in the kitchen ceiling, 'But how come you have a gas cooker?'

'It's bottle gas. A pipe comes in through the wall. A chap comes every month and changes the bottle. Not that I'm here that often and when I am I don't bother with much cooking if I'm working so the one he takes away is never empty – sometimes it won't have been used at all. But

71

if I altered the arrangement I might find I'd have to fix it myself.'

'I don't expect it's very complicated.'

He shrugged his shoulders. 'Not to some folk, I dare say. Anyway, I've no intention of finding out.'

To some people his approach to a simple task might have lost him respect, but to love-struck Tessa it was yet another example of how removed he was from the world of lesser men.

'Do you know about grilling?' she asked. 'Or would you rather I did the steak and you peeled the mushrooms and fried them?'

'Steak I can do. The frying pan is in that cupboard and you'll find oil on the end of the bench. How do you like your steak? I have mine a bit charred on the outside and very rare in the middle. But you can have it as you prefer. My cooking talents are limited but I can cook steak to perfection.'

'Do mine the same as yours. But let me get going first, or give me a hand peeling the mushrooms.'

'OK, that's the best plan. Let me pour us a glass of wine while we're slaving at the hot stove.'

Often enough Tessa prepared meals at Chagleigh Farm just as when she hadn't been working at the hotel she had cooked for her grandmother and herself, but never had she experienced an atmosphere as there was in the tiny kitchen of Hideaway Cottage. She noticed that when her wine glass was half empty Giles topped it up, just as he did his own. Was that why she had such a warm, *complete* sort of feeling, as if all her life had been leading to this moment? But her feet hadn't quite left the ground and when she saw Giles coming towards her glass with the bottle for yet another top up, she shook her head.

'You go ahead, but don't give me any more. You see, at home – on the island, I mean – Gran and I only drank wine with our meal at Christmas, Easter and birthdays. I hadn't thought about it, but I don't think they ever have it with meals at the farm. So I mustn't let you take me home tiddly! Gosh, doesn't this smell *good*! Lunch feels like hours ago. Shall I cut some hunks of this crusty bread?'

A couple of minutes later she carried their glasses as he led the way with the tray of food. The lamplit living room, the warmth of the flickering flames of the burning logs, the none-too-neatly-folded morning paper on the couch left there as if confirmation that Giles hadn't a natural eye for tidiness despite the effort he said he had made in readiness for her visit, all of it added to an atmosphere Tessa felt to be perfect.

'It's a lovely cottage. But, do you know, it isn't a bit the kind of home I expected you to have,' she said as she waited while he carried a small gate-leg table topped by the tray of food to the fireside.

'And what sort of a home would that be?' he asked, his tone making her feel childish and out of her depth.

'I don't know that I'd really given it any thought,' she answered, determined not to give a hint of the hours of each day when he filled her mind. 'I suppose modern, perhaps a service flat. This is homely, the sort of place that makes you want to kick off your shoes and curl up on the sofa.'

'What a delightful idea. Perhaps we'll try it after we've eaten our supper. More wine?'

About to refuse, she remembered her effort to appear sophisticated. 'Thank you. The result of our labour deserves wine.' But she must keep control of herself. How much wine would it take to make her 'tiddly'? She had an uncomfortable feeling that Giles could read her thoughts. 'After we've eaten and cleared up the mess, will you show me your workroom?' Then with a chuckle that escaped before she could hold it back, 'It's the sort of maternity ward for all my friends in Burghton.'

'Labour ward might be the more accurate description. Yes, if you want to see it. But I fear my clearing up didn't stretch that far.'

But when, the meal eaten and the dishes washed, he opened the door leading off the living room and ushered her into what she thought of as his private sanctum, she was disappointed. It was surprisingly tidy, no papers left around, nothing to show that this was where the inhabitants of Burghton saw the light of day. The typewriter was covered and by its side a machine she couldn't identify.

'Where do you keep what you type? The room looks as though no one uses it.' She couldn't keep the disappointment from her tone.

'The good folk of Burghton are safe in the top draw. And that, I'm afraid, is how things will be for a while. Someone from Deremouth cycles

74

over to do my typing. I dictate on to this machine and leave it for her. Mrs Johnson has been very reliable, until this last week she's never let me down. She lost her husband a year or so ago and must have quite a struggle to bring up their four children on her own. Now one of the brood has gone down with measles, no doubt to be followed in quick succession by the other three. So until she can come back I have no typist.'

How could she keep the admiration out of her gaze as she looked at him? A man of national repute – national and international, she corrected herself – and yet he made no mention of getting rid of this Mrs Johnson and engaging a replacement; already Tessa had held him on a pedestal, but what he said raised him even higher.

'I have an idea,' she said, speaking even as it formed. 'If you don't want to engage a proper typist – and I think it's splendid that you'd rather wait for this Mrs Johnson, who must need the work – what about if I keep your work up to date?'

'You? But I thought you were a carer-oblique-friend to Deirdre. What time do you have to take on an extra job?'

'This wouldn't be a job. Don't you see? I know Burghton as if I lived there. I told you, the folk there are like family. When I was at school I wasn't in the really clever set – just ordinary and average. So when for the last year the really bright ones did extra maths and languages, all that sort of thing, I was with the lot who did more practical things. Typing was one of my choices. Just like in the sewing classes, some

75

chose to do embroidery, but I preferred dress-making. Then at the hotel, although they called me deputy manager, I was really a general dogs-body and I did most of the typing. I wouldn't be as fast as your lady from Deremouth, at least not at first, but I would save there being such a mass for her to catch up with, don't you see?' Imagine if she could end each day listening to his voice. 'Please say I can do it. I'm quite careful, I don't make lots of mistakes.' She was conscious that he was watching her closely; if only she knew what was going on in his mind. Perhaps he thought she had an awful cheek and was wondering how he could refuse her offer without hurting her feelings. After all, a proper professional typist would work so much more quickly than she could. Had she spoilt the evening by suggesting it? But imagine hearing stories of the lives of the people from Burghton spoken in his voice, spoken just as he thought of them. He *must* say she could do it.

'And what do you think your uncle and aunt will have to say about it? But Tessa, you would be doing me a great favour; that I can't deny. I've had dealings with the agency in Deremouth in the past: once they sent me a girl who was frightened of the solitude down here and I'm sure, on the occasions when I stayed in the house, expected I would try to rape her. Then, the second time they sent a middle-aged woman, a good typist once she got started, but she never stopped talking. You're different, I suppose because you know the characters already. But it's out of the question that after you finish work with Deirdre

76

you cycle over here in the dark and come to what would often be an empty house. No, I can't let you do that. And, as I say, I'm often out in the evenings.' Yet she could tell from his expression as he looked at her that he hadn't quite put the idea out of his mind. 'I look on you as a friend. Friendship and business don't go hand in hand.'

Tessa looked at him squarely, frightened that her hero might have feet of clay.

'You don't have to waltz around the point,' she said, ashamed of her hostile tone. 'If you don't think I'd be quick enough, or type well enough, I'd much rather you just came out with it. I don't make scenes if I don't get my own way. I suppose I just felt that if I typed what you dictated it would make me part of the book. Silly of me.'

'Not silly at all, except that I'm sure your aunt and uncle would worry to have you here alone on these dark winter evenings. If you want to take on extra work, then what I pay Mrs—'

'I'm not looking for a job and if you talk about paying me, then forget the suggestion.'

'I don't want to forget the suggestion. I like the idea that you should be involved. Now how about this for an idea . . .'

And so it was that when he delivered Tessa back to the farm he drove along the narrow lane right to the gate, then went in with her to meet Naomi and Richard. There was nothing in the manner of their greeting to suggest just how different he was from the picture they'd formed of him. Tessa had implied he was a friend of Mr Masters, someone probably Richard's age. Giles was forty, good looking in a rugged way and

77

with a voice that was evidence of an expensive education. Naomi had borrowed the first of the Burghton series from Tessa's collection and made time to read it. This wasn't at all the sort of man she had envisaged. The writer had the gift of taking the reader into the psyche of each character, every one of them different and yet the whole bringing to life a mixed community that was utterly believable. And this man? He might bury himself in Downing Wood to escape the hubbub of town life, but he struck her as very much part of the modern post-war world.

'Before I accept Tessa's kind offer to help me I want to be sure it has your approval,' he said with a warm and friendly smile at Richard and Naomi. Then, having gone through an explanation of the plight of his usual typist, he rested a hand on Tessa's shoulder as he said, 'Instead of reading in bed as she says is her habit, this work-thirsty niece of yours has offered to spend the last hour of the day typing up what I have been recording. Sometimes there will be nothing, and sometimes more than she can do in one end-of-day hour.'

'I shall enjoy it. It'll be even better than reading the book to feel that I had a hand in its preparation. And it'll be good for me to have some typing practise.'

'But you haven't a typewriter,' Richard objected.

'Everything's in the car, Uncle Richard. Giles insisted that was where it all stayed until he was sure you and Aunt Naomi thought it was a good idea.'

'We're not your gaolers, my dear. It'll only be

until measles has run its course so the late nights won't hurt you as long as you're sure your typing will be up to the job.'

Tessa felt she stood outside herself looking at the scene. Giles Lampton actually here in the kitchen of Chagleigh Farm, then he and Uncle Richard going outside to the car to fetch the things she would need and carrying them up to her bedroom. The thought of Giles in her bedroom was both exciting and embarrassing; he would be bound to notice that between two bookends on her bedside cabinet she kept her treasured collection of all nine volumes of the Burghton series. The thought of it seemed to tell him her most private thoughts. She felt gauche, frightened to look at him as he and Richard came down the stairs, expecting to be met with that teasing expression, his brows raised, his eyes leaving her in no doubt.

'I'm eternally grateful to you, Tessa. There is enough there to keep you busy for a night or two. After that, Mrs Pilbeam, perhaps I could occasionally drop off some dictation while this poor child is with Deirdre. If you find it too much, Tessa, you promise me you'll tell me. I look in at Fiddlers' Green most days.'

Tessa nodded, smarting under the description 'poor child'. 'Naturally, but really it's no trouble and good for me to get some typing practise.'

'Well, thank you, anyway. Let's hope the rest of Mrs Johnson's brood don't get measles, then she should be back in a week or so.'

Not without a feeling of guilt, Tessa hoped the germ would spread.

After he'd gone she expected either Richard or Naomi would be sure to refer to her rush to get out for the evening. Fate was on her side though; it seemed they were satisfied that she had been occupied with something which involved Fiddlers' Green where they knew Giles was a frequent visitor. And so started her first night of sitting at her dressing table, listening to his voice and typing his words. A little older, a little more worldly, and the magic of it might not have been so intense.

Next morning Deirdre wanted to sort her clothes and put aside anything she was discarding to be taken to the church jumble sale. While she sat in her chair deciding which pile each item should be put in, what more natural than Tessa should tell her about the typing arrangement?

Immediately Deirdre's easy, friendly manner vanished to be replaced by the old tight-lipped, angry expression. 'You think he's the cat's whiskers. I know you do. Every time he comes in I can feel it – and I bet he can too. Has he tried any hanky-panky with you yet?'

'What a funny thing to say! Hanky-panky? Of course he hasn't. Anyway he didn't ask me to do his typing, I offered. I don't want my typing to get rusty; I don't know what I might need in my next job.' It was hitting below the belt and she knew it. As soon as she'd spoken she wished she could withdraw her words.

'If you're any good he might give the Deremouth woman the push and take you on full time. He can see you've got a crush on him and he fancies you; I've seen the way he watches you sometimes. But don't be a sucker, Tessa; he's had years of practise. Mind he doesn't try and have it away with you.'

'Where in the world do you pick up your expressions?' Tessa said with a laugh, hoping to steer the subject away from what she didn't want to hear.

'I wasn't always stuck in this blasted chair. I had some good times. Dad was wrapped up with the business when I first left school and it was easy enough to pull the wool over Miss Sherwin's eyes. I had a lot of friends. Bet I've done more with my life than you ever did with yours, living with a grandmother.'

'Maybe. Now what about this jumper? It's cashmere. You ought to keep it.'

'OK, if you say so. But I was telling you about Giles. Miss Sherwin used to chatter a lot to me about him. She doesn't like him, that's for sure. Perhaps there was something between him and my rotten mother. They must have been two of a kind.'

'But if that's true, why does your father give him the run of the place like he does?'

'Search me, I don't know. I don't even know if there was really anything going on between them – can't remember back that far. She must have been horrid – and stupid. She went off with some stinking rich American before the war started. Miss Sherwin saw it all. Giles served in the navy. I don't remember any of it, except that when he was on leave he used to stay with us. Well, he stayed with us unless he had any more inviting bed to sleep in. Poor old Giles, stuck on a ship with only chaps. When I was a kid, say fifteen or sixteen, I used to look forward to when he came. You remember how, at that sort of on-the-brink age you want to find out about all this sex business. I instinctively knew it wouldn't be wasted on him if I sort of flaunted myself. Miss Sherwin kept an eye. If he'd tried anything on, she'd have pounced.'

'What does it matter to us if he likes the ladies?' And of course that was true, Tessa told herself as she made sure her tone gave nothing away. 'He's old enough to be our father. Anyway, I'm glad to be able to do his typing until his regular typist is able to start work again. He's going to bring his recordings to the farm and collect what I've done while I'm here each day. You don't want this blouse, do you? I've never seen you wear it.'

'Crumbs, no. I shouldn't think even at the jumble sale anyone would want it. Miss Sherwin chose it for me before the accident and couldn't understand why I hated it. I was sixteen and longing to look as glam as Betty Grable.' Deirdre went back to talking about those halcyon years between leaving school and her accident. Tessa suspected that some of the tales of parties and near seductions were exaggerations of the truth, but she looked with real affection at the pretty girl imprisoned in her chair.

All the Johnson children went down with measles so for the next month most of Tessa's days ended with the sound of Giles' voice. But there were others when he brought no work, instead collected what she had ready for him and, with courtesy that earned him Naomi's and Richard's respect, asked them if they would agree to his suggesting to Tessa he might take her out to dinner. Soon she would be twenty, quite old enough not to ask permission, but they appreciated what they considered to be his old-world charm.

Tessa was in seventh heaven. Giles filled her every thought and he would have to have been blind not to realize it. She was a delight to be with. He enjoyed her open adulation; when he read her silent message, almost begging him to love her, he prided himself on having the will-power that stopped him taking advantage of her naivety. Tessa had no idea what went on in his mind and imagination. Early in April, leaving enough dictation to keep Tessa busy for two or three weeks, he returned to London to see his publisher – and to get back into the merry-go-round of living. He had plenty of friends, both male and female; it was crazy to hang around in Devon because of a young girl with her head full of dreams and no experience of reality. So he told himself. And there were times when he believed he had succeeded in putting her out of his mind. His friends were in many walks of life, and it would have surprised Tessa if she could have listened to the discussions he had with some of his more serious-minded acquaintances. She believed the man she knew was the *whole* man but the truth was more complex.

Try as he would, the vision of her was never far below the surface. In an attempt to put her out of his mind he would take one or other of his willing acquaintances to dine, to dance and home, either to his apartment or to hers, both of them anticipating they would have the whole night before them. This was the way he wanted his life; this was the way it had been for years, neither ties nor responsibilities making demands on him. When Tessa pushed herself to the forefront of his thoughts there was one truth that wouldn't be ignored: he wanted her, he wanted to be the first man to show her the wonder that could be found in natural, uninhibited sex. But what was she but a sweet, adoring child? Did she have the slightest idea of what was in his imagination? Not for the first time he likened her to a volcano waiting to erupt, unaware of the passion that waited to be awakened. That inner voice whispered to him of the joy there would be in teaching her how to use her body, hers and his, too. He made no contact with her while he was away, nor yet with Julian Masters. Tessa was secretly disappointed when on her twentieth birthday there was no word from him; but reason told her that he probably didn't know the date and, even if he did, to contact her would be because she had let it be so obvious how much he meant to her. A birthday message belonged to her dreams and it was high time she faced reality.

Then, in the second week of May he returned to Devon, stopping at Chagleigh Farm on his way to Hideaway Cottage to collect any typing Tessa had been saving ready for him. A few minutes chat with Naomi and Richard, then as he put the folder of typing on to the passenger

84

seat of the car and prepared to leave, as if it were an afterthought, he said, 'If she has nothing better to do this evening, how about if I collect her and take her out to eat? She has been remarkably good over all the hours she must have spent typing up my dictation.'

'I can answer for her,' Naomi replied. 'She'll be thrilled. What time shall I tell her? About seven? That'll give her time to pretty herself up.'

If he could have heard the remarks between Richard and Naomi as the sound of his car grew fainter, he would have been reassured.

'Young Tessa mustn't spend her life being a companion to Deirdre Masters,' Richard said thoughtfully. 'There's no future in it for her and what chance will she have of meeting anyone? Even Lampton, he's a good enough chap, but how can he lead her to meet young men?'

'Is that the chauvinist in you talking?' Naomi teased.

'It's the realist. Can you see Tessa happy with no husband? She may like to feel she's inde-pendent, but she's no career girl. I do worry about her in her present job; there's no future for her there.'

'Working at Fiddlers' Green is better for her than working here with us, although I do miss having her around. I'll give you a hand with the afternoon milking if you like, shall I?' Then, thinking back to where their conversation had started, 'Anyway, it was caring for Deirdre that put her in touch with Giles Lampton.'

'Hardly the same thing as a young man she might share her future with. He's a sound fellow though, and all this typing has been good practise for her. Come on, love, let's go and drive our old ladies into the milking shed.'

'Where would you like to go? Deremouth? Exeter? Or would you rather we looked for a country pub with food?' Giles asked as he held the door open for her to get into the car. She didn't answer immediately so he walked round to his side and got into the driver's seat. 'Still thinking?'

'Let's just go home and do something for ourselves.' Until she'd arrived back at the farm from Fiddlers' Green she had imagined him still to be in London and here she was, dressed in her new dirndl skirt and the blouse she had bought at the same time because the pale green of the silk was exactly right with it. All that, and an evening with Giles. No matter how she tried to compose her face, it insisted on smiling.

'Then I hope you aren't hungry. Don't forget I've been away. Milk, bread, cheese and a tin of soup, that's the extent of the shopping I did.'

'I expect it's silly, but I've missed the cottage. I just want us to be there again.'

He took her hand and raised it to caress it with his cheek as he drove. 'Do you?' And there was something in his tone she'd never heard before. 'Do you, sweet Tessa? Yes, we'll go home. You can make us a jug of coffee, and later we'll go to Deremouth and buy fish and chips. How does that appeal? It's not too cold, we'll eat them in the traditional way straight from their newspaper wrapping. I've missed you and your simple delights.'

And when she didn't answer, 'You're supposed to tell me that you've missed me, too.'

'Oh, but I have. Every morning I hoped it would be the day that Deirdre would say you'd phoned them to tell them you were back. Then every evening when I got home I hoped Aunt Naomi would say you'd collected the typing. Then, today, she did.'

It wasn't until he'd turned into the narrow lane to the cottage that he spoke again. 'I'd told myself I wouldn't bring you here again,' he said, looking straight ahead of him. Yet without turning to her he could sense her hurt. 'It's no use, Tessa, the thing you want, the thing I want. You are just twenty, I'm twice your age and lost the innocence of youth more years ago than I can remember.' Making a turn into the area of scrub near the cottage, he switched off the engine and turned to her. 'What do you think brought me back from London? You did, you precious child. I couldn't get you out of my mind. Never a moment when you weren't there.'

'I thought of you all the time, too. I kept imagining what you were doing; I pictured you with glamorous women, sophisticated, successful, lots to talk about. How could I expect you would want to come back to Devon and me?'

Holding her under the chin, he raised her face looking directly at her and willing her to meet his gaze. What she read in his eyes banished every coherent thought from her as her lips parted knowing that he would move closer, then feeling his mouth cover hers. 'Damn this gear stick,' he muttered, barely moving away from her.

'Let's go indoors,' she whispered. Yet she couldn't bring herself to move away from him. She moved her fingers through his wavy hair, caressing the nape of his neck.

'Indoors.' He spoke with mock authority, his tone telling her that moving away from him and getting out of the car was taking her nearer to – to what? As happened to her so often when she was with Giles, she felt gauche and uncertain; and yet she longed to get into the cottage, alone with him. Was he saying he was in love with her? Of course he was, hadn't he told her it was thoughts of her that had brought him back?

Once inside the cottage he closed the front door, then standing behind her with his hands on her shoulders, leant against it, pulling her nearer. 'You said, "Let's just go home". And here we are – home.' It seemed to her that his voice was a caress.

Lowering his hands from her shoulders, he cupped her breasts in his palms. Could this really be happening to her? He sensed the change in her breathing – shallow, quick breaths as she moved into realms unknown. Although it was only May the day had been warm and coming out in the evening she had thrown her cardigan on to the back seat of the car. Under the silk of her new blouse there was nothing except a satin bra. She closed her eyes, leaning against him as the movement of his thumbs worked its magic. 'Giles. Giles,' she whispered so softly it was hardly a sound at all, 'never knew . . . want . . . want . . .' But she hardly knew what it was she yearned for, only that she was being lifted away from all coherent thought and longing for something just out of her reach.

'You want . . . I want . . . but we can't Tessa, not here, not like this in some stolen furtive few moments.'

'It couldn't be furtive, not if we love each other.' She turned towards him, her arms tightly gripping him, her body pressed against his. 'You want, I want . . . I've never felt like this, sort of tingly all over my body. Is that what happens when people make love?'

'We could find paradise together, you and me. And we will, my blessed Tessa.' He moved his chin against her head. 'But when we make love I want us to go to sleep in each other's arms and to wake to a new day, and to love again, again and again.'

'I want that too, but . . . but . . . now . . .' Taking his hand she drew it again to her breast, longing for what she had felt before and yet half frightened of the sensation she couldn't control.

'Tessa, no. We shouldn't have come here. I could pick you up and carry you to my bed. God knows it's what I want. I want to bring your beautiful body alive. I want to be the man who teaches you the joy of loving. But not here, not like this.'

'Now – this year – next year – and *always* – it has to be you. I could never be with any man but you.'

Giles held her away from him, looking at her in the fading light inside the low-ceilinged cottage. Outside it would be an hour before dusk but here, surrounded by trees, night was already falling. If Tessa had experienced a sensation new to her, it was one born of nature; what Giles felt as he looked at her was something he had never before experienced. She was so young, so untouched, her eyes shining with love, her body silently crying out for him to satisfy the hunger he had aroused in her. It had never been in his character to let himself be steered off course, so what was different with Tessa? Forty years old, a confirmed bachelor, could it be that he had fallen in love? He seemed to stand outside himself as he heard himself reply to her.

'This year – next year – always . . .' Raising her face to his, tenderly he kissed her forehead. 'But this isn't the time or the place. We'll go away. Take a holiday, even a week. You haven't made arrangements yet, have you?'

'No. But Giles, can you imagine Uncle Richard giving his blessing for us to go off together? Even if we tell him we mean to always be together. He'd say I can't marry until I'm twenty-one. You see, they don't guess how I feel about you, and they suppose you think of me as just someone who works for an old friend of yours.'

'So I imagined. I'm not asking his permission. We'll put all that aside until you've had your twenty-first and can make your own decisions. Tell them you're going on a walking holiday with some friend or other. That won't surprise them, you've done it before.' Then with a satisfied smile, 'And am I not your friend? We shall go for walks, perhaps in North Wales. How would that be?'

'You mean stay together, properly stay together?'

'Didn't I say I wanted to go to sleep holding you, and wake up loving you all over again?' he said softly. Then, as if casting the mood off, 'Now then, Tessa, my sweet, we'll forget that coffee and go straight to Deremouth. Cod and chips for two, how's that?'

She nodded. 'Perfect,' she assured him. 'So perfect I'm almost too frightened to think about it.'

'Such a funny child,' he said with false mockery, 'starry-eyed at the thought of cod eaten from newspaper.'

In fact, even though he said it to tease her, he wasn't far from the truth. The thought of sitting on the sea wall with her newspaper packet of supper was the perfect way to celebrate the joy that was almost too much to bear. A smart restaurant, a meal with wine or even champagne, would have emphasized the difference between her life and Giles'. *Al fresco* cod and chips would be a new experience, probably for both of them.

And as if to put a blessing on where her life had brought her, without conscious thought on her part, she suddenly saw the image of her grandmother and seemed to hear her voice. 'Rejoice!' Oh, but she did rejoice. She never knew there could be such joy.

She had always believed that if anything was worth having it was worth fighting for. But the holiday plans fell into place like a perfectly cut jigsaw. Julian Masters immediately agreed to her taking a fortnight's holiday and neither Naomi nor Richard considered there was anything unusual in her planning to join Natalie Wells, her old school friend, just as they knew she had on previous occasions when she had lived with Gran. The only cloud came in the shape of Deirdre who, for one whole day, reverted to her earlier self, unsmiling, sarcastic, resentful and thoroughly sorry for herself.

Four

Giles met Tessa as she got off the bus in Exeter, stowed her case in the boot of the car and within minutes the city was behind them as they headed north.

'You're quiet. Are you having regrets?' he said, not turning to look at her as he drove.

She gave him a quick glance, but his expression told her nothing.

'How can I have regrets? It's just that I felt so mean not telling them the truth. I know I couldn't but I wish it had been different. If only I were a year older and we could have let everyone know how we feel. But I know you're right, Giles. It's just that I hate not being open. Uncle Richard insisted on carrying my case to the Exeter bus stop at the end of the lane. It made me feel wretched.'

'I wonder he didn't consider it heavy for someone intending to spend a holiday on the move.'

'I told them that Natalie was making the arrangements either in a B and B or at a youth hostel.'

She sensed a change in him – or was it her imagination?

'And where is this fictitious Natalie supposed to be meeting you?'

'I didn't make Natalie up. She's real. We were

93

best friends at school and since then we went away together twice when I was still living with Gran. I rang her up from the phone in the village and told her what I was doing. I had to be sure she didn't write or telephone while we were away.'

'You told her you were coming away with *me*?'

'Yes, of course I did. She's my best friend; of course I wanted her to know. Anyway, I hate deceit.'

There was very little traffic as he slowed the car to a stop by the grass verge, leaving the engine running.

'You hate lies and deceit and yet you say you have no regrets. That must be a lie.'

'It isn't! How can it be a lie?' Forgetting all of her intentions to behave in a calm, utterly adult way, she couldn't prevent the words rushing out. 'Coming away with you is like a miracle; I've thought about you every day and every night since we first met, but even when I let myself imagine something like what is happening to us, I always knew it was a dream, not part of real life – no more likely than going to visit the man on the moon.' She was frightened; she could feel the beat of her heart and heard the way her voice was rising. Something about him was different. 'Giles, what is it? What have I said? Is it that you're only here because you didn't want to disappoint me? If so, just put me out at the next railway station and I'll go home. I'll tell them that Natalie couldn't get away, I'll tell them—'

'I don't act out of fear of disappointing other people. You'll realize that when you know me better.' Yet his words did nothing to reassure her. The first magic of setting off on their journey had gone. 'You're such a child—'

'I'm *not!*' Then, hearing the dangerous croak in her voice, she shouted in defiance. 'I'm a woman! Lots of girls of my age are married and have babies. I'm not a child.'

'Dear, sweet Tessa. Age isn't just years. That you are twenty and I am twice that isn't what's important, it's what our lives have done to us. I'm *used, soiled* if you like; you are pure, honest, beautiful, full of dreams.'

'Full of nothing, that's what all that means. Full of dreams just means empty-headed. And I'm not! I know how I feel! I thought you knew, too. I thought it was the same for you. We're spoiling it all.'

'No, Tessa, nothing can spoil it. I will tell you something that I swear is God's truth: no woman has ever touched my heart as you do; no woman has ever filled my mind as you do and God knows why – it's not your intellect, it's not your worldliness. I didn't mean this to happen, didn't want it to happen. But the thought of your belonging to any other man but me is – is—'

His words drove away all her fears. Leaning towards him she put her arms around his neck. 'I could never belong to any man but you; it's as if I'm part of you. If you weren't here I – I just wouldn't be a whole person.'

He drew her close and just as her spirit had

plunged, now it soared. Then, releasing her with a sudden movement, he slipped the car into gear and they were on their way. It was as if the last ten minutes had been the dividing line between the past they had left behind and the future that awaited them.

At Marlhampton, Julian Masters stood at his study window watching Deirdre staring sullenly at nothing in particular as she sat in her wheel-chair. It was a long time since he had seen that expression on her face. He ought to load her into her vehicle and take her out somewhere, perhaps buy her lunch in a country pub. Yes, that's what he'd do. First he must finish looking at the monthly report from his factory in the Midlands.

He'd guessed it was the thought of a fortnight with no companionship of her age that had put such a sullen, discontented look on Deirdre's face. But the lack of companionship was only half of it. She felt hurt and rejected, imagining Tessa 'swanning off' with her girlfriend, walking the hills, laughing, running, doing all the things which were normal to everyone but to her. She wished Tessa had never come to Fiddlers' Green; without the months they had shared she would have been settled in her rut of misery not realizing how much fun was still out there for her if only she could get from one place to another. Aimlessly she manoeuvred her chair to face the other direction and started slowly across the lawn. With her back to the drive she didn't turn when she heard a car. Her first

96

thought was that it must be Giles, quickly followed by *He won't stay, not when he finds Tessa's on holiday.* Quick on the heels of that came another thought as she remembered he had said he was going to London and wouldn't be back in Devon for a few weeks.

'Deirdre!'

Her cares vanished as she recognized the voice. This time she turned remarkably deftly and with renewed energy started towards the parked van as quickly as she was able to turn the wheels of her chair.

Watching, Julian frowned, his protective instinct aroused at the sight of a stranger approaching his helpless daughter. He hurried from the study and in seconds was heading across the grass towards where he could see an animated conversation was going on.

'I don't think I've had the pleasure,' he said as he came within earshot, his tone making it clear that he felt no pleasure.

'No, we haven't met. You must be Mr Masters. I'm Naomi Pilbeam, Tessa's aunt – and Deirdre's friend.' Naomi held out her hand to him.

'Ah.' Hardly a sound at all as his manner relaxed and he took her hand in his. 'Deirdre has talked of you and of the pleasure she has had in trying to help you in your dairy. I'm glad of the chance to thank you.'

'I don't need to be thanked for doing something that gives me pleasure. I was just putting a suggestion to her. You tell him, Deirdre.'

How the girl had changed, he thought, looking at the bright smile she turned on him. Her eyes were shining with excitement, and her face held its smile as if it was the only way it knew how to be.

'Mrs Pilbeam has come to fetch me, Daddy. She says if I have nothing better to do – as if I might have – I can help her this afternoon. She says she can lift me into the proper seat in the van and put my contraption in the back. She says I can go back with her now and have lunch at the farm before we get down to work this afternoon.'

For the first time he looked at Naomi with interest. Until then all he had seen was a thin, middle-aged woman with a lined and weathered face, wearing clothes that had seen better days. Now he looked deeper and was aware of something he couldn't put a name to. It had to do with the direct way she looked at him when she spoke, and the soft, deep tone of her voice.

'She and I work very well together. A busy afternoon will turn into fun, won't it, Deirdre? I suppose I have a cheek coming to beg for a volunteer to help with the work.'

He raised his hand in a sign to stop her speaking as he answered, 'If she'd been able to get there, I think she would have volunteered first thing this morning. She's going to miss Tessa.'

'Richard – that's my husband – he and I are going to miss Tessa, too. But a fortnight will soon go. I'm afraid I shall need to bundle her into the van now if you say she can come. I've taken my morning delivery to the village, but there's still lunch to see to.'

'I'm all ready, Daddy, I don't need to go

indoors.' It was as if Deirdre feared that if they hesitated the wonderful opportunity would be lost.

'Then I'll lift you into the van and put the chair in the back,' Julian said. 'Will your husband help you at the other end?'

'Of course he will, if we need him. But Deirdre and I can manage most things without his help.'

Deirdre chuckled. 'Aunt Naomi and I are a working partnership.' At the farm it had felt natural for her to call the Pilbeams Auntie and Uncle just as Tessa did. The first time she had said it, it had slipped out by mistake, but when she'd opened her mouth to correct herself, Naomi had given her a broad smile and simply said, 'That's nice. Richard'll like it too.'

Now Deirdre's words weren't lost on either of the others. Taking the handles of the chair ready to push it to the van, Julian caught Naomi's eye, the 'Auntie Naomi' in both their minds. Naomi remembered hearing him spoken of as an aloof man, surely a man who would suppose she had suggested herself as an honorary aunt to gain favour. Instead as he pushed the chair, over the top of Deirdre's head just for a second, he held Naomi's gaze and mouthed the words 'Thank you'.

'What time do you workers expect to finish? I'll bring her car down and fetch her.'

'She's fine with us, so come when you like. If we've done our chores in the dairy, we'll occupy ourselves with something else.' And again that broad smile that spoke to him of contentment

99

with her lot. 'We bumble along from one thing to the next; there's no clocking on and off at Chagleigh.'

Julian noticed the admiration on Deirdre's face as she gazed at this newly acquired Aunt Naomi. But was it simply admiration? As the question sprang to mind, so too did the answer. And he was ashamed. How could he have let it happen that the daughter he loved could have felt herself so isolated that she turned to comparative strangers to bestow her affection? With Deirdre on the front passenger seat of the van and the wheelchair stowed where half an hour ago had been the daily deliveries, he put out a hand to hold Naomi back as she turned from closing the back doors.

'With Tessa away, are you sure she won't be an encumbrance?' he whispered.

'If I weren't sure, I wouldn't be here. I'll collect her again tomorrow unless she doesn't want to come. There's so much she can do there – and what better therapy than being useful?'

Then, her quick smile telling him that her mind had moved on, their brief association already faded into the past, she climbed into the van and switched on the engine. Julian Masters wasn't used to being brushed aside in that way; he didn't like it. Grateful though he was on Deirdre's account, he had no intention of being beholden to the Pilbeams. So as the van disappeared he took the hybrid and set out for Exeter.

That was how he came to buy Deirdre's electric wheelchair, her gateway to independence. They spent the evening in the garden while the 'learner driver' became accustomed to her new mode of transport. Miss Sherwin stood by, clucking in fear of the harm that could be lying in wait. With growing confidence, Deirdre became adept at handling her new acquisition, turning in circles first to the right, then to the left, braking suddenly, stopping and starting. Already he could picture the look on Naomi's face when she surprised them by arriving unaided and 'ready for work' in the morning.

Every emotion was heightened for Tessa. She wanted to cling to the glorious feeling that she was a woman in love, yet even as she thought it she knew she wasn't being honest. Of course she was in love, so much in love that she couldn't believe what was happening, that her idol wanted her as much as she wanted him. It was so wonderful that it was beyond the realms of possibility. But that silent voice that wouldn't be ignored reminded her that, although she was twenty, she was uncertain of what was ahead of her. She was going on a fortnight's holiday with the most wonderful man in the world; they would make love. But what would that be like? It must be wonderful; if it weren't it wouldn't be so important to people, they would just do what they needed to get children if they wanted them. Of course she knew all about what you had to do – she had discussed it many times with Natalie – and then there was that almost frightening feeling she'd had when Giles had done what he had when he'd been holding her breast. Even thinking about it made her clench her teeth. This time tomorrow she would be different: she would no longer be a virgin.

'You're not going to let yourself miss anything.' Giles laughed, his voice cutting across her thoughts. 'I've never had a passenger so interested in the scenery.'

'Of course I'm interested. Giles, don't you see how exciting it is? Except for during the war, when the school was evacuated to a huge manor house in Berkshire, it was in London – no, not even as exciting as being actually *in* London; it was stuck in the suburbs. Not that it makes much difference where you are, there's no chance of being let out and seeing much if you're at a girls' boarding school. Apart from that I lived on the Isle of Wight until I came to the farm, so I want to see every single thing. Last year Natalie and I went walking in Derbyshire, but I got there by train. Some of the countryside we went through was lovely, it wasn't all drab by any means, but train journeys are so miserable, don't you think? You see hundreds and thousands of houses from the back, mean little back gardens, yards, some with bath tubs hanging on the wall, everything looking so dingy. In a car you see the fronts, you see people. I don't want to miss any of it. I've never been north from Devon.'

Giles took a quick glance at her. She was like a child going to her first party. Was he being fair to take advantage of her juvenile crush on him? For he had no illusions: she was in love with

102

love; she was in love with his association with Burghton and the characters who had peopled her unnatural existence living with an elderly grandmother.

'I was brought up not ten miles from here,' he said.

'You've never talked about your family. Are they still around here? Is that why you've come this way, so that you can take me to meet them?' Her interest in the village they were passing through evaporated; he wanted to take her to see his roots, to introduce her to his family: '. . . my fiancée, Tessa.' She could almost hear him saying the words.

'I don't remember my father. He was killed on the Somme and my memory doesn't go back that far. My earliest recollections are of living with a bachelor uncle, my mother's brother, but mercifully I was sent to boarding school when I was eight. My uncle was the vicar of Saint Agnes church in Moorbrook, over there to the left some ten miles, and my mother kept house for him.' He didn't answer her second question.

'Did you base any of your characters on him in Burghton?'

'Most certainly not. From what I learnt from him, I just trust he didn't get the chance of catching a choirboy alone.'

'Did he beat you? But he could never do that to a choirboy; there would be awful trouble in the parish.'

'Beat me? Good God, no. Smarmy, over-kind, then when he thought he had my trust – but never mind.'

Tessa frowned, knowing there were things implied which he assumed she understood.

'Are they alive, he and your mother?'

'My mother moved out while I was at university. She never told me why and I didn't ask. She was still relatively young and got a job as a sort of personal assistant to Julian Masters' secretary. In those days Julian used to live in the village and I dare say he took her on to give her an escape route. Anyway, she was still quite young – she'd married at eighteen so must have been in her thirties. She married a captain in the Canadian Army in nineteen forty-three and lives in Alberta. I haven't heard from her for years. We hardly knew each other; she was no more important in my life than I was in hers. I did have a letter about a year after she went to Canada, saying she had a daughter.'

'And your uncle? Has he retired?'

'Gone to the home in the sky for clergy. I dare say he'll find companionship.'

'I don't understand. You sound so bitter – so, almost, full of hate.'

Taking his eyes from the view ahead on the fortunately straight road, he turned to look at her.

'I hate hypocrisy, pretence.' But was that true? The question sprang into his mind uninvited. Was he not being hypocritical in his treatment of this precious, innocent girl? No. He *must* genuinely love her or why would his conscience trouble him? Through all the affairs he'd amused himself with over the years, never once until now had he looked to the future and felt guilty. Aware that

Tessa was waiting, uncertain of what was behind the story he had told her, his expression changed. Looking straight ahead at the still-empty road, his face broke into a smile and, peering at him, she felt reassured. 'I know just the place for lunch,' he told her. 'A pub I've known since I was first old enough to frequent such places. They do remarkably good food.' Taking her hand in his he raised it to his lips and gave it a kiss that held more pleasure than passion. 'We're on our holidays and what better to set us on our way than a pub lunch in the garden of the Cat and Fiddle?'

'Two weeks, Giles. Today it feels like eternity. Do you know what I'd like more than anything? I'd like us to just keep driving until we got to Gretna Green. Two weeks would turn into all the years of our lives.'

'No, Tessa, it wouldn't bring happiness. You couldn't start the rest of your life knowing you had deceived people who love you.'

'But for two weeks we can pretend.'

Giles imagined the cottage that awaited them at journey's end. This certainly wasn't the first time he'd booked it, and neither was Tessa the first companion he had taken there. But he had never felt even the slightest twinge of guilt. Don't look ahead to things that may never happen, he told himself. Even though Tessa's adolescent love was something he'd never known from anyone else, surely it was up to him to make sure that tonight was so rapturous for her that hero worship was turned into mature love.

'Here we are,' he announced as the swinging

sign of a cat playing a fiddle came into view. There were one or two bicycles leaning against the side of the building, just one car already in the car park and, completing the rural scene, a pony and trap. As Giles got out of the car a portly, middle-aged man wearing a butcher's apron tied round what at one time had been his waist, came out of a side door then, recognizing him, waved a greeting.

'That's Jack Milton,' Giles told Tessa, 'the landlord. Just wait there. He and I go back a long way.'

She waited as he said, watching in the driving mirror as he and the landlord shook hands. In a minute Giles would bring his old friend over to the car to be introduced; in anticipation she glanced in the mirror to make sure she looked her best. She heard their voices but not their words, and there was no sign of their coming towards her. She frowned, her confidence again threatening to desert her. Then Giles came back alone.

'Out you get,' he said, opening the door for her. 'I told Jack I wanted that table by the stream and he's seeing that we have an umbrella to shield us.' Ever the optimist, Tessa's spirit rose. 'Jack's wife is Swiss. I said we'd have fondue; she makes the best sauces I've ever tasted.'

Once they were seated at their table, a barmaid brought out the umbrella, which Giles took from her and fitted into the table. While they waited for the fondue they strolled by the stream and then out came the same barmaid carrying the pot of hot oil, the flame from the heater flickering in the breeze. She was followed by a girl too young to have left school, who must have been employed to do a Saturday job, bearing a tray with a selection of home-made sauces, two long-handled forks and two dishes of raw meat cut into cubes. So the feast commenced. It was Tessa's first experience of fondue and she forgot her disappointment at not being presented as the future Mrs Lampton as they cooked their meat, sometimes losing it in the oil and catching the wrong piece, dipping their catch inelegantly into the delicious sauces.

'This is the best possible start to a holiday,' she said as she dug around in the oil for her lost piece of meat. 'So much more fun than ordinary food with a knife and fork, don't you think?'

'That, my dear Tessa, is why I brought you here.'

'We've made a memory. When we're very old we shall look back and remember every second of it.' Not the most tactful remark she could have made, as she realized when she saw his sudden frown. 'When we're very old' was a reminder to him of the gap in their years, and even more of the gap in their experience. The words seemed to hang between them.

At two o'clock The Cat and Fiddle closed, but it was nearer three and the other tables in the garden were empty; whether there to eat or simply drink the occupants had all gone.

'Here's the car key. You can get in while I just go round to the kitchen to say hello to Heidi. She's lost none of her skill.'

Tessa felt like a child. 'You run out and play

while the adults talk,' he might have said to her. Watching him walk away, the joy of the last two hours evaporated. She wished she could hate him for being so insensitive but she couldn't – it wasn't in her power to hate him. So, alone, she walked back to the car and sat waiting. In fact, he was only two or three minutes, even though to her it seemed much more. Then he appeared; his smile as he got behind the driving wheel was all it took to chase away her momentary blues.

In Bridgnorth they stopped again and wandered around the delightful old town where they found a tea room and ate scones with jam and cream. Pouring the tea banished any lingering feeling of inferiority and when, as they walked back towards where they'd left the car, he disappeared into a florist's with a brief 'Wait here', emerging a minute or two later with a bunch of hothouse roses, her happiness was plain to see.

She had never before seen the hills of Shropshire.

'So lovely, you can see for miles. It's gentle and yet it's – what's the word? – strong, that's it, it's *strong*. Devon is gentle with its narrow lanes. Craggy places are harsh, don't you think? But this is, yes, it's strong, strong and kind. Have you been here before, Giles?'

'Many times. The cottage is isolated, but it's a far cry from my work place in Downing Wood. It's centuries old but has been thoroughly modernized, mostly before the war but they have done a few things since. It has its own generator for electricity and a bathroom as good as I have in my London flat, but the low ceilings have their original beams, and there's the original open fireplace. You'll like it.'

And when, half an hour later, he opened the heavy ancient front door, he only had to look at her expression to know he'd been right.

'Giles,' she turned to him, so full of emotion that she could find no words. 'Giles,' she said again, putting her arms around his neck and burying her head against his shoulder.

He held her close against him, then raised her head so that he could see her face.

'You think this can be our home for two weeks?' he asked softly, a teasing note in his voice.

'I think I could stay here forever and ever. It's so *right*, all the lovely old oak furniture and such comfy-looking chairs. It's a proper home. You like it too?

'Come upstairs and see the rest. It's not large but I agree with you, it's so *right*. And so it should be; the owner is an interior designer. He lives in London but has this for when he wants to escape. I've known him for years. He only rents it to friends. Come up and see the bedrooms. I'll bring the cases.'

He'd said 'bedrooms'. Did he mean that they wouldn't share? Again she felt unsure of herself, out of her depth. At the top of the narrow staircase he dumped their cases and steered her towards one of the bedrooms, stopping on the way to open the door of a modern bathroom with off-white tiled walls and bathroom fitments.

109

'This is bedroom number two,' he said, ushering her into a delightful room in total keeping with the living quarters downstairs.

'It's beautiful,' she said hesitantly then, holding his gaze and feeling her nails biting into the palms of her clenched hands, 'but Giles, we don't want two rooms. Isn't that why we came away? I thought that was what you wanted.' There! She'd said it. Now she turned her face away, feeling so uncomfortably hot that she was sure he must notice. She felt his hands on her shoulders, then drawing her close he tilted her face.

'Did I will you to say that?' he whispered.

'Tell me, Giles.'

'Tell you I want you more than I thought possible to want any woman? We'll find paradise together, Tessa, my sweet Tessa.'

'Show me our room,' she whispered, her mouth so close to his that he could feel the warmth of her breath.

'I want to take you there now, this minute. I want us to feel the warmth of the evening sun on our bodies. I want to be deep, deep inside you.'

'Why do we have to wait?' She guided his hand to her breast, silently begging him to do what he'd done before. If only she knew more about what would make it wonderful for him too, but she only knew about kissing and that people made love to get babies. Nothing had prepared her for this aching yearning that made her legs feel like jelly.

Without releasing their hold of each other they

moved towards the main bedroom, Giles walking – shuffling, rather – forwards and Tessa backwards. Once inside he kicked the door closed, not because there was any chance of their being interrupted, but because it seemed to shut the rest of the world away. Then he unbuttoned her blouse and slipped it off her shoulders. Next came her bra before together they pushed the rest of her clothes to the floor and she kicked off her sandals. She seemed to stand outside herself, savouring every second yet not completely part of it all. Her sheltered life had left her unprepared for the sensations, both physical and mental, that made a stranger of her even to herself. Already she was unbuttoning his open-necked shirt. The situation held a quality of unreality; it belonged in her dreams. Yet even her dreams hadn't prepared her. Giles pulled off his undergarments, letting them fall to the floor next to hers. Shoes, socks, and then, like her, he was naked.

'The sun's gloriously warm still,' she said softly, frightened of breaking the spell. How trite her words sounded. Would he know that she had hidden behind making the first comment to come into her head rather than let him guess that the nearest she had even come to seeing a naked man was in pictures of statues? Perhaps he understood her sudden discomfort. No, the spirit he was sure lay dormant waiting for him to bring it to life would know nothing of false modesty.

'And you're gloriously lovely. You're just as I've imagined,' he said softly, drawing her closer.

Her momentary unease had gone as suddenly as it had come. Leaning against him she felt the warmth of his body.

'I can feel your heart beating . . . bump, bump, bump,' she muttered, her lips moving against his shoulder as he held her.

'Every pulse in my body is beating, throbbing.'

'And mine,' she breathed. She had the strangest feeling: half fear, half yearning. Taking his hand she carried it to her breast, longing for him to do what he'd done that evening in the cottage. Instead he dropped to his knees, pressing his head to her groin. Involuntarily she gasped. This was something she hadn't expected; momentarily she was lost. As his warm mouth caressed her she was taken over by something out of her control; she pressed his head closer, closer. Then he raised one hand to her breast.

'Want . . . want . . .' she breathed.

Kneeling up straight he leant against her, gently moving her backwards to the bed.

'And I want you.' He was breathing hard, as if he'd been running. 'Now . . . now.'

If Tessa was on strange territory, so too was Giles. His life of casual affairs had satisfied him physically; there were no sex games he hadn't played. But no woman had excited him as Tessa did, even though in experience she was little more than a child. As he moved her further on to the bed he looked down at her, so perfect, so eager. He must be gentle, he told himself; the first time would hurt. But there was nothing gentle in the need that drove him.

In her nightly imaginings she had never felt

112

this strange aching feeling that tingled even in her arms and legs, a yearning for something still unknown.

And then it happened. Yes, it hurt, but the pain was exquisite, it was as if he were branding her, making her his own, now and forever. She was filled with joy as, with her legs wrapped around him, she arched her back to force him ever nearer. There was something primitive and wild in the way she moved beneath him. Then, for both of them, control was gone, nature was supreme. She had been born for this moment.

Afterwards as they lay close, fighting for breath, she managed to force out the words, 'Was like – was like – never knew – be like that.' Then, after a huge gasp, 'Sort of sacred, glorious.'

He didn't answer. They were free agents; there was nothing to get up for. So, as the sun started to sink behind trees on a faraway hill, they both slept.

Much later, bathed and dressed for the evening, he took her out to dinner. White damask table-cloth and napkins, champagne, candles; it was an evening like no other.

Back in the car, before he switched on the engine he held his cigarette case to her, then lit first hers and then his own. For a few seconds they sat back in their seats, seeming to savour the moment.

'This evening . . .' she began, groping for the right words.

'Yes? This evening?' He turned to look at her, his eyebrows raised as he waited.

'It's hard to find the right words.'

113

'This evening . . .?' he prompted.

'Well, don't you see, it's made me a different person? Even though I knew you were wrong when you used to say I was just a child, I can see now that I wasn't really a proper *woman*. There was so much I didn't know, don't you see? I was a young girl and now, even though I'm only a few hours older, I'm a proper woman.' In the darkness she couldn't see his expression, but she took his soft chuckle as agreement. 'I'm glad about it, though, Giles. I mean, we really *know* each other now.' Never in her life had she experienced such a feeling of contentment and certainty. She wound down the window to let the cigarette smoke go out and the scented air of summer come in, so sure of the rightness of where she was that she didn't notice Giles had not replied.

'Just the two of us,' she said, just as she had earlier. He understood what was left unsaid.

As the days of their fortnight passed all too quickly, she made two or three phone calls home to the farm; she even gave them accurate descriptions of where they had walked on the Shropshire hills and, during the second week, of the trip 'she and Natalie' had taken to Shrewsbury.

On their last morning she brought all her hotel training to bear as she cleaned the cottage before they left.

'They'll send a cleaner in; you don't want to bother mopping the floors.'

'Yes, I do. We walked an awful lot of mud in after yesterday's storm. I won't be long. What

114

time do you want to be on the road? Oh, Giles, it's all gone so quickly.'

'Too quickly,' he said, coming towards her.

'Don't walk on the wet floor. If you get the cases down I'll be ready in five minutes. The floor is the last thing.'

'I never doubted you were a Mary; don't tell me you are a Martha after all.'

She chuckled, carrying her bucket out of the back door to throw the water by the hedge, then took off her shoes once she was back inside. 'I'm a bit of both, I expect. Don't you think most women are?'

'Not those of my acquaintance. I'll pack the car.'

Was it because she'd insisted on leaving the cottage looking as inviting as she had found it that he was so quiet on the drive south? It wasn't that he was bad-tempered or angry with her, but he seemed withdrawn. Perhaps he was just sad to be going home, she told herself and, as if to console him, laid her hand somewhere near the top of his leg as he drove. For a second he covered it with his, the action driving away her doubts.

'Doesn't it seem silly that you have to put me down in Exeter so that I go home by bus, when you will be passing the end of the lane? I hate going home to lies and deceit. Can't we tell them, Giles?'

'Tell your uncle that I've taken his ward away a child and delivered her home a woman? Wasn't that what you said that first evening? No, my sweet Tessa, what is between us is just for us.

Soon you will be a free agent and until then I'm not chancing the wrath of an irate guardian because I've deflowered his ward who's young enough to be my daughter. In any case,' he went on firmly as she tried to interrupt, 'I'm not going back to Downing Wood at the moment. After I've left you I shall get straight on to the London road. I must check into the apartment and see my mail, then I'm going down to Spain for a brief visit.'

'Spain?' He might as well have said he was going to the moon. 'What? Another holiday? Or is it the setting for a new book or something?'

'Neither. It's my retreat from the fleshpots.'

'Fancy you having a faraway house like that.' She was determined not to let him guess how hurt she was that there were things in his life he didn't share with her. 'Deirdre never mentioned it.'

'I doubt if I've ever talked about it to them. Why should I? I told you, it's a retreat.'

She wanted him to know her every thought and yet, even now, she was on the edge of his life. 'We could have gone there for our holiday,' she said, horribly aware that such an idea wouldn't have occurred to him.

'Indeed we could if you'd had a passport and the freedom to live your own life.'

His answer took away her feeling of being isolated from him. She turned to him, her eyes bright with excitement. 'Next year, Giles. As soon as I'm twenty-one I shall apply for a passport, and anyway by next summer we shall already be married.'

'Bugger!' He swore softly as he rounded a bend in the narrow lane and saw a herd of cattle ahead of them being driven home for milking. 'I should have stuck to the main road. I know the district well around here and thought I'd take this as a shortcut. Damn it, just when I've got a long drive ahead of me.'

'You can dump me off before we get right down to Exeter if you like. I'll get a train or a bus.'

'I'll put you off at the bus stop in Exeter as we arranged. There's no point in trying to get to London cross-country. From Exeter I shall have main road all the way.'

There were so many questions she wanted to ask him. Whereabouts in Spain was his retreat? Was it a house or an apartment? Who looked after it when he wasn't there? What was he doing in Spain when he found it? Did he drive all that way or go on a train? Yet there was something about his expression that prevented her questioning him further.

An hour later he drew up at the bus stop in Exeter. Leaning close to him she wound her arms around his neck. 'The end; once I get out of the car it's really all over. Now I have to go home and tell fibs.'

'It's their own fault. They should realize you are old enough to make your own decisions.'

'Will they know I'm different? It's all been so wonderful. Was it wonderful for you too, Giles, darling Giles?'

For a moment he was silent, his expression inscrutable. Then, looking at her very directly, he said, 'It has been a fortnight I shall remember

117

all my days, if I live to be a hundred. Out you get, sweet Tessa.'

'How long will you be away?' she asked, not loosening her hold of him.

'I don't know. There are things I have to arrange. I'll come back as soon as I can.' Then, kissing her very gently on her forehead, he unwound her arms from him and got out of the car to get her case.

It was all over. In that moment as she climbed out and held her hand out to take her luggage, she seemed to see the fortnight flash through her mind. She too would remember it for the rest of her life. And soon he'd be back; at the thought her imagination took her to the cottage in Downing Wood and the hours they would spend together there. Before the holiday she had known nothing of love, not as she did now. As she watched him get back into the car, her memory carried her to the moments when their love-making had brought them to that pinnacle of joy, a sensation that each time had been more than physical: it had been a union of their bodies and their spirits. She wished the car door wasn't shut and Giles already looking over his shoulder to make sure he was safe to pull out into the traffic; she wanted to remind him, to rekindle the wonder of it in his mind. But the car was moving away and she was left at the bus stop with her case.

If only she could talk about it to someone. But she mustn't. And in any case, who could she talk to? She believed Naomi would have understood

118

what she meant, and yet surely there was no logic in her thinking. Naomi and Richard were ancient, thought the twenty year old, and yet there was something about them that told her they would understand the wonder of what she had discovered. But she knew she couldn't. And if she were honest with herself she knew she wanted to hear herself put it into words and yet she wanted to hug it to herself. Soon Giles would come home from Spain and then there would be no need to find the right words; for him as well as for her what they had shared had been glorious. She thought of Amelia and seemed to hear her familiar voice: 'Rejoice'. Yes, Gran knew.

Back at Fiddlers' Green, Tessa's routine was very different from before her holiday. In two short weeks Deirdre had found an independence that had changed her life.

'Your aunt and uncle have been amazingly kind,' Julian told her when she put her bike in the one-time carriage house just as he was getting his car out. 'A day hasn't gone by when the child hasn't taken herself down to the farm. I could have bought her an electric chair before, but on her own where could she have gone with it? It was her lucky day when you came here, my dear. Without you none of it would have happened.'

'Aunt Naomi is very special. From the first time I took Deirdre down there they took to each other. It's being useful that's important, don't you think? And she is useful. Aunt Naomi doesn't make concessions because Deirdre's in a chair;

119

she works as hard as anyone.' Then, laughing, 'A bit of a cheek, really: you pay me to be a carer-oblique-friend and I take her down to the farm to be an unpaid worker.'

'There are things more important than money,' he answered. 'You had a good holiday, I hope?'

She nodded. 'The best ever.' She made sure her voice gave nothing away; 'best ever' had a hearty sound to it, the sort of comment that might come from a girl who had spent a fortnight hiking with an old school friend.

And so began what she thought of as a new period in her life, for it could never be simply a continuation of what had gone prior to the glorious fortnight. The thought of it coloured her every minute; no matter what she was doing it was there at the back of her mind. She felt loved; she felt that everything that had gone before had been leading her to the glorious fulfil-ment of sharing her life with Giles. Each morning when she arrived at Fiddlers' Green she hoped to hear that he was back in Devon. But one week, then a second passed. Please, please make today be the day he comes, she pleaded silently, for with every passing day it became more imperative that she talked to him. She knew so little and he was the only one she could talk to. Could it be that her period had gone out of kilter because she had made love for the first time? Perhaps she would just miss a month. If only he were here he would make everything right, and even if she wasn't twenty-one no one would stop them getting married.

She had been home for five weeks when, as

she was laying the table for their evening meal and Richard was scrubbing his hands in the outer scullery, Naomi said, 'Fancy your forgetting to tell us about Giles Lampton. They must know at Fiddlers' Green.'

'Know? Know what? I think they said he was away. Is he back?' Please, please let him be back. Now it'll be all right. He'll talk to them and make them realize we love each other and he'll get a special licence. Please, please . . . But her silent sentence didn't get finished.

Five

At Naomi's announcement Richard came back into the room, still drying his newly scrubbed hands.

'So Marlhampton has lost its nearest claim to celebrity,' he said casually. Then, with far more interest, 'I say, that smells good. Are you ready for me to start carving?' Food held priority over the comings and goings of Giles Lampton.

'Yes, I think that's everything.' But Naomi couldn't dismiss Giles so easily. Perhaps it was feminine intuition, but she sensed that his departure would upset Tessa more than she would let them see. 'How funny that they didn't tell you at Fiddlers' Green, Tessa. Or perhaps they did and you didn't think to mention it. When he's around he spends so much time there. I'd have thought that Deirdre would have said something to me, too, for that matter; she knew you did all that typing for him not so long ago.'

'They must have got it wrong in the village, Auntie. He's been away for some time so I expect they are putting two and two together.' It took all Tessa's acting ability to sound no more interested than the other two while her heart was banging so hard that she wondered they couldn't hear it.

'Oh no, it's true enough. Mavis Bright saw the notice in an estate agent's window in Deremouth.

She said she was pretty certain it was his cottage, but when she took Herbie, her spaniel, for a walk she drove that way and let him run in Downing Wood. I wonder the agent wasted a For Sale board on it; no one much ever walks that way to see it.'

'Giles has a house in Spain,' Tessa threw in casually. 'He calls it his retreat, just like he did the Downing Wood place.' But this was stupid. Why was she pretending that he was no more to her than just a friend of the Masters? Anyway, if what she was getting more and more certain about was true and she was to have his baby, even they couldn't raise objections to her getting married without waiting until her birthday. But for the present, the baby was *her* secret, hers and, as soon as Giles got in touch with her, his too. 'He's out there now.'

'So Marlhampton will have to interest itself in someone else,' was as far as Richard's interest stretched as he deftly sliced the home-produced topside of beef.

Naomi was uneasy. There was something in Tessa's expression that warned her that she didn't believe he wasn't coming back to Downing Wood. But she said nothing, simply passed the vegetable dish across the table to Richard . . . and waited.

'Look,' Tessa blurted, her voice coming out louder than she intended and taking the couple by surprise. Naomi instinctively held herself in readiness. Whatever was coming spelled trouble. 'I wanted to tell you but Giles said I must wait until my birthday. He thought you would be

123

against our getting married because I'm a lot younger than he is.'

'Married?' Richard put down his knife and fork and turned his full attention on her. Naomi's mouth felt dry, her heart was thumping. His voice was as cold as steel; surely Tessa must sense the change in his manner? 'Married? To a man you hardly know? I've never heard such utter rot! Just be thankful he's cleared off. You may be sure he won't come this way again.'

'But he *will*.' Tessa gave up all pretence of eating her food. Her voice was strident as she looked first at Richard then at Naomi, then back to Richard. Was it fear or anger that drove her? She put Naomi in mind of a trapped animal. 'He will come back. And I *do* know him. I lied to you about Natalie. Giles rented a cottage in Shropshire. *That's* where we spent the fortnight, just as if we were married.'

'Bloody man!' Richard shouted. His voice was as beyond his control as the tic in his cheek. Pushing his plate to one side he glared at Tessa. She saw his expression as being full of hate; only Naomi understood his hurt and disappointment. 'To take an innocent young girl—'

'I'm not stupid.' First he'd raised his voice, now Tessa raised hers. 'I knew just what I was doing. So now you know. Just because he's decided to sell the cottage doesn't mean he's getting rid of me too. Of course he isn't.'

'And you try and make me believe you're not stupid! Use your sense for Christ's sake and see him for what he is. If he'd thought of you as anything more than an easy companion for a

124

holiday he would have talked to us about his intentions.' Only Naomi noticed the sudden change in him, and even she couldn't put a name to it. He seemed more distant. Tessa was still talking but what she was saying didn't register with either of them . . . If Giles was giving up the cottage in Downing Wood he would spend more time in Spain . . . after they were married that would be their main home. Words, just words, while Naomi's mind concentrated on Richard, and Richard seemed unaware of both of them. His eyes were closed and his breathing was fast and shallow.

'Richard?' she said softly, reaching to lay her hand over his. 'Let it go, Richard. Eat your food, darling.'

Opening his eyes he looked at her. It was as if Tessa wasn't there at all.

'Bloody indigestion,' he said breathlessly.

'You started to eat too quickly. Take it slowly. You said you hadn't had a proper meal all day.'

He shook his head.

'I think there's a drop of brandy in the sideboard cupboard,' Naomi said. 'Tessa, can you get it?' The previous conversation might not have happened.

'No. It's easing. Doesn't last. Had it in the market.' He opened his eyes and looked directly at Naomi. 'Frightened me, I'll tell you. But it passed. Then later, I had to stop on the way home. Better now – almost gone.'

'You've been too long without food. There's some soup from yesterday I can warm. Would that be easier to digest? Or porridge?'

Recovering, he looked at her with an expression that made Tessa feel uncomfortable to witness. 'Better now,' he whispered. 'I'll have that brandy and sit out in the fresh air for ten minutes. Can you keep mine warm for later?'

Outside he sat on the five-bar gate gazing unseeingly at the lower field, a field that rose to the stile leading into the High Meadow. They assumed his thoughts to be on what Tessa had told him. She let herself imagine that he was seeing reason and when Giles came back from Spain and got in touch with her she would not only tell him about the baby but, also, that she had talked to Richard and he was in agreement for the wedding to go ahead.

Naomi's mind had no room for Giles Lampton. She had never known Richard to be ill. You couldn't say he was ill, she corrected herself; a twinge of indigestion was nothing to worry about. She wanted to follow him outside to reassure herself that the fresh air had put him back on form but believed he needed to be by himself to think about what Tessa had told them.

It was with relief that she saw him coming back across the yard.

'We've had ours –' she greeted him – 'but I've kept yours warm in the oven. Can you manage it now?'

'I feel fine again. I'll eat it slowly this time,' he said. Then, putting his arm around her in a casual embrace, 'Sorry, love. Where's Tessa gone?'

'Out on her bike. Oh dear, what a mess. It's

all his fault. Tessa would never have deceived us.'

'Poor kid. Things hurt so badly when you're young.'

'We're so lucky.' She nestled her head against his shoulder. 'Now, I'll get your dinner out of the oven and you mind you don't bolt it.'

As she had so many times, Tessa took the Deremouth road then, just before she came to the long bridge over the Dere estuary, she turned right towards Otterton St Giles and Downing Wood. She knew it was crazy but she felt she would see his car on the patch of wasteland by the side of the cottage. But there was nothing, only the estate agent's For Sale board. Pressing her face to the window she saw the living room was still furnished. Perhaps that was how he had bought it. Nothing there had been of his choosing and so he would sell it on.

He must have phoned the estate agent. Or perhaps he had put it all in the hands of his solicitor in London before he left for Spain. Yes, that must have been what he'd done. As soon as he got back to England he would come to Devon – or, even better, he would phone her at Fiddlers' Green and suggest that she meet him somewhere. She could easily make an excuse to Mr Masters that she needed a day off. Richard and Naomi would assume she was working as usual . . . then she pulled her thoughts up short. More lies, more deceit. But now there would be no need – already she'd told them at home about him. Imagine their surprise – especially Richard's – when she arrived with Giles. She didn't doubt him; she was certain that one day soon, even if it didn't work out in exactly the way she'd been imagining, Giles would come back to her. Sitting on the wooden bench in the porch of the cottage she closed her eyes as she let her mind go back over that wonderful fortnight. Memories crowded back to her: the glory of the nights, a glory more wonderful than she would have believed possible. And at home they thought he wouldn't come back! Of course he would. It had all been as wonderful for him as it had for her. Hand in hand they had walked for miles on the open hills. Giles had known the district well. Long Mynd, the Devil's Seat, and what was the name of that hill she had called the top of the world? No one could approach unseen, they'd been utterly alone, cut off from the world and yet part of the nature that surrounded them on that overcast June afternoon; with her eyes closed she could still seem to see the clouds scudding fast above them as she'd lain on her back, gazing upwards; then the pageantry of nature was complete. That was the only time they'd made love with their clothes on, yet the wonder of it had been just as intense. They had been at one with the rolling hills and the wild sky. Except for that first afternoon and that one time on top of the world, Giles had been careful he wouldn't make her pregnant – so he'd said. So that was when she must have conceived their child.

It was getting dark even though the days were at their longest. It would take her more than an hour to get home even if she pedalled her hardest.

So many evenings when she'd been out with Giles, she had lied to them and said she was keeping Deirdre company, but this time she'd not said where she was going. She mustn't be late: they would worry about her and think she was upset and frightened that Giles wouldn't come back to her. She wasn't frightened; of course he would come. Perhaps he was on the train travelling through France even now. Once out from the shelter of the porch, she raised her head and looked up at the darkening sky, then closed her eyes again as she pleaded . . . Let him come soon . . . I want to tell him about the baby . . . don't make us wait for months . . . the baby would be born if I had to wait until my birthday . . . Let us be together, please, please . . . I'm not frightened. Then she wheeled her bike out on to the dusky lane and set off for home.

She rode as fast as she could, aware that Richard and Naomi wouldn't want to go to bed while she was still out. On the one or two occasion they'd known she was being taken out to dinner by Giles by way of a thank you for the work she had done for him they hadn't waited up. But they'd see it as different for her to be riding alone after dark.

'I'm glad Tessa's out,' Naomi said as she finished clearing all traces of their meal. Such a lovely evening. I'll help you shut up outside and, after that, there's no one here but us.'

Richard's mouth twitched into a hint of a smile. 'Would the woman be tempting me?'

'And if she is?' She stood very close to him, moving her face against his neck. 'Do you feel

129

better now you've had a proper meal? Tessa has her own key – we don't need to wait up.' As soon as she said it she regretted it; she could feel his body grow tense.

'If I could get my hands on that sod, I'd beat the living daylights out of him. She's just a kid; she would have trusted him, that's what is so beastly.'

'Perhaps she's right, darling: she's not a stupid girl. Come on, let's go outside and get the place put to bed.'

Even when Tessa had been on holiday they had never gone to bed with the sinking sun. The last long rays streaming through the bedroom window heightened their anticipation. Through all the years of their marriage, sex had been important to both of them. Young and with abundant energy they had loved each other so completely that every avenue of eroticism had been explored; as the years had melted gently into the happy and complete relationship where nothing they desired was out of bounds to them, scarcely a day ended without the act of love-making. Seldom could it be described as erotic, rather it was a silent and loving way of sharing the last minutes of each day.

But, on that late July evening, the scene at the meal table had something to do with the emotion that drove them. It wasn't gentle love they needed, it was something wilder, something that would drive away the shadow of what they both feared and leave no room in their thoughts for anything except themselves and each other. This would be no tender affirmation of their abiding love; their bodies were as familiar to each other as to themselves, but dull habit had no place as they brought each other to the limits of desire. They wanted it to last for hours even while they raced towards the climax that neither of them could hold back.

'We're so lucky,' she breathed, still holding him fast, 'so blessed.'

'Blessed . . . thankful.'

'There aren't any words.'

'We don't need words, you and me.'

Short sentences, spoken in whispers, as if any sound would break the spell that held them. Then he rolled off her and she heard a change in him. He had been breathless, indeed they both had, but the unnatural gasp broke through her euphoria.

'Richard?' She wasn't even sure if he heard her. Frightened, she reached to turn on the bedside light. 'Is it that pain again? We ought to keep something in the house, something for indigestion. I'll go and get the brandy – that helped earlier.'

She slipped her feet into her slippers and put on her dressing gown, then as she reached the door turned to look at him expecting to be met with a silent message that somehow would combine the moment with what had gone before. But she might as well not have been there; he was staring unseeingly at the ceiling, his face contorted with pain. Forgetting her mission for the brandy she went back to the bed and dropped to her knees by his side.

'Try and sit up a bit, darling. If I rub your back it might help.'

'Arms . . . shoulders . . .' It was hard to be sure, but she thought that was what he said. His fists were clenched and his face was contorted with pain.

'I'm going to ring for the doctor,' she said, as much to herself as to Richard. It was only as she ran down the stairs that she realized with surprise and fright that he hadn't attempted to stop her. A glance at the hall clock told her it was not quite half past ten. At any other time she would have worried that Tessa was still out on her bike even though it had been dark for some time, but her thoughts didn't go as far as Tessa, nor did she feel sympathy for poor Dr Harding who was just on the way up his stairs to go to bed at the end of a busy day when the phone rang. But, true to his profession, after hearing what she told him he said he would come immediately.

Then he took her by surprise and rocked the foundations of her world when he added, 'I shall call for an ambulance to come out from Deremouth. You go back to your husband, Mrs Pilbeam, and I'll be with you in five minutes.'

It couldn't be happening! In all their years together she had never known Richard have even a day in bed. Hospital? No, he'd hate it. Even if he needed care, somehow she would manage to look after him and the farm too. Just like the pain had eased earlier, perhaps she would find he was recovering already.

Back in the bedroom her first reaction was a flood of relief; the colour of his face was heightened, but at least the expression of pain was gone.

'The doctor will be here in a minute,' she said, forcing her voice to sound positive so that he wouldn't know how frightened and out of her depth she felt.

'It's dying down,' he whispered, frightened to breathe deeply. 'Oughtn't to bring him out – it's late – I'll be all right . . . minute.'

'He'll give you something. We ought to keep a better medical chest.'

She moved to the window to watch for the light of Dr Harding's car. No need to mention the ambulance, for now that Richard was starting to feel better the doctor would be certain to send it away.

But he didn't. The next half hour was like a living nightmare. An involuntary cry from Richard just as the doctor was examining him; the arrival of the ambulance with three attendants and a stretcher, then the sight of Richard, his naked body covered with a sheet, being lifted to the stretcher and carefully carried down the stairs. He didn't look at her, he didn't even seem to realize she was there or what was happening; his world went no further than the pain that filled his chest, his arms, his shoulders and his jaw. A pain that seemed to be squeezing the life out of him.

As they carried him out of the house Naomi tore off her dressing gown and dragged her clothes on, taking no heed of appearance. She moved so fast that before he was safely in the ambulance and the men ready to set off for Deremouth she was in the car ready to follow. It was only as the cavalcade moved slowly down the narrow, potholed lane that she remembered she hadn't left a note for Tessa.

There was a storm brewing. The still air had suddenly whipped itself into a frenzy and in the distance Tessa heard thunder. With the back tyre of her bicycle completely flat she had already been pushing it for nearly four miles, hurrying as fast as she could and knowing that at home they would be worrying about her. The scene at the meal table had receded into the back of her mind, pushed into insignificance by those few minutes at the cottage.

She was almost home. As she came to the turn into the lane she could see the lights from the farmhouse. It must be well after eleven o'clock, past Richard and Naomi's usual bedtime that was based on his early milking time in the morning. They must have gone to bed and left the down-stairs lights on to welcome her home. The thought gave her a feeling of comfort, and right on cue she remembered the words in Gran's letter telling her that it was a house filled with love. There was no logic in her certainty that when Richard got over the hurt that she had lied to them about her holiday he would give his consent to her marriage, but logic had nothing to do with the welcome she saw shining in the lights from the house.

Then her rambling thoughts were brought to a halt by the sound of a vehicle coming towards her down the narrow lane. She stood right back, pushing her bike against the prickly hawthorn hedge as it came near. When she recognized that

134

it was an ambulance she felt a stab of fear. Of course it wasn't from the farm; there were two or three more properties further along. But even before she could start to hope, she recognized the van following behind.

Naomi saw her pushed against the hedge and pulled up, leaving the engine running. Opening the door she called, 'They're taking Richard to hospital. But he seemed better. Heart attack, they said. Silly taking him. He would have been better in bed. I forgot to lock up. I'll be back as soon as they let him come home. We both will.' Her short, disconnected sentences were so out of character, as out of character as forgetting to turn off some of the lights and lock the door.

'I'll leave my bike here in the hedge and come with—'

'Look after things.' And taking her foot off the clutch pedal Naomi started forward with a jolt, then put her foot down, determined to catch up with the ambulance.

There could be nothing more certain to take Tessa's mind off her own affairs than this. She imagined the scene at the dinner table: Richard's anger, her own anger, Richard going outside for air – and she had imagined that there alone he would have been starting to understand about Giles and her. If he were ill, was she the cause of it? No, he'd said that he'd had indigestion during the day. She tried to believe that when he got to the hospital they would examine him and find there was nothing wrong with his heart and it had been indigestion all the time. She tried to concentrate her mind on formulating a plan of action for the morning. She would have to phone Mr Masters tomorrow morning and explain that she couldn't come to Fiddlers' Green – but even then she would be left with the animals to care for. The dairy work she understood, but she didn't even know how much food any of the animals had and, as for milking a cow, she'd never even watched as Richard attached the milking machine to a cow's udder, and equipment like separators and coolers were an unknown world to her.

Knowing tomorrow demanded an early start she went straight to bed, setting the alarm clock for half past six. But how could she sleep when she could see Richard so clearly . . . Richard . . . Naomi . . . the disruption to their lives . . . guilt at her own part in what had happened? Running Chagleigh Farm demanded all his health and strength, something that they had all taken for granted. She remembered how Naomi had talked to her of the life she and Richard shared, her fears for him during the Great War and her thankfulness when he came home unscathed. Thankfulness she felt every day of her life, then and now, too. Please help them, Tessa begged silently. I didn't realize until now how dear they are to me. I know I was cross with him earlier but deep down I really love him, I love both of them. Please help me find out how to do things and be really helpful.

The night seemed endless and the dawn chorus was already in full song when she had an inspiration. Adjoining Chagleigh was Wendover, a mixed farm owned by Geoffrey Huntley. She had never met him and perhaps it was like Chagleigh, run by just him, or him and his wife. She had seldom heard him mentioned at Chagleigh, but that he was there at the back of her mind gave her comfort enough to help her drift into sleep.

Whatever the circumstances, Tessa had never let care for her appearance slip. So just after half past six she ran her bath, making a mental note that she must remember to see to the fire. That was another job that had never concerned her; Naomi looked after it and hot water was always on tap as if by magic.

By five to seven, with her make-up and hair ready to face the day, she was collecting the eggs so that they would be in the basket on the bench in the dairy ready for Deirdre to get to work on later in the morning. Next came the pigs; she had no idea how much food to give them or even what they were used to eating. Somehow she *must* manage, she would beg for help from wherever she could find it, she would work from morning till night herself, anything rather than let Naomi and Richard down.

Looking out across the lower field that rose towards High Meadow she was faced with the hardest task of all. It was well past the hour when Richard would have driven them down to the milking shed. The thought of milking them, one by one, she felt she could master, not with the machine but by hand. A long and laborious task, but once she got the hang of it she would manage. But the milk from the pail didn't get poured straight into the churns that were collected from the gate and so she would have to fathom out how to use the cooler and the separator. She looked around as if by magic some inspiration would appear. Suppose the cows wouldn't come in a herd like they did for Richard, suppose they wandered in all directions. Yet she knew simply by looking at their heavy udders that they were overdue for milking.

Taking her courage in both hands she went through the gate and started up the field. The cows looked at her balefully but made no attempt to form a group and walk down the slope as they did for Richard. She had never felt so helpless, helpless and useless. On the rare occasions when Richard couldn't be there for milking she had seen Naomi usher them down through the gate and into the shed. The milking machine wasn't for her either; it was the memory of seeing her sitting on the three-legged stool, her head against the cow's flank, her hands working steadily and purposefully, that made Tessa feel she could do it too. But first she had to bring them in from the field.

Glancing at her watch she saw it was still only half past eight. Too early to telephone the unknown Geoffrey Hunter and throw herself on his mercy for help or, at least, for advice.

I'll leave the cows until I've explained to Mr Masters why I can't come to work, she thought. Somehow the idea of sharing her problem helped her as she hurried back indoors and dialled the number.

'Hello.' Miss Sherwin's voice seemed to tell

her that to disturb a household so early was either bad manners or bad news.

'Miss Sherwin, it's me, Tessa. I know it's early but I want to speak to Mr Masters.'

'I don't know if he'll come to the phone at this hour of the day.' Then, curiosity making her relent a little, 'Is something wrong? Are you ringing to say you can't come to Deirdre?'

'Yes, my uncle has been taken to hospital. My aunt is with him. I have to look after the farm.'

'Oh, my dear, what a to-do. He's coming into the hall now; I'll give him the phone and you tell him all about it. It's Tessa. She's in trouble there at the farm.'

On any other occasion Tessa might have been surprised and touched by the unexpected concern, but the pressing demand of the cows was too near the front of her mind.

'Trouble at the farm?' Julian Masters' voice was like a lifeline to cling to. So Tessa poured out the story, or as much of it as she knew. She explained how she'd been late home from her bike ride because of a puncture and had just seen the ambulance disappear with Naomi following.

'I wanted to go with her. He's never ill. It must have frightened her terribly. But she said for me to stay at home and look after things. She said they might let her bring him home today, but after a heart attack they won't do that, will they? I wish I'd learnt to drive the cows in – I went in the field and tried but they just stood there looking at me. It's way past their milking time. I must go and try again—'

'Let me think what we can do,' came his calm

voice. She felt as if a great weight had been lifted from her. No longer was she alone.

She waited, trying to imagine how his mind was working. There was no logic in her feeling of relief that he was sharing her problem for, after all, he knew even less about farming than she did. So when he spoke again, he surprised her.

'You've seen young Gerry Baker, the lad who started working here a few weeks ago doing odd jobs and helping the gardener? He was new to the district when he came here, but he was brought up on his grandfather's farm in Hampshire. I'll send him down to give you a hand. Tessa?'

'Sorry,' Tessa croaked, 'I never cry.' But the snort proved this was an exception to the rule. 'Just, I was so worried I'd do it all wrong. I mustn't let them down. He's never ill.'

'My dear, you won't let them down. Baker will be with you in no time – I'll run him down in the car.'

And, true to his word, in less than five minutes Julian's car drew up and the burly young man got out.

'I can't believe it,' she said as her eyes followed Gerry climbing up to where the cows stood, watching him with mild interest. He'd noticed a long stick against the side of the milking shed and was carrying it for guiding and steering the herd. 'I didn't take a stick. I forgot that's what Uncle Richard uses. It sounds sort of stilted to say that I don't know how to thank you, Mr Masters, but it's the truth. I don't mind how hard

140

I have to work but I was so frightened of making a mess of it.'

'I fancy that young Baker is in his element. He only left his grandparents' farm because his girl-friend works for a family who moved down this way. He's a good worker; he won't let you down. Your aunt may be right in thinking they'll be home today but, like you, I should think it highly unlikely. No doubt she'll let you know what's happening, but I'm sure if his condition is serious – and I hope it isn't – she will want to be there as much as they allow. So' – and as if with a change of mood his face broke into a rare smile – 'it'll be all shoulders to the wheel. Today I'll see that Deirdre doesn't bring herself down, I'll drive her in her car – her 'hybrid', I think she says you call it. You'll need that to take the orders to the village if your aunt has the van. Use Baker as you like, but he's only on loan, he remains on my payroll. Now I'm off to collect Deirdre. Will you both come up to the house for your lunch as usual?'

'No, there's plenty of food in the house. We'll all three of us eat here.'

He imagined the three young people gathered around the table, all of them proud of the part they were playing keeping the wheels turning, and for a moment he envied them their youth and enthusiasm.

At about three o'clock Naomi phoned. 'The night staff were very kind and once the doctor had seen him, the night sister let me sit with him all night. I'm sure it's not usual, but I suppose she knew I had nowhere to go.'

'What do they say, Auntie? How is he now?'

'He ate some lunch and this afternoon he does seem much more like himself. I doubt if they'll say he can come home until after the doctor's morning round, but I should think we'd be back by the afternoon. How are you managing?'

So Tessa explained about Gerry Baker. 'He knows an awful lot and loves having the chance to be on a farm. So you mustn't worry. Deirdre and I may only be learners, but Gerry makes up for it – and we're willing workers. And I've not forgotten that today is the day for the order for that retirement place.'

'Well done. Try and get it there in good time this afternoon. They only give the old dears a light supper and sometimes they are waiting for the eggs.'

'It's all boxed up ready. Have a word with Deirdre while I put it aboard the hybrid, then we're on our way.'

The Sunshine Home was about six miles from the farm, a home for the elderly no longer able to care for themselves but not ready for the geriatric ward of the hospital. It had been built by Deremouth Rural District Council and opened some three years ago when the order for eggs and butter had been given to Chagleigh Farm. In Tessa's early days with Richard and Naomi, before she had found the job at Fiddlers' Green, she had enjoyed delivering the butter and eggs twice a week. So when she arrived instead of Naomi no one thought it was odd or enquired whether there was something wrong. Tessa was sure that Richard wouldn't want his health to be a topic of general interest, no matter how kindly meant.

'We've done well.' Driving homeward Tessa turned her head to call to Deirdre, who sat behind her in her chair.

'Makes you feel good, doesn't it?' Deirdre agreed. 'I wish we could tell Aunt Naomi. Perhaps she'll phone again.'

'I expect she will tomorrow morning. She said he wouldn't be able to come home until after the doctor had done his ward round. Then she'll tell us to get out the red carpet.'

'Funny, isn't it?' Deirdre said thoughtfully. 'A couple of days ago who would have thought that their happiness could come from having him home? And probably told he mustn't do much even then. Yet now it sort of fills you with a thankful feeling – not so much for us, although of course we're thankful, but it's hard to imagine how they must be feeling – especially her, because he probably didn't know how scary it was for her to have him taken off like that.'

Tessa mulled over Deirdre's words as they continued on their journey. 'Nearly home. Shall I put my bike in the back with you and drive you to Fiddlers' Green?'

'Can't I help with anything? We ought to make sure the dairy is spic and span so she sees how well we've done things.'

But, in the event, the dairy had to stay as it was. For just as Tessa wheeled the chair down into the yard, Julian's car drew to a halt behind them. There was something in his expression that warned them they weren't going to hear anything good.

'I'm glad you've got back,' he said, getting out of the car and slamming the door. 'When Mrs Pilbeam couldn't get an answer from you, she tried ringing me.'

'I spoke to her just before we went out,' she told him, 'and she said she expected to have to wait until the morning to be told he could come home. Has the doctor given him the OK this afternoon?'

'I'm afraid the news I have is about as bad as it can be.' He hoped that would prepare Tessa for the shock to follow.

She held his gaze steadily, steeling herself to hear – to hear what? She wouldn't let her thoughts carry her down the road she was frightened to imagine.

'You mean he had another heart attack? But he was resting in bed; he wasn't even using any energy – and look at the work he's always done here.'

'This time there was nothing they could do.' There was no easy way of breaking the news, but Julian found it hard to tell what he knew she was hiding from hearing. He couldn't escape the memory of Naomi Pilbeam's voice, deadly calm as if the life had been drained from her: 'I rang Tessa but she must be out. Will you tell her that I will be home later. I will be on my own. My husband – they couldn't revive him – nothing they could do – dead. Richard is dead. I shall sit here for a while. I have the van. Tell her not to worry. I don't want to come home yet.' Then, as if she only then realized she was talking, 'Silly, isn't it? I just thought I'd stay here for a bit longer.' He had known exactly why she wanted to stay. It wasn't that she had realized she was in no mental state to take a car on the road; it was because as long as she was in the hospital where Richard had probably already been taken to the mortuary, she didn't have to face the emptiness of home.

'I told her to sit and wait where she was and I would drive you over. She ought not to bring herself back on her own.'

'It's not fair.' Deirdre's voice broke and at the sound of it her control was lost. 'It's not fair. What will she do without him? They were . . . were . . . complete together. Without him she will be half dead. Why couldn't it have happened to some other couple? Lots of people quarrel but *they* never did.' She sobbed. 'You know what I mean, don't you, Tessa? You could sort of feel there was something making them like one person.'

Tessa nodded. 'A house filled with love, that's what Gran called it.'

Julian gave his daughter his 'for decoration only' silk handkerchief from his breast pocket so that she could mop up, and then she set off for Fiddlers' Green in her electric chair. With Tessa sitting at his side, he drove slowly behind Deirdre until they reached the road, then while she turned to the left he went the other way on the Deremouth road.

For a while they drove in silence then, as if picking up from Deirdre's tearful outburst, Julian said, 'This is going to be so hard for your aunt. Not only losing a partner so deeply entwined in her life, but somehow she will have to make a decision about the farm.'

'Except for an occasional milking session, she has nothing to do with the animals. Uncle Richard was saying a day or so ago that Tammy was due to calf. Will she – Aunt Naomi, not Tammy – know what to do?'

'Let's hope Tammy manages without help. I believe that's quite usual. Animals are much better at this sort of thing than humans.'

At his words Tessa realized that since arriving back from the Sunshine Home, her own affairs had been pushed out of her mind. Now, though, she seized the opportunity of confiding to Julian, at least in part. 'Mr Masters, I've been meaning to ask you: do you have Giles' telephone number in Spain? Or do you know when he's coming back?'

Julian laughed. 'Coming back? Who knows? I've known him to go off for pretty well a year with no word and then wander in as if he'd been gone no more than a day. And, no, I doubt if he even has a telephone.' Then, giving her a quick glance, 'Has he gone off without collecting the typing you've been doing for him? That would surprise me. The one thing he takes seriously is his work and, of course, that's why he cuts himself off when he goes to Spain. No distractions, no invitations, no admiring females queuing for his favours. Even though he's selling the cottage, believe me, he'll wander back one of these days when he's finished dictating whatever it is he's working on.' Another quick glance told him that Tessa had more than a superficial interest. Poor child, he thought. At her age it's so easy to give your heart to someone out of reach: a film star, actor or, apparently, even a writer.

As if she read his thoughts, Tessa found herself unloading her worries. 'I'm not a stupid, adoring fan. I was, I expect, before I met him. But Giles and I are going to be married.'

Julian frowned, not liking what he heard. 'You say he proposed marriage? Tessa, my dear, fond as I am of the man – not that we have a great deal in common, but one can't help being drawn to him – I am always aware that he is utterly undependable, a will o' the wisp.'

'No, deep down he isn't like that at all, Mr Masters.' She took a deep breath and he knew there was something important to follow. 'When I took my holiday it wasn't to go walking with an old school friend. I went away with Giles. We stayed together – you know what I mean – as if we were already married. He was frightened that if I asked Uncle Richard's consent to marry me it would create trouble; better to leave it until next spring and then I shall be free to make my own decisions.'

'You lied to them?'

'I didn't like doing it, honestly I didn't. But I knew Giles was right and they wouldn't have agreed. They really don't know Giles. Well, not properly.'

'So when did Giles go to Spain? I didn't even know that's where he was.'

'Straight from our holiday. He brought me back as far as Exeter so that I could go home on the bus like they were expecting. He said he had to go out there, but would be back as soon as he could. But, honestly, I don't want to disturb him when he's working, I know how important that is to him. But you see, it's *vital* that I talk to him.'

Julian asked no question, but his heart went out to her. He thought of Deirdre, how her life had been changed in a few seconds when she'd been thrown; now there was Tessa, a girl he'd believed to have a wise head on her shoulders. But if he weren't mistaken, her own life had been thrown just as firmly off course. Somehow they *must* make contact with Giles and he must learn a lesson that he'd avoided all these years: a man must take responsibility for his actions.

'Here we are,' he said as they turned into the gates of the hospital. 'We'll work something out, Tessa. But in the meantime, your aunt must come first. I won't intrude today. As soon as I see you are with her I'll go.'

A minute later they walked up the side steps to the front entrance and saw Naomi's solitary figure sitting in the foyer, her eyes closed even though she was sitting in far too upright a position to be asleep. It wasn't until much later that Tessa realized she hadn't even said goodbye to Julian, nor thanked him for bringing her.

'Auntie,' she called softly, as if she were frightened of disturbing Naomi's private thoughts. Then, sitting beside her on the bench, she took her in her arms, holding her close as if her strength would drive away the numb misery.

'They've taken him away.' Naomi might have been talking to herself. 'Here somewhere . . . don't know where.' She looked at Tessa and yet she might have been any stranger; there was no light of recognition in her eyes.

Tessa had never felt so inadequate, so out of her depth. And yet she desperately wanted to find a way to give comfort. Rightly or wrongly she found herself speaking in a firm, practical way, surprising herself that she did when her heart ached for the desolate figure before her. 'Mr Masters brought me over so that I could drive you home.'

'That was kind,' Naomi responded, standing up as she spoke.

Together they walked out of the building, Naomi with her head high, her face showing no expression. She let Tessa lead her down the hospital steps, too numbed by shock and misery for tears.

Six

'Auntie, it's so awful. I can't believe it. I want to help, to say something that would . . . would . . . Oh, but there's nothing.'

'No. Don't say anything.' Naomi's voice was flat, her face expressionless. It was as if she were going through the motion of polite conversation with a stranger – if it could be given the name of conversation – while her innermost feelings were numb.

'Mr Masters has been a real brick.' Tessa tried to follow her lead. 'I don't know what I would have done if he hadn't lent Gerry to us. We can hang on to him until we sort ourselves out, but he – Mr Masters, I mean – insists that Gerry is on *his* payroll.'

'How kind.' The reply only emphasized that no matter what Tessa said, there was no way of breaking the protective armour of Naomi's calm politeness. Both of them found it easier not to talk at all. And so, in silence, they covered the miles from Deremouth to Marlhampton.

As they came along the lane towards the farm, Tessa glanced at Naomi, expecting that surely the sight of Chagleigh would break through her defences. And perhaps it did, but the effect wasn't what she expected. The expressionless mask dropped and in its place was a look that was hard to read. Was it determination? Was it hope? Then something that might even have been a slight smile as the older woman turned her head to look across the lower meadow where the cows were happily grazing.

'He'll help me, give me courage,' she said, seemingly speaking her thoughts aloud. Then, looking at Tessa as if she had only just realized she was there, 'I won't fail him.'

'We'll help with the dairy work, Auntie, Deirdre and me. I know Gerry is only on loan but I expect Mr Masters will let him stay a while. Perhaps he might even leave Fiddlers' Green and come here to the farm permanently. He's very keen.'

Naomi shook her head. 'I'm going to do Richard's work. He'll help me. He won't leave me, he knows . . .' But whatever it was Richard knew was lost in a sob that refused to be held back a second longer just as they turned into the yard. Switching off the engine, Tessa instinctively put her arms round Naomi, but her action was met with no response. She felt rejected.

'Auntie, it's so awful. He was . . . well, he was a . . . a rock.'

'Don't! Let's go indoors.'

In the lobby were their wellingtons set in a neat row just as they were always left. Naomi kept her chin high and looked straight ahead as she unlocked the door to the kitchen. Tessa wasn't so brave. She looked at the neat row of boots and was filled with foreboding. Soon she wouldn't be there to support Naomi; she would be utterly alone.

'You must be starved,' Tessa said, thankful that with Deirdre's 'help' she had prepared a cottage

151

pie with the remains of last night's beef before they took the delivery to Sunshine House. Her idea had been that it would be ready to cook as soon as she heard Richard was being brought home. 'It won't take very long to cook the supper. Why don't you have a nice warm bath while you wait? You must be tired and hungry.'

Like an obedient child Naomi did as suggested and returned half an hour later wearing a night-dress and dressing gown. The cottage pie was brought from the oven looking good and smelling even better, bringing forth a loud rumble from her empty stomach.

'I didn't have time to prepare a vegetable. We'll have to have tinned peas. Is that all right?'

'Of course.' It would have taken more than unappetizing processed peas to break through Naomi's reserve. As soon as her plate was put in front of her she took up her fork and started to eat, bolting her food as if she were starved. The last meal she had eaten had been the previous evening, although she had been given two or three cups of weak, sweet tea at the hospital.

They made no attempt to talk and Naomi had more or less cleared her plate when, with no apparent warning and making no sound, her body jerked convulsively. With her hand over her mouth she got up from the table so suddenly that her chair fell backwards with a crash as she rushed through the adjoining scullery to the outside lavatory. From the kitchen Tessa could hear her retching and then the sound changed. There was nothing restrained in Naomi's crying. She howled, she wailed, she called Richard's name. Feeling utterly helpless, Tessa followed her and found the lavatory door wide open.

'You were hungry and ate too fast,' she said, putting her arm round the shaking figure that leant against the whitewashed wall as if it hadn't the strength to stand alone.

'Like Richard, last night.' Naomi's words were hard to understand. 'Please God, take me like you've taken him.' No longer protected by the armour of numb reserve, she gave up the battle for control.

A house full of love. Amelia's words came back to Tessa. What would she say of it now?

The night seemed endless. Naomi's mind jumped from the present, to the recent past, then back down the years. Since she'd been a schoolgirl all her hopes, dreams and aspirations had been shared with Richard, just as his had been with her. Suddenly she was alone, frightened to look ahead to an abyss of loneliness. Her near-hysterical bout of crying had left her weak and drained.

'Richard,' she whispered, 'Richard, please hear me, please give me a sign, tell me you'll be with me.' She remembered the fear she had felt through the first of those awful wars, the Great War as it was known; she had prayed with all her heart and soul that he would be safe. But now, lying alone in the bed where they had turned to each other with love that was too much part of their lives to need words, she couldn't pray. She could form the words in her mind, but that's all they were, just words while the anguish of her spirit cried out to Richard.

Wriggling over to his side of the bed, she rested her head on his pillow as if she expected that would bring him closer. Instead it forced on her the reality she couldn't bear to face. Richard was gone. Burying her face against his pillow she felt the burning tears sting her eyes and made no attempt to hold them back. *I can't bear it. If you're not here, Richard, there's nothing. I want to die. How many years have I got to get through? Help me. How could you leave me? You're my life.*

Tessa crept along the corridor and listened. Ought she to go in? She wanted to, she wanted to hold Naomi close and share her grief, yet as her hand reached for the doorknob she knew she mustn't. She was an outsider. How could she possibly give comfort to a woman whose very heart had been torn from her? Turning away, she crept back to her own room, but sleep was a million miles away.

Any day Giles would come back and when he heard that they were to have a child they would be married as soon as it could be arranged. Then what would happen to Naomi? Even if Gerry worked for her instead of for Mr Masters, she would be alone in the house. Tessa imagined her sitting at the meal table with no one to share the food, no one to speak to; she'd bank up the fire to give hot water and there would be no one to use it except her. There *must* be a solution. Lying in bed, haunted by the memory of Naomi's muffled tears, into the gloom of Tessa's thoughts came something so simple that she couldn't believe she could have been so stupid as not to see it sooner: if Giles came back quickly, before anyone bought the cottage, or if she could find a way to contact him by phone, she could persuade him to take Hideaway Cottage off the market. Then, even after they were married, she could still be nearby and Naomi wouldn't be so dreadfully alone. The trouble was, she and Richard had never looked beyond each other for friendship. They had plenty of acquaintances in the village, but no intimate friends.

Satisfied that she had found a solution, Tessa slept. And, despite herself, exhaustion got the better of Naomi, but not for long. As dawn broke she was again awake. If she put her hand under Richard's pillow she could feel the cotton material of his pyjamas; and yet here in the room that had held so much of their lives she couldn't bring him close.

It was nearly seven o'clock when Tessa woke, hearing the sound of movement in the yard. It must be Gerry bringing the cattle in for their morning milking. Getting out of bed she grabbed her dressing gown to cover her nakedness, then went to the window. What a mercy Mr Masters had let them borrow him; it would give them time to advertise for someone experienced to take over the work of looking after the animals – the bread and butter of the farm, as Naomi called them.

So went Tessa's thoughts until they were pulled up sharply by the sight in the yard. The cows were ambling out of the milking shed while Naomi kept them in a group with the help of the stick Richard had always used. But that wasn't the only thing of his she had taken as a boost to her determination: dressed in her usual workman's overalls and wellingtons, on that first morning without him she had taken his battered felt hat from the hook in the lobby and put it on her head. As she steered the cattle into Lower Meadow and shut the gate on them, Gerry arrived. Tessa watched as the two talked; even from that distance she could see that Naomi's shut-in expression was back. No doubt Gerry was expressing sympathy, something she was still too shocked to acknowledge. Would the young man understand her cool, withdrawn manner? Or would he feel rebuffed? Tessa felt that her presence was required and hurried to run her bath. Even working at high speed it was twenty past seven when she ran down the stairs. She, too, wore workman's overalls and in a minute would be pushing her feet into her wellingtons, but her face was made up with care and her short hair shining from the ministrations of the brush.

And so started Day Number One on Chagleigh Farm with the ghost of Richard everywhere, bringing no comfort.

The morning was half over when a shadow fell across the open doorway of the dairy. 'Hello?' Tessa called enquiringly.

Into the open doorway stepped a portly man of some sixty years, rosy faced and with greying, bristly sideburns and hair of the same hue which curled to frame the back of his tweed cap.

'I take it Mrs Pilbeam won't be on the farm

today? My name is Huntley.' The visitor introduced himself. 'You may have heard of me; I farm next door.' He was certainly nothing like the working farmer Tessa had conjured up in her imagination. His booming, jovial voice was in keeping with his expensive tweeds, and she was sure his highly polished boots knew nothing of mud and worse in the farmyard. Her immediate thought was thankfulness that she hadn't called on him for help the previous morning. 'And you – you'll be the niece, I dare say. Shocking thing to happen. How is the poor lady?'

'You've heard about my uncle?'

He gave a bark of a laugh. 'My dear, the whole of Marlhampton will have heard. In the country news travels with the speed of a heath fire. I got out my pen to write to Mrs Pilbeam, but then I pictured her predicament and I thought – no! Better to call and have a word with her. She'll be in the house, I expect? Although I did ring the front bell and no one answered, that's why I walked round here. Dreadful for her, dreadful, dreadful. I always marvelled how they managed with just the two of them.'

'They managed perfectly.'

'Where did you say I shall find her? Or has she gone into Exeter? So much to do with all the arrangements. One thing you can be sure of with death: it leaves plenty for other people to deal with; and perhaps that's as well, and it gives less time for grieving.'

'You'll find her up in the top field. If you don't want to walk you can drive through the lower meadow as long as you take care to shut the gate going up and coming back down. Then there's just the stile so you have to leave the car and walk the last bit.'

The visitor beamed affably. 'You've got me sized up right enough. I'm not the man to walk up a hill if I can drive. A pity the same couldn't be said for Pilbeam. Worked himself into the grave – and she'll do the same if she isn't made to see reason.'

'To them it was never work. It was a life they loved.' She thought of herself trying to drive the cows for milking the previous morning and how near she had come to calling on this tailors' dummy of a countryman for advice. From there her mind took a sideways jump and she pictured Richard in clothes more suitable for a scarecrow and a heart belonging to the work he and Naomi shared. Perhaps she ought not to have let Geoffrey Huntley carry his condolences in person; it might have been less painful for her to read his message of sympathy.

She heard the car start on its way up the hill, and ten minutes or so later heard it stop as he let himself through the gate from the lower meadow, then when he'd closed it the sound of the motor told her he was leaving Chagleigh. That would be the first of so many who could try to bring Naomi comfort by their words of sympathy.

Naomi seemed metaphorically to have stepped into Richard's shoes (or wellingtons, rather), for she made no attempt to break off her work and organize lunch. So when Tessa and Deirdre returned from taking the daily delivery to the village, they went indoors to see what they could find. There were still plenty of vegetables and so it looked as though it would be soup and bread. It was evidence of how removed Naomi was from normal living when she accepted without comment that there were four places laid.

'You'll have to fill up with bread,' Tessa told them as she carried the tureen to the table and started to ladle out the soup. 'I'll need to do some shopping this afternoon, Auntie. Is there anything else you'd like me to do?' She didn't want to put it into words that there was the death to register. 'I expect you'd rather stay and work with Gerry.'

'We've been checking the sheep's feet,' Gerry said when Naomi didn't answer. 'Mrs Pilbeam said she'd never done it before, but she's a real natural. Learnt to sort of sit the animal on its behind and get it between her knees so it couldn't move a darn sight quicker than I did when I came to do it first. It's a knack and to see the way she tackled it she might have been doing it for years.'

Tessa's glance met Naomi's and a silent message passed between them, both remembering what she had said as she looked towards the fields. Could it be that Richard was giving her the strength and courage to do what she had to? All Naomi said was, 'We've got more than half of them done and penned separately. It's something I've learnt to do, and I'd like to get it finished this afternoon. I'm grateful to Gerry for teaching me.'

'Today I've looked after the pigs,' Gerry told them, 'but come tomorrow Mrs Pilbeam will take over. I tell you, you'd never guess she'd not had dealings with the livestock side of things, she's a real natural, like I said.'

'There's plenty of soup, Gerry. Pass your bowl and let me give you some more.' Tessa reached her hand to him and he gladly passed his bowl for a refill. It brought home to her just what a change there was in Naomi. This was *her* farm kitchen, they were eating *her* food, yet there she sat, crumbling her bread, making a pretence of eating her soup, making sure she kept her face set in what was almost a smile, and all the while her world was falling around her. Was she finding comfort in the belief that Richard was watching over her? Let it be like that for her, Tessa begged silently.

'You two workers get back to the top field,' Tessa said as she collected the dirty plates. 'Deirdre and I will see to these things and then, after we've finished weighing out and wrapping the butter – the wrapping is Deirdre's job, she does it so well, the words "Chagleigh Farm" always come right in the middle just like they should – well, when we've done that we ought to do some shopping. There must be other things I can do, Auntie?' Surely she didn't need to spell it out. She remembered exactly what she had had to do when her grandmother died, but it was as if Naomi wouldn't let herself think of any of it.

'No. There's nothing today. You know where my purse is for the shopping.' Then to Gerry, 'I'll see you in the top field in about ten minutes. If I'm there first I'll see if I can get started on my own. Have a cigarette or whatever you want; you needn't hurry.' It was all said in a friendly manner as she pushed her chair back under the table and turned to go upstairs. Tessa and Deirdre looked at each other, knowing that they both recognized the charade she was playing. Only Gerry, who had met her for the first time that morning, accepted her tone as normal, although he did think it was odd that a woman who had lost her husband less than twenty-four hours before could carry on so calmly.

An hour or so later Deirdre was concentrating on getting her half pound of butter placed on the wrapper in exactly the right position when she stopped, sitting very still, and listening. 'Sounds like Daddy's step in the yard. Have a peep, Tessa. What could he want me for?'

The high window of the dairy looked towards the gate to the lower field and, as Tessa strained to make herself as tall as she could, she saw Naomi coming towards it down the slope. Then, approaching her from the yard, she saw Julian Masters.

'Yes, it's your father,' she reported, 'but he's not coming this way, he's going to speak to Aunt Naomi. That's kind of him but, Deirdre, it must be so hard for her to have to bear people's sympathy.'

'Dad's never a mushy sort of man,' Deirdre answered defensively. 'See how he helped yesterday, taking you to the hospital.'

'I was so grateful. She was in no state to drive herself home.'

So the dairy work went on while both girls were secretly wondering what was being said outside. However, they were to be left in ignorance as Julian didn't come in to speak. They heard his car drive off – and how were they to guess that he had seen his passenger seated and closed the door firmly before getting in himself and slamming his own?

Driving towards Deremouth Julian glanced fleetingly at Naomi, who sat at his side gazing straight ahead and, he was sure, seeing nothing of the passing landscape. To say she was pale told only half the story; her complexion was an unearthly grey hue except for the dark shadows under her eyes. The lines had been there on the day he had first met her, but now they seemed to pull her mouth down, adding years to her. She was probably younger than he was himself, but on that summer afternoon she looked old – old and tired of living. Her voice cut through his thoughts, taking him by surprise.

'I ought to have done this myself this morning. Why should you bother? I ought to have done it for him myself. You didn't even know him.'

'You ask why? No, I never met your Richard, but you and he have shared the dinner table with Deirdre and me for many weeks and I shall never cease to be grateful for what you two have done for her. She wakes up looking forward to the day ahead. You are her adopted Aunt Naomi and Uncle Richard, and each night she chatters about you both.' Both? Purposely he said it, just as purposely he used the present tense, as if that way he could help keep her memories alive. 'And if you were happy to be her aunt and uncle, doesn't that give me the right to be something more than a stranger who lives a mile along the lane?'

'You're very kind.' She answered like a child determined to be on her best behaviour.

'Kindness has nothing to do with it. I wish I'd known Richard, but from what I have heard of him he wasn't a man who would want *you*, the woman who shared every aspect of his life, to have to deal with the administrative necessities at a time like this. Talk to the vicar yourself but leave the rest to me. Please, Naomi. I feel certain Richard would want you spared. Do it for him. Humph?'

'Don't!' He'd been looking at the road ahead and her stifled gulp caught him off guard. 'Mustn't start crying.' She clamped her teeth firmly together but she couldn't control the spasms in her thin face.

'Cry, my dear. You will find him more surely in tears than in the pretence of winning the battle you have to face.'

She felt that for the first time she was seeing behind the aloof but courteous front he put up. 'Was it like that for you when you lost Deirdre's mother?'

The question took him by surprise. 'Certainly not. I believed I was head over heels in love with Chloe. Until then my life had been filled by the business I was building. I was forty-two, she eighteen. Her parents willingly gave consent to the wedding and, fool that I was, I thought heaven had fallen in my lap. Deirdre must have been conceived on our honeymoon, for that's all it took for me to realize I had been married for my money. The country was arming ready; anyone with any sense could see what was ahead. So, like many more in that field, I was accruing the sort of wealth a peaceful England would never have made for me. We'd been married just nine months when Deirdre was born and by the time she was taking her first steps Chloe had gone.'

'How awful for you.' He knew from her tone that his story had momentarily cut through her own misery.

'No. All I felt was relief. And that, I suppose, is the sadness. We had no marriage, no common ground, no friendship. A broken marriage gives one such a sense of failure. I soon realized that my feeling for her was no more love than hers for me. Yet, you know, the feeling of failure is always there; the slate can never be wiped clean.'

'Such sadness – and for Deirdre, too, to be deprived of a mother. Richard and I were so blessed.'

He nodded. 'I know. I could tell that from what you both did for Deirdre. And be sure of one thing: just as I can never wipe the slate clean, neither will you. What you and Richard built into your marriage will always be with you.'

'Will it? If I couldn't find him I don't know what I'd do. But today when I was learning to do the sheep's feet – I'd never done it before, you see; all that was Richard's work – I could feel he was there for me. Gerry was wonderful, he showed me what to do, but it was Richard who gave me confidence. I couldn't have done it without him.'

'You must hang on to Gerry. At heart he's a farmer.'

'If I can keep him a few more days.' Her voice was strong again; Julian knew she had conquered that wave of misery which had nearly brought her down. 'Richard and I never had any help,' she was saying, 'no outsiders working there. When Tessa came she helped in the dairy, but we never employed anyone. It was our pride that we did it ourselves. And he will be there for me; he will help me. He *must*.'

'Daddy, why didn't you come and speak to Tessa and me this afternoon?' Deirdre said at dinner that evening.

'Because it was Mrs Pilbeam I came to see. There were things she needed to get done; I drove her.'

'I'm glad. She's much more upset than she wants us to know. If you catch her when she forgets you're there she looks . . . different . . . sort of despairing. But I saw her later and she was still wearing her overalls. She didn't go to town in her working clothes, did she?'

Julian remembered his own surprise when she had got into the car still in her workman's overalls and wellingtons. Now, though, a smile played at the corners of his mouth as he answered, 'Not entirely. She took off her hat. But Deirdre, we should never judge people by their clothes. Mrs Pilbeam is a lady in the real sense of the word, be she in working togs or a model gown.'

Deirdre laughed, partly at the image of Naomi in a model gown and partly out of sheer happiness

165

that her father should speak as he had about her beloved Aunt Naomi.

But what Julian hadn't told her was how his ill-clad passenger had acquiesced when he had offered to leave her in the car while he registered Richard's death and then called on the undertaker.

Only as he opened the door for her to get out when they got back to the farm did she meet and hold his gaze. 'Thank you – can't tell you how grateful I am. The things you did for me – for Richard – I dreaded doing them. Silly, I know. I ought to have gone to town this morning – kept putting it off. The last thing I could do for him – and I couldn't do it.'

'Do you imagine he doesn't know that?' Then his tone changed as he spoke more forcefully, trying to lift her spirit before her insecure grip on control was lost. 'And my actions weren't entirely altruistic. Everyone needs to serve, whether it's the community, the family, someone you love. I have Deirdre, thank God, but I do so little that's useful these days. Promise me that if there is anything, anything at all I can do for you, you will tell me.' Then, with a sudden smile, 'Retiring too young can be tricky.'

She promised, shook his outstretched hand, then watched him drive away. She was thankful and grateful that he had relieved her of the things she had been too cowardly to face; but there all thought of him ended, for she was hardly likely to ask help from a retired industrialist to whom the mysteries of farming were a closed book.

* * *

166

Routine had to be Naomi's medicine. She got through each day determined not to be beaten and, each night, went to bed almost too weary to climb the stairs. And yet once alone in the dark bedroom sleep always eluded her. There were nights when she would reach her hand to his side of the bed, almost making herself believe that she would feel the warm, familiar body. Night after night she fought her tears, but misery and exhaustion always won. She mustn't let Tessa guess she was crying, better to pull the covers over her head, to bury her face in the already damp pillow. *Richard, Richard, how can I go on without you? I'm nothing, not even a whole person. Just want to die* . . . And so her days ended until at last sleep carried her away. By morning her determination was back again. Through the working hours of the day it took all her energy and concentration to carry out the tasks Gerry had taught her during the week or so they had worked together. Now she was on her own and it didn't enter her head to worry about Tessa or the fact that there had been no mention of Giles coming back.

But for Tessa the passage of time couldn't be ignored. It was the beginning of August, more than eight weeks since she and Giles had driven north to that paradise in Shropshire. From her collection of books about the people of Burghton she found that his work had been published by the same firm for many years. If she were to write a letter to Giles and send it to the publisher in a sealed envelope explaining that she had typed for him when he'd been in Devon and asking that it could be forwarded to his address in Spain, that must surely get her a reply in about a fortnight. She couldn't hide her secret much longer; in fact, she was amazed that Naomi hadn't noticed a change in her already.

Three days later she had a reply, not from Giles but from the publisher, regretting that he had been unable to forward her letter as all that was known of Giles Lampton's whereabouts in Spain was that his nearest town was Llaibir. Any contact during his periods in Spain was always made by Giles himself, and if he should happen to ring, he would be advised that there was a letter waiting for him from her.

By the end of the day Tessa had read it so many times she almost knew it by heart. Her imagination was working overtime as she stripped off the last of her clothes and, naked on this warm night, started to get into bed. Then she caught sight of her reflection in the long mirror on the wardrobe door. Forgetting bed, she stood gazing at it, turning sideways first one way and then the other; it wasn't that she had a 'bump' yet, but her figure was different. Her breasts felt heavier as she cupped them in the palms of her hands, and did she imagine it or had she lost her youthful appearance of agility? She shivered – certainly not because she was cold. She had faced most things without fear, but there had never been anything like *this*.

Despite her worries, once in bed she soon fell asleep. What time it was when a sound woke her she didn't know, but she was sure she heard movements downstairs. In an instant she was pulling on her dressing gown. Creeping on to the landing she saw that Naomi's door was pulled to and her room in darkness. If there was an intruder she couldn't have heard. In the dark Tessa crept barefoot down the stairs, relieved to see a streak of light shining under the kitchen door. Surely a burglar wouldn't have switched on the electric light. Even so, she squared her shoulders and took a deep breath before throwing open the door to face whatever was before her.

Naomi turned at the sound. 'Do you want some tea?' she asked, as if middle of the night refreshment was the normal thing.

Tessa nodded. In that moment she made her decision: she must tell Naomi the whole truth. Yet as she took a cup from the hook on the dresser, at the front of her consciousness was what had happened to her aunt in these last weeks. Always thin, but usually fully clothed, it had never been as apparent; tonight, wearing just a thin, cotton, sleeveless nightdress, there seemed to be no flesh on her bones. Her figure had always been saved because she had retained the firm breasts of her youth, which now seemed just to emphasize her bony frame. Her face was gaunt, the only colour the dark shadows beneath her eyes.

'I woke you. Sorry,' she said as she poured tea into Tessa's cup.

'I couldn't sleep either,' Tessa lied. 'Auntie, I have to talk to you. Is now a good time?'

For a second something akin to a smile flitted across Naomi's face. 'Why not,' she said, 'no one is going to interrupt us.'

'It goes back to my holiday with Giles . . .'
And so she told her story: the holiday, her absolute trust that Giles meant them to marry as soon
as she was twenty-one, her fear that he must have
met with an accident or fallen ill – and finally
that she was expecting their child.

Naomi let her talk without interrupting, yet all
the while she seemed to hear Richard's voice
saying what, in her heart, she believed to be true.

'Even his publisher doesn't know his address,'
Tessa explained. 'But he knows the town. Auntie,
I know what I have to do: I have to go to Spain;
I have to find him. Not just for me and the baby,
but for *him*. I know, positively *know*, that if he
could he would have been back long before this.
He loves me just like I do him. I'm not some
silly love-struck child, and I know him better
than any living person. I know he's always been
a Casanova but that was because he was just
amusing himself. With me it was different.
You've got to believe that.'

The news had cleared Naomi's thoughts of
everything else; even Tessa could see a subtle
and nameless difference in her. Her eyes seemed
to look and really *see*.

'Have you spoken to Mr Masters? Surely an
old friend like that must know where he is?'

'He doesn't know. He says that Giles has always
disappeared for months at a time, then come back
as if he'd been gone no time at all. But this is
different. Aunt Naomi, we are going to be married
after my birthday, but the baby must be due at
the beginning of March.'

'How can I let you make a journey like that

on your own? But I can't possibly leave everything to come with you.'

'I bet you've never been abroad any more than
I have. I'm not stupid and I'll phone each day if
you like while I'm looking for him.'

'But you don't speak Spanish. And you'd have
to go on a ferry to France, then get a train to
goodness knows where, then on to Spain. How
can I let you go off like that, especially when
you're pregnant?'

Reaching across the kitchen table Tessa took
Naomi's hand in hers, looking at her earnestly.

'I *must*. And I'm ever so well; I've not felt
sick, not even once. Don't you see – even if I
weren't expecting our baby, I simply have to find
out what's wrong? He promised. The last thing
he said was "I'll be back as soon as I can". He
must have been in an accident; perhaps he's ill
or lost his memory. Anything might have
happened. He's alone out there.' Then, knowing
she wasn't being fair, 'Supposing it were Uncle
Richard. You'd move heaven and earth to get to
him.'

'You'll need a passport. Get the application and
I'll sign it. But Tessa, are you sure, *one hundred
per cent sure* that he wasn't just running away?
Suppose you get out there and you find he had
no intention of coming back?'

'But I tell you, he *did*. I know there's gossip
about him, but that's not the Giles I know. Auntie,
I never knew there could be such joy as we found
together. It wasn't just me, it was him, too.'

Naomi sat gazing into space, her hands wrapped
around her half-empty teacup. '. . . never knew

there could be such joy . . .' What right had she to cast doubt on Tessa's trust? If she stopped her going, all it would do would put an insurmountable barrier between them. But if she made the journey – a frightening thought for a young girl alone in a strange country and with no knowledge of the language – and if she found Giles not ill nor with a lost memory, simply wanting to put time and space between himself and his entanglement with her, it would be an unbearably hard lesson to learn. Then there was the complication of the pregnancy. The longer the journey was delayed, the harder it would be for her.

'Get the form tomorrow and we must think about money.' Then, seeing Tessa was trying to hold back her tears, 'My dear, you shouldn't have kept this to yourself so long. I'm sorry. I've been selfish; I've not looked beyond myself.'

'You've got enough troubles.' Tessa snorted. 'It's so good to have told you.'

'Mother – your grandmother – left money for your keep. Each month Richard paid it into an account he opened in your name. I've got some savings in the post office—'

'No, Auntie. I won't need much more than my fare. Once I get to the town in his region, someone will know where he lives. Then I'll be fine.' She didn't say how often she had felt resentful, believing that Richard had been paid to give her a home.

'How much did you tell them at Fiddlers' Green?'

'I've only told Mr Masters – but not about the baby.'

Naomi nodded. 'We must go back to bed, my dear. It'll be milking time before we know it.' For a moment she shut her eyes as if she would escape the world.

Watching her, Tessa was aware of just how fond she had grown of her. 'Auntie,' she said, almost timidly, 'when I find Giles, I shan't come back until after we're married. I feel awfully mean. That's the one thing that has worried me, thinking of you here. But I have a plan.' And so she told Naomi her thoughts on Hideaway Cottage being taken off the market so that she and Giles could live there. 'That way I could still come and help you here.'

'Dear Tessa, it doesn't do to look ahead and plan. Live your life, my dear, grab every bit of happiness you can. And if you and Giles have found real love, then give yourself to it heart and soul.'

'That's what you did, you and Uncle Richard.' Even as she said it Tessa thought how strange it was that in the middle of the night it was easy to say things that would remain unsaid by daylight.

'Yes,' Naomi answered softly, her thoughts going on a journey of their own. 'And nothing can ever take away from you the joy you've known.' Then, drawing a line under a conversation that had become uncharacteristically emotional, she stacked their empty cups and carried them to the sink to rinse them.

Then together they mounted the stairs, knowing that this time they would sleep.

* * *

It was late in the afternoon the following week when Julian walked across the lower meadow where Naomi was coaxing the Jersey herd into some sort of group to start their leisurely walk to the milking shed.

'You're busy.' He greeted her. 'I know I mustn't hold you up, but I wanted to take the opportunity of our having a word while the girls are out. Having finished in the dairy they said they were going into Deremouth – Deirdre wanted shoes.'

'Deirdre loves shoes, doesn't she?' Naomi answered, smiling a welcome at her unexpected visitor.

'If only she could wear them out.'

'Amen to that. Has Tessa made a clean breast of things to you?' For any day the passport would arrive and then, although it was hard to imagine how Tessa would manage in a country where she didn't speak the language and, even worse, what the outcome would be if she did track down the elusive Giles Lampton, the sooner she started out the better.

'She has. But to be honest, I never doubted the situation. That's what worries me. Did Lampton realize what could have happened and decided to go while the going was good? If I could lay my hands on him . . .' And there was no doubt what he would like to do to the younger man.

'That's exactly what Richard said. But all we knew then was that they'd been on holiday together. If it weren't for the coming child I'd have refused to sign her passport application. How could I, though, as things are? If only I could go with her. Not that I'd be any use. Even if I could leave Chagleigh, I don't even have a passport.'

'Fortunately, I do. And so does Deirdre. So this is why I wanted to talk to you.'

By this time the cows had ambled as far as the gate to the yard. Once there, they knew exactly where they were heading and in their uninterested way they plodded to the milking shed. While Naomi was sorting them out and fixing the tubes of the milking machine to the swaying udder of the animal in the first stall, she needed her full concentration on what she did. She hadn't overcome her dislike for the contraption, but using it made an enormous difference to the time it took to do the milking. At the steady rhythmical sound of the rich fluid spurting into the pail, she turned back to Justin.

'What are you saying?' she prompted.

'Deirdre knows nothing and that's the way I mean it to stay for the present. However, my idea is that I drive the two girls to Llaibir, the nearest town to wherever Giles has his house. A holiday in Spain, what could be more natural now that I have time on my hands? We'd travel in the hybrid so that Deirdre would have the independence of her chair. Once we're there Tessa could make enquiries, as indeed I would as well. We'd play it as it comes. There must be a hotel in town or somewhere to rent. I promise you I'd see she was all right.' Then, after a slight hesitation, 'And if the swine has been playing with her affections and doesn't mean to be caught, then at least she wouldn't have to face it alone.'

He saw how hard she clamped her teeth on the

175

corners of her mouth while the muscles in her face twitched and jerked out of control. Even on a 'good day' she had lost the looks of her youth, and over these recent weeks overwork, misery and an increasing dread that she was failing in her attempt to maintain Chagleigh had left their mark.

'My dear,' Julian put his hand on her shoulder, 'you don't approve.'

'Relieved . . . grateful . . . been so worried . . .' One word at a time she had managed, but to string three together was her undoing. 'Sorry. Just seem to cry for nothing lately.' She found herself looking at Julian with complete honesty. He was almost a stranger and yet she made no attempt to hide from the truth. 'I'm so tired, tired to death. I wanted to do well, to do all the things that Richard did so easily. Last night I went to bed meaning to listen – I knew the calf was ready to be born. But I didn't even hear the cow calling. Richard always heard if one calved in the night, but I didn't wake. When I went outside just after six, that's when I heard the cow in distress. I tried to remember what I'd seem him do. I tried to pull the calf out but I couldn't turn it, I just made things worse and had to call for the vet. But it was too late. Poor little thing was dead.' She took a man-size handkerchief from her trouser pocket, a handkerchief she had last used to clean the windscreen of the van.

Watching her, Julian was conscious of a strange sensation. He wanted to hold her close and comfort her, to strengthen her with his strength.

Instead, he took out his cigarette case and held it to her, took one himself and flicked his lighter.

'Thanks. Sorry about that exhibition. I ought to be seeing to the milking.' And as if to draw a line under the last five minutes, she rubbed the grey and murky handkerchief across her face then took a deep drag on the cigarette.

'You know, don't you, that young Gerry would like nothing better than come back to give you a hand.'

'He was splendid. But I can't, I *won't* take someone on to do Richard's work. Perhaps I'm going silly – do you think I am? But as long as I'm looking after the animals I can feel he's still with me. It's just that I don't do things as well as he did – everything takes me so much longer and I can't hide from the truth: I'm failing Chagleigh. I'm failing him.'

'I think you are attempting the impossible – and if Richard could hear this conversation I'm sure he would agree with me. Do you think he'd want you to wear yourself to death? No, of course he wouldn't. And here I am, hindering you and being utterly useless.'

For a while they stood leaning against the wall of the barn, smoking in silence. Then she threw down her half-smoked cigarette, trod on it firmly then picked it up and put it in her trouser pocket.

'I must see to those poor old ladies,' she said, turning towards the milking shed. 'You've done me good. Thank you. And thank you for what you're offering to do.'

'She may not agree,' Julian warned. 'She may think we're implying she isn't capable.'

'It's not that. Tessa is a remarkably capable girl.' Then, with something akin to a smile, 'As she tells me, she learnt French at school and Latin too, and most Mediterranean languages are based on Latin. It's just this dread of how she will cope if she's been living on dreams. You know him so much better than I do. Do you think he means to marry her, a girl half his age and with no experience?'

'I've known him a long time – and yet I don't know him at all.'

Long after Julian had gone, those words echoed and re-echoed as she became ever less certain of the trustworthiness of the charming Giles Lampton.

From Dover they took the car ferry to Calais. Each hour Tessa's spirits rose in line with her confidence. How exciting it was to hear a foreign language – for if she were honest with herself, it could have been any foreign language for all that she understood of it. When they broke their journey for a meal it was easier. Julian surprised her by speaking fluent French but when the waiter spoke directly to her she was pleased that he understood when she asked him to *parlez lentement, s'il vous plait*. After that she at least got the gist of what was said to her. Deirdre looked on with admiration, but without enough confidence to open her mouth.

They stopped off three nights on the way, time when Tessa's emotions carried her from confident anticipation to relief that she wasn't facing the journey with its language difficulties alone, to appreciation of Julian, to inability to focus on a future that she was frightened to plan lest she should be tempting fate. Then on the evening of the fourth day of travelling they came to Llaibir. She had expected a bustling town, but she soon found how wrong the images she had built had been. The buildings were tall, opening straight on to narrow footpaths; the shops were all small, almost as if they had started as front rooms of houses. As a holiday destination for Deirdre it was completely unsuitable; she could never negotiate the narrow paths and steep kerbs.

Leaving the girls in the car, Julian went into a general store – for despite being nearly nine o'clock in the evening the shops were open. Peering out from the hybrid they watched as he talked to the shopkeeper, a squat woman who smiled and gesticulated as she talked.

'Delightful,' he announced as he got back behind the wheel. 'Most helpful. There is a restaurant around the next corner and somewhere we can spend the night almost next door to it. It may not be the Ritz but she assures me it is well run and we shall find all that's necessary. For one night what more can we ask? And who knows what tomorrow will bring, eh, Tessa?'

On that evening, the long drive behind them, Tessa's optimism was at its highest. Tomorrow she would go to the post office where Giles collected his mail; they must know where he lived.

But by the next day she had to face the difference between dreams and reality. Her school

179

Latin wasn't going to help her with her enquiries, so Julian wrote a card in Spanish for her to take with her: 'I am looking for Giles Lampton, who has a house near here. Can you please help me? Thank you very much.' He and Deirdre were going to the coast some ten miles away, so with hope in her heart Tessa set out on foot. Perhaps by the time they met up at the end of the day Giles would be with her.

She went to the post office; she went to the police station; she enquired in various shops. That evening from the post office she telephoned a weary Naomi.

'No one has heard of him, Auntie. At the post office one man spoke a bit of English and he said Giles hadn't been in for post for a long time. They didn't know where he lived.'

'Perhaps you ought to try in the surrounding district. Giles would never actually live in town if he wanted to get away from people.' Then, after a silence, 'Tessa, look, love, if you can't trace him, don't worry about the baby. You and I will give it all the love it needs.'

Tessa felt a hot tear escape and roll down her cheek. 'That won't happen. If something dreadful had happened to Giles surely someone would recognize his name. But –' she hesitated, wanting to tell Naomi how much her support meant, but frightened of words that would give emotion the upper hand – 'but some of the people in the village would cold shoulder you as well as me. I'd never want to do that to you.'

'Bugger the people in the village.' A comment so out of character that they both laughed. It may have helped them through the moment of emotion, but it did nothing to change the situation.

'In the morning I'll buy a bicycle. I shall be OK where we're staying – they're nice people. Deirdre wants her father to find somewhere near the sea for them to stay; it's only a few miles on and it's not fair to have them hang around here; this is their holiday. With a bike I can get to the sort of out-of-the-way places Giles would be likely to bury himself in.'

Neither of them put into words the truth that couldn't be ignored: if he had been as sincere as Tessa said, why would he have gone to earth in some isolated spot where he couldn't be found?

Seven

Julian and Deirdre's day proved more satisfactory than Tessa's. Not only did they rent a house close to the harbour for a month, but the owner agreed to come each day and 'look after things', which included doing the laundry. Deirdre was delighted with the plan: meals out every day, everything new and strange to her. It was hard not to think of Naomi and worry that she wouldn't have time to look after the dairy as well as everything else. But Deirdre found it impossible for anything to cast a shadow on her suddenly changed world.

Julian didn't dig too deeply into his own feelings. If he let himself reflect on his being in Spain with no companionship except two young girls – or young by his approaching-sixty standard – he was surprised that he wasn't frustrated. Yet he felt his life had found a new purpose. And here he would let his thoughts go no further.

Tessa had expected to stay on alone in the bed-and-breakfast establishment in town, but when Julian showed her the large-scale map he had bought she realized that Llaibir was the only proper town for miles. Giles could be living north, east, south or west, but if he wanted a post office box for his mail it would have to be in Llaibir. So each morning as soon as she'd cleared away the breakfast – the only meal they ate at home – she was away on her bicycle, always exploring a different area and taking with her the card that Julian had written with the question in Spanish. As her confidence grew she called at any shop, café, or even house if it was in an isolated situation and made her enquiry. But the answer was always the same: a shake of the head and words she came to recognize as meaning they knew no Giles Lampton. In the hybrid Julian and Deirdre played their own part in the search. He called at engineering workshops, at a building site; he stopped the car to ask a group of walkers and on another occasion a party of road builders. But each evening when they reported on their day's activities they could find no glimmer of hope.

Deirdre had always envied Tessa her lithe, slim figure, so naturally she noticed there was a change.

'With all your cycling you ought to be getting thin, not fat,' she said, catching Tessa off guard as they settled for the night in the twin-bedded room they shared. Then, with a sly look that belied the teasing note in her voice, 'I bet you're pregnant. All that talk of having to find Giles because you're scared something has happened to him – and the tale that you and he are secretly engaged. I bet you've come to Spain to find him because he's miked off and left you in the club.'

'He *didn't* "mike" off as you so crudely put it. And "in the club" makes it sound horrid.'

'Ah.' Deirdre breathed, her expression changing as she looked at Tessa with real affection. 'So you *are* pregnant. I've been wondering for days.

Well, I'll tell you one thing: we'll find the bugger and see he does the right thing.'

'It's not like that, Deirdre. Honestly it isn't. When he went away I had no idea I was pregnant. It's just that if he doesn't come home until the time of my birthday – that's when we planned to get married – the baby will already be born.'

For a minute or two neither said anything, each pretending to be drifting into sleep. Then Deirdre reached her hand towards Tessa's bed. 'Tessa,' she whispered, 'I suppose it's wicked of me to hope he's hidden himself away where we can't find him. But when the baby gets born, think how nice it could be. It would sort of belong to *us*. Can I be godmother? Wonder what it'll be, a boy or a girl . . .'

Tessa moved her hand across her slightly swollen stomach. Over the weeks as pregnancy had developed from being a suspicion to certainty, her mind had concentrated just on Giles. How strange it was that this was the moment when, for her, the small embryo became a real person.

'I don't mind which it is. And wherever Giles is now, even if we don't find him, he will be back in England almost as soon as it's born.' Hearing her, Deirdre thought she said what she did because she was frightened to face the truth. But she was wrong; Tessa's trust in him never wavered.

But after another week or so Tessa was getting more despondent than she allowed anyone to guess. And she was frightened, too. Each day she cycled for hours, increasingly aware that she was no longer the slender, lithe girl she had been at the beginning of summer. Cycling in the extreme heat was exhausting, but on a day in September although it was hot and sultry, there was a change from the brilliant sunshine. It was the second Monday of the month, an afternoon when the sky seemed low and every turn of the pedals an effort. Although they had no storm, cycling through the quiet countryside she could hear the distant, long rumble of thunder. She guessed that she was about seven miles from 'home' when, without warning, her usual stamina deserted her. Her back ached, her legs felt like lead – and the thunder was getting louder. She was riding through an area of almond groves. She knew that's what they were, not because she would have recognized an almond tree, but she could see where men were working, shaking the branches and letting the nuts fall on to the net they had laid around the base of the trunk. She ought to walk across to them and recite the words Julian had taught her. But she couldn't. All she wanted to do was sit on the ground, to sit there and weep from sheer weariness. There was no real grass verge, but a foot or two of rough, dry stubble before the wire fence that separated the almond grove from the road. First she laid her bicycle down then, feeling clumsy, unattractive and anything but agile, she lowered herself to the ground.

And that's where she was when, a few minutes later, a truck rounded the bend and stopped. The driver, a dark-haired young Spaniard, wished her, '*Hola, buenas tardes,*' and she forced a smile to her face and repeated his greeting.

'Ah! You are English,' he cried with a beaming smile and managing to crush her confidence that she spoke like a native so long as she stayed within the small vocabulary she knew. 'My English not good, but I try to use. My *abuela*, she is of your country. Are you in need for help, señorita? Or do you not enjoy the storm that will soon be here?'

'I was just resting. Then I will cycle home. But I am looking for a friend.' She spoke very clearly and much louder than was normal, then felt embarrassed that she should have done so to this young man who prided himself on being able to speak her language.

'I will be your friend you seek.'

At that Tessa laughed. 'You will certainly be my friend if you can tell me you know where I can find Giles Lampton.'

'So!' He held up his hands in a most un-English manner. 'These almond trees where the men are working belong to your friend's finca. There it is at the top of the hill behind them. That is where you find Giles. But, I do not comprehend, what is your trouble? Why do you weep?'

'Don't know.' She gulped. 'I've asked dozens of people and no one has heard of him. Just so relieved.' This time she forgot to speak with that bit of extra clarity used to foreigners. Digging in the pocket of her pleated shorts she brought out a handkerchief and proceeded to mop up. 'I'm so grateful. Thank you.' Then for good measure

186

she threw in, '*Muchas gracias*,' which earned her a warm smile from her new friend.

'It gives to me much pleasure to help you.' Then, opening the door of the truck, 'And I am happy to have your acquaintance. I am Timus Rodriguez and my home is on the land which joins to that of your friend.'

'I am Tessa Richards, Timus. If you own the land next door to Giles I expect we shall get to know each other.'

Timus looked bewildered. Perhaps the pretty girl had come to work for Giles in the making of his books. But staying to a subject he knew, he said, 'I have made you not to understand. The land that joins to that of Giles is not owned by *me*, but by my father. He and my brother – and me also – we work with the almond trees.'

She only half listened. She wanted to find the gate on to Giles' land. Her thoughts were racing so fast she could scarcely keep up with them. Imagine his expression when he saw her . . . but perhaps there was something wrong, some reason why he hadn't come back to England . . . but why should he have come back yet, when he didn't know about the baby? And why had he never told her he grew almonds?

'Where is the gate? How do I get up to his house?' She got to her feet with more energy than she had felt for weeks and, picking up her bicycle, was ready to be off. Timus pointed to a track just beyond the field where two men were busy harvesting the nuts.

'*Gracias*.' Never had she wished she knew

more words than she did at that moment, but Timus seemed content with her poor effort.

'If we acquaint together, you and me, I teach you my language. Yes?'

'Oh, yes. Of course we will know each other now that I've found Giles. I must go. When I've seen him I have a long way to cycle back to where I'm staying.' And she was on her bicycle and away before he even started the engine of the truck. Watching her go, Timus smiled, the incident impressed on his memory to be relived later. But by the time Tessa turned into the track towards the finca, for her it was already slotted into the past.

The track was too steep for her to pedal so she abandoned the bike, leaving it on the stubbly verge, and continued on foot.

Nothing had gone right for Giles that day. Right from the beginning he had felt at odds with what he was doing. Ten minutes of dictation then, as he played it back and listened, he had erased it and restarted, not just once but time and time again. That had been the pattern of his working day. He would go for a walk, put the whole thing out of his mind and start again this evening. The first heavy drops of rain were splashing on the ground, but that didn't deter him.

That's how it was that as he crossed the court-yard in front of the house he saw someone coming. It couldn't be . . . was it? But how had she found him? He ought to have got in touch with her. It would have been easier in a letter. Tessa . . . his little Tessa . . . His heart was racing and yet he seemed unable to move as he watched her walking up the hill with her head bent in the effort. Then she looked up and saw him. He wanted to maintain a reserve, make it easier for both of them to see that their lives were poles apart. They'd had a wonderful fortnight . . . but then, he'd had plenty of pleasurable weekends – weeks, even – often in that same cottage . . . When he'd been in the mood for female company he had never been left wanting. He'd told her he was going to Spain and didn't know when he'd be back – why couldn't she have understood that was his way of telling her it was over?

And why, as she approached as fast as the steep hill permitted, did he find himself hurrying to meet her? He hadn't been able to get her out of his thoughts. It was crazy and yet he had no power to stop himself as he held her close.

'Giles, I knew I'd find you. Now everything will be all right. Been asking . . .' But her words were lost as his mouth covered hers. Talking was for later; in those first minutes neither of them wanted anything more than this. And only half acknowledged there was the thought at the back of his mind that if she'd come all this way to find him it would be cruel to send her away. Shropshire had given them a glorious fortnight; just imagine the joy they could find shut away from the world here. That would give him time to make her see how different their lives were from each other, lead her gently to realizing that the consuming passion they shared had nothing to do with the day-to-day routine of living. Where was she staying? Wherever it was they must go and collect her things – she would stay here with *him*.

But the next words she spoke pushed everything else from his mind. 'I had to find you, Giles. You see, we can't wait for my birthday. Before that we are going to have a child.' She carried his hand and laid it on her not-quite-flat belly.

'Christ!' The word, and the way he said it, escaped before he could hold it back. Whatever he had expected, it hadn't been this.

Tessa drew back as his hold on her slackened. 'You're not pleased.' It was a statement, not a question, but it gave him time to answer as he knew he must. She had been an innocent child; why in heaven's name hadn't he taken more care that this shouldn't happen?

'I'm in a state of shock,' he murmured, trying to force a laugh into his voice. He rubbed his chin against her head partly out of sympathy for where her unleashed passion had brought her – hers and his, too – and partly so that she couldn't read his expression. He needed a few moments to adjust to where the news had brought them. 'Come indoors and see your new home. It's too late to do anything today, but in the morning I'll go into Llaibir and arrange for a wedding.'

For all his fine words, she was still uncertain. 'Giles, be honest with me. Do you mind about the baby?'

'I'd never contemplated fatherhood.' Then, smitten with guilt when he glanced down at her face and realized he had wiped the radiant joy from it, 'What we found together was so perfect,

I suppose I didn't even consider it might reach beyond just the two of us.'

It seemed she was satisfied with his explanation. And by the time they reached the house and he ushered her indoors, her momentary uncertainty had deserted her. They stepped straight into a vast living room, its high ceiling with the original beams. Books lined one end wall and at the other was an enormous open fireplace. The off-white marble floor and the heavy dark wood of the furniture were in perfect keeping.

'It's perfect – right for the house and right for you, Giles.'

He raised his eyebrows, mocking laughter in his eyes. 'Perfect? But there's not a highly polished brass in sight nor even chintz curtains at the windows.'

'But this is Spain, silly. Brasses and chintz are for the thatched cottages of England.'

'And you think you could be happy here amongst the almond groves?'

'I could be happy in the poorest hovel, so long as we're together like we were in Shropshire.'

He drew her close, holding her against him. Again he did it rather than let her guess his thoughts, but this time he felt ashamed and humbled. He must treat her fairly; he must never destroy that trust.

An hour later, the storm having passed round them and the rain stopped, with her bicycle propped on the back seat of his open-top car and she sitting by his side, he drove down the steep and rutted path to the road.

'You never told me that you grew almonds. Do

191

they look after themselves most of the time? You're usually in England, aren't you?'

'Tell you the truth I think I'm something of a butterfly – or a common moth, maybe – I flit from place to place as the spirit moves me. I fear you'll find me a most unsatisfactory sort of husband. Will you mind upping sticks at a moment's notice? That's the way I've always lived.'

Ignoring his question, she returned to the almonds. 'I suppose you're back here now because the nuts are being harvested. Then what do you do with them?'

'God knows. Personally, I do nothing with them. A neighbouring family, Marcos Rodriguez and his sons, have most of the land round here. There's just a field opposite owned by a bit of a crank and the five acres down the hill belonging to my place. Rodriguez approached me with a view to taking the land off my hands, but I refused. I like to look down on it and know it's mine. But I told him I had no use for the trees – he could do what he liked with them. Can you imagine me scratching around picking up wretched nuts? Oh, no. So Marcos adds my meagre offering to his own crop.'

'But Giles, it would be great to look after the trees. It would make one feel as though one *belonged,* don't you know.'

Glancing sideways at her he thought, as he had so often, what a delightful creature she was. 'You'll shortly be Señora Giles Lampton; you'll need no trees to make you belong.'

'Just a typewriter and a set of headphones,' she

192

said with a laugh, the cares and worries of her weeks of searching swept clean from her mind – just as was all thought of the almond trees.

Once the excitement died down Julian poured them all a glass of local wine to drink a toast to the happy couple.

'All I can offer, I fear,' he said. 'This is just a place to sleep in. Sheer chance that we even have this. But the sentiment is the same. We raise a glass to wish you a long and happy marriage, and by way of congratulating you, Giles, my friend, for your choice of a wife.'

To Tessa it was like living a dream. Then her thoughts jumped to Naomi. What would she be doing, alone there at Chagleigh? Ashamed, she realized that she hadn't telephoned since they'd been living by the harbour.

'I must ring Auntie,' she said, putting the chunky wine glass belonging to the house on the table. 'I haven't spoken to her for ages and I promised I would keep her in the picture.'

'I supposed you must have found a telephone somewhere when you'd been cycling,' Julian said. 'However, I call her most evenings.'

'Did she tell you I hadn't spoken to her? I feel awful, letting the days go like that.'

'I tell her that you are busy helping Deirdre to bed. She always understands. She probably has too much on her own mind to even notice; too much for any of us to be much help to her, I fear. If you ring her with your news, tell her I shall phone shortly. Today she had a helper starting, a woman who served in the Women's Land Army

193

during the war. She can't go on as she is, and she refuses to engage a man to take on your uncle's work.'

'*You* tell her about Giles and me, Mr Masters. Say that I'll speak to her tomorrow when we have a date fixed. I know she'd love to be here for the wedding, but it's just not possible.' Tessa remembered how resentful she'd felt towards Richard when his mother was dying. Her understanding had come a long way in a year and a half.

So Julian went off to use the coin-operated telephone in the porch of Pedro's, a local café frequented by the fisherfolk. No one referred to what he'd said about speaking to her most evenings; uppermost in Deirdre's mind was the excitement of a wedding, while in Tessa's imagination were the years ahead of her when they would make that lovely house on the hill their home.

'I need a cigarette,' Giles said. 'Are we supposed to obey that inelegant notice?' He pointed to a card stuck to the wall above the mantelpiece on which was written in bold letters, PROHIBIDO FUMAR.

'Afraid so,' Deirdre chuckled. 'Señora whatever-her-name-is was really insistent, and she comes in every morning and Daddy says she warned him that she has a nose like a bloodhound.'

'I'm off to look at the sea and have a cigarette.' And that's where he was when Julian retuned from talking to Naomi.

The storm had blown away and the evening

194

was still. In the lamplight he could see the fishing boats swaying gently in the harbour. Out with the dawn, home with the setting sun . . . did that make for a secure, peaceful, contentcd life? For him it wouldn't. He needed the stimulation of a changing scene, new people to meet, new challenges. Christ, but he'd got a challenge now! Of course he loved Tessa. Physically she filled his every desire, just as he'd known she would from the day he'd first set eyes on her. Sex – surely that had to be the most important thing in any marriage. Imagine being tied to a woman of intellect, a woman with interests in world affairs, even all that and beauty, too – it would ultimately count for nothing if she hadn't a sexual appetite akin to his own. But marriage . . . unchanging routine . . . faithful to one woman – could he make himself adjust to that way of living?

So deep in thought was he that he didn't notice Julian approaching, realizing he was there only when the flame from a cigarette lighter made him turn his head.

'Didn't hear you,' he said. 'I was just thinking.' Then, hearing his worried tone, he flourished the hand which held the cigarette. 'And obeying instructions.'

Julian laughed. 'And you haven't even met the lady. I wouldn't want to cross her. Why in heaven's name didn't you contact Tessa in all these weeks?'

Just for a moment Giles hesitated, tempted to give a truthful answer. But what would be the point? 'You know me, Julian – I never tie myself to dates. And to be honest, after our being together for a fortnight earlier in the summer, we couldn't go back to living as we had before. We both knew Richard Pilbeam wouldn't see me as a suitable husband for her – and perhaps he would have been right – that's why we decided to wait until she comes of age. She deserves someone her own age, not a man old enough to be her father and pretty soiled with living.'

'What she deserves is a man who will be faithful to her and give her the love she needs and deserves. Whatever you've done in the past, that was before you knew her. She's a very special girl and you're a lucky man.'

'You and Deirdre will stay for the wedding? I'll get things sorted out in the morning. Meanwhile, I'd better be getting home. Here comes Tessa to say goodnight.'

Julian left them, making the excuse that he was going to say goodnight to Deirdre.

'Now that we've told them everything, come back home with me tonight. In no time we'll be married; what's the point in your living here and me there?' He was standing behind her, holding her close. His hands cupped her breasts, breasts that had changed more than the rest of her body in these early weeks of pregnancy. There was urgency in his words as he spoke softly, his chin moving on her head, his thumbs working the magic he knew she couldn't resist. 'Come home with me. He can't stop you. Think of the night we can share.'

'More than anything it's what I want. I've longed and longed for it. But I can't come home with you now.' Turning suddenly, she put her

196

arms around him. 'Loving together is the most beautiful, wonderful thing. But I can't say to Mr Masters that we don't want to wait, we want to sleep together tonight. It would be spoilt because we'd know they'd be thinking about us, imagining. It would make it horrid instead of – of something sort of sacred.'

'My sweet Tessa. I really do love you.' And in that moment it was the truth.

That same evening at Chagleigh Farm the atmosphere was very different from that in the little house by the harbour. Naomi sat alone, her elbows on the kitchen table, a half-eaten plate of scrambled egg, cold and unappetizing, in front of her. She had carried the daily paper through and laid it on the dresser on top of yesterday's, neither of them even unfolded. If her conscience would allow, she would tell the newsagent not to deliver them any more, but once she did that she knew she would be on a slippery slope to opting out of society. Society? To what society did she belong? She had even had to take her name from the flower rota at church, her one afternoon away from the farm.

Richard, I'm making such a mess of it . . . such a bloody, bloody mess. Today it was afternoon before I took the things to the shop – and could I wonder that Bert Louch there told me he had been approached by Geoffrey Huntley's manager? Of course they would be more reliable, they're not a one-man band. What can I do? But I can't, I won't, have some other man doing your things. Oh, Richard, why did you leave me? I'm no use;

197

I don't know what to do. When Geoffrey called
hassling me I sent him packing just like you had
when he offered before. I can't *sell Chagleigh, I*
won't. It's what we made it. No, that's not true.
It's what you *made it. Richard, everywhere I look*
I see you. And if you're watching me, what must
you think of the mess I'm making? Just so tired
. . . so tired . . . miss you so much . . . don't know
what to do . . . nothing matters without you . . .
sitting here blubbing . . . where's my backbone?
I can't give up. But suppose – I won't do it, but
just suppose – I agreed to Geoffrey Huntley's
offer, I'm so frightened. If I moved away, to the
village perhaps, would I still hold you close? And
if I am holding you close, if it's true and not that
I'm going barmy, what must you think of what
I'm doing to our Chagleigh?

Oh, look at me, won't you, gone to bits like
some silly kid . . .

And that's when her miserable thoughts were
interrupted by the shrill telephone bell. She blew
her nose then rubbed her eyes with the palms of
her hands before she took a deep breath and
unhooked the receiver from the phone on the
wall.

'Wonderful news, my friend,' Julian's voice
greeted her. 'Tessa has found the missing bride-
groom. He's about seven miles inland from where
we are staying on the coast.' Then, when she
didn't answer, 'Naomi, are you still there? My
dear, you're crying,' as he heard a telltale snort.

'Rubbish. It must be a bad line. Is everything
all right with them? About the baby?'

'Everything seems remarkably wonderful;

198

you need have no fears. He's going to town in the morning to make arrangements for the wedding. Tessa will ring you herself tomorrow to tell you what's happening. She's anxious about you, how you're getting on. It must be a weight off your shoulders to have a one-time land girl with you.'

'Julian' – and he could tell by the sudden change in her tone that her defences had slipped – 'I don't know what to do,' she croaked, her battle lost. 'I look around and all I see are things that I haven't done. Geoffrey Huntley was here this morning trying to persuade me to sell – he tried to persuade Richard about a year ago, but of course he wouldn't. This was our life; now he's gone and it just – just mocks me.'

'Do you not think that Richard might want you to accept Huntley's offer? He'd certainly not want you to wear yourself out trying to do his job and your own too. What about this one-time land girl? She must make a difference.' Purposely he spoke in a matter-of-fact tone, knowing that was the only way to help her find her control.

'She's very willing. But she knows nothing about animals. She spent the war growing vegetables in East Anglia.'

'And she didn't say when she applied?'

Naomi started to laugh, although there was no humour in the sound. 'I didn't ask and she didn't say. But she's OK, she'll learn, or rather she is keen to learn but I'm only learning as I go myself.' This time there was no disguising her snort. 'I'm behaving disgracefully. Richard would be so ashamed.'

199

'I think not. I think he would be wretched to see the situation, but never ashamed. As soon as the wedding's over Deirdre and I will come home. She may not be as useful as an able-bodied helper, but she has all the enthusiasm and she misses you.'

'I love having her here and she is a huge help. But I have so little time for the dairy. She'll be by herself a lot.'

'Unless I engage someone to replace Tessa she'll be by herself at home, too. And I don't think she'd want to replace Tessa. Now she has her own transport of a sort, I'm sure she'd rather be working in the dairy. She needs to feel useful; we all do. To be honest I find retirement hard to take.'

'Funny life, isn't it? When things are going well we imagine it will stay that way forever.'

'Perhaps it's time for change. Why don't you give Huntley's suggestion consideration?'

'I couldn't.' Her answer was positive and immediate. 'Please don't talk about it.'

'Very well, it's forgotten. But when I get back to Marlhampton would you think I was intruding if we talked about your way forward? Because for you, for me, for everyone, the future has to be lived and we have to make of it the best we can.'

A few minutes later, leaning against the sea wall, smoking and talking to Giles, no one could have guessed that Julian's mind was miles away in a farmhouse kitchen in Devon. What was there about Naomi Pilbeam that made it so impossible to put her out of his mind? Was it because for the first time his days were empty? A wealthy man – and although he didn't add his appearance to the equation, there was something very distinguished about him with his slim, upright build, his iron-grey hair and moustache, his rather courtly manner that was a natural part of his personality – who if he'd been looking for a wife would have had no trouble in finding one. But he wasn't looking for a wife and what he gave to Naomi was undemanding friendship. Yet she was always there at the back of his mind. No one could see her as a beauty, with her thin face etched with lines, her hands hardened with work. She was painfully scrawny, yet there was an underlying strength about her. He hated to think she was there alone, alone and miserable.

That was when Tessa came out of the house and he went indoors to say goodnight to Deirdre.

At Chagleigh, Naomi scraped the remains of her scrambled egg into the scraps to be made into pigswill, rinsed her plate, banked up the fire and went to run a bath before bed, for there wasn't time for such luxuries in the morning with a herd of cows to bring in for milking.

Lying in the warm water she longed to be soothed, comforted; but all it did was make her more aware of her loneliness and aching misery. Talking to Julian she had purposely given the impression that it was because she felt she was failing Richard in her care of their farm. And of course that was part of it. Not to anyone could she share the anguish that filled her. Everywhere she looked she could imagine Richard there. She'd close her eyes and feel that if she put out her hand she would touch him; she seemed to hear his step in the yard just as she heard an echo of his voice. Jealously she guarded her memories, frightened that they would dim with time. But how could they when he held her heart just as he had ever since she'd been a schoolgirl? Now look at her, ageing ahead of her years, tired to death, and yet . . . and yet . . . With her eyes closed she soaped her hands and moved them sensually on her body, pressing them against her groin as if to conjure up the weight of him. Richard, Richard, help me find you, want you . . . help me find you . . . As she arched and lowered her body the water swirled over her shoulders, her breathing quickened with excitement . . . make it be wonderful . . . always wonderful with you . . . stay with me . . . stay with me . . . now, yes now.

As she opened her eyes the cold light of the bathroom showed her just what she was – a lonely woman in a bath of cooling water. Climbing out, she dried herself without looking in the steamed mirror, then scrubbed her teeth and went to her lonely bedroom. She seemed to hear her voice echoing from hundreds and thousand of nights as it whispered 'Glorious'; just as she remembered the feeling of contentment and thankfulness. But not tonight. Perhaps she had satisfied the physical need in her, but she didn't want to think about it. There had been nothing glorious about that final moment, only confirmation – if confirmation were even needed – of just how alone she was.

Later, believing herself too tired to sleep, she lay staring out of the window into the dark night. Had she been awake some ten minutes later she would have realized that her day's work wasn't over; she would have been faced with yet something else beyond her ability.

By morning when she went out to climb the slope of Lower Meadow to drive in the milking herd, she glanced to her left to Brook Field where the cattle grazed who were not in milk. Something was wrong. She knew it from the sound of a feeble lowing. Milking must wait. As she climbed the stile into the field, that all-too-familiar sense of failure flooded her. Why couldn't she have realized last night that the poor creature was going to calf? And even if she had realized it, what could she have done? At what point do you wake the vet in the middle of the night?

The calf was dead; the weak and anguished cow standing over it with hardly the strength to lick the still form. This was the second calf she'd lost. If things went right it was just luck; if they went badly it was because she was incapable. And so another day started with the reminder of her inadequacy.

The wedding was timed for eleven thirty as Julian and Deirdre were starting their long drive home as soon as it was over. The ceremony was brief, the bride wearing her favourite dress, which was on its second summer, and Giles looking elegant and distinguished in a cream-coloured linen suit. There wasn't a buttonhole in sight. But the agreement was just as binding and the promises the same as would have been made had the day had all the festivity it merited. Then, as soon as it was over and they were outside again saying their goodbyes, Julian opened the double doors of the hybrid and prepared to wheel Deirdre aboard.

'Let me do it, Mr Masters,' Tessa said. Then including Deirdre she added, 'We've had such good times in this.'

'That's why I told Daddy that I don't want another – what was it you were? – a carer-oblique-friend. I can manage most things for myself – much more than I used to before you came. It's really good that Aunt Naomi is so overworked; it means she will give me more responsibility. I bet I could manage to do the cream if she wrote down exactly how – and cut and weigh up the mushrooms. Eggs and butter, they're no problem.'

Julian looked down at her with pride. Then he remembered Geoffrey Huntley's offer which, surely, Naomi would be a fool not to accept. If she clung on to Chagleigh she would wear herself out. And probably come to hate it into the bargain. But if she sold, there would be a tremendous void in Deirdre's life – and what of his own? He turned away from the question before it had a chance to take root.

For Tessa everything was just as she'd dreamed. And the first few weeks held all the wonder of their Shropshire holiday, all that and more. For now there was no end in view, no need to count the days knowing parting was looming ever closer. During his time there alone, Giles had been dictating another book of the people in Burghton, intending to have it typed in its entirety when he returned to London. Instead, Tessa typed it for him, working for hours and loving every minute as she listened to the doings of her friends. It was something else they shared; she felt ever more involved in his life. The smooth running of the house didn't require help from her. Maria, a middle-aged Spanish woman, arrived early each morning on her bicycle and kept the house immaculate. She ordered the shopping, cooked the meals and didn't pedal home until after the evening meal was cleared away. So Tessa had no worries on that score and was always ready and willing when Giles suggested they could go out. All that and the joy in knowing that pregnancy did nothing to lessen her sexual appetite – indeed it enhanced it – and in those early months she believed nothing could change the wonder of where life had brought her.

But time doesn't stand still and with each month she grew larger and heavier.

'What's happened to that lithe, petite child I took to the Shropshire hills? You must be exhausted. Why don't you have an early night?' He spoke kindly enough, but there was something in his manner that made her feel ashamed of her burgeoning body. Still, his suggestion of an early night excited her; she must have imagined his increasing aloofness. By daylight they were good companions, but their last two attempts at love-making had been unsuccessful and for more than a month he had drawn away from her touch.

'An early night? That sounds the perfect end to the day. Let's, shall we?'

'I said "you", not "we". I want to go through the final chapter of my book. When you've got it typed I was thinking of taking it rather than trusting the post.' Then, after pausing as if uncertain whether to continue, 'Don't you ever feel you *must* get away from here for a change of scene?'

'Yes, but I can't go to England now. The baby isn't due for a month, but supposing it came early and started while we were travelling? Maria was telling me this morning that her second son arrived at eight months. My Spanish is really coming on, you know. We talked for ages and I managed really well. She spoke extra slowly but I understood most of it and could answer – well, it must have been understandable. You'd have been proud.'

'Good girl.'

She walked to where he sat, then bent to move her cheek against his.

'Let's creep off to bed, Giles.'

'I can't. I'm sorry, Tessa, I can't. It's not right with you like you are. Your body's not your own and its most certainly not mine.'

'I've been pregnant for months and it didn't use to stop you.'

'I'm sorry.'

She felt rejected – and worse. When had he

ever shown any interest in the coming child? Maria had talked of men's pride in seeing their wives blossom into pregnancy. But Giles had never been like other men. He'd avoided touching her as her body changed. She hated feeling clumsy and heavy; she longed for them to find each other in loving as they always had. Didn't he love her any more? In every other respect they were as close as ever they had been. Yet he avoided any physical contact as if she had some unclean disease.

She spent the next day typing and the following one he left for London, promising to be back before the end of the following week. Tessa wasn't a bit nervous to be alone in the house but he insisted someone should be there with her and Maria was happy to leave her husband in charge of their family. Afterwards Tessa wondered whether Giles had had a premonition of what was ahead and that was why he had escaped to London. Whether or not that was the case she couldn't tell, but she was thankful to have Maria with her when in the middle of the following week, after a busy and interesting morning in the almond grove helping Timus Rodriguez spraying the trees, she went into labour. The first violent pain just as she reached the house after climbing the steep driveway to the first cry of the child was less than four hours.

With five children of her own, Maria made an efficient midwife. Secretly she thought that men were superfluous on such occasions and they could have managed very nicely without the doctor, but Timus had insisted on calling him.

Once he had gone and mother and baby had been spruced up, she laid the tiny bundle in Tessa's arms.

'Have you ever seen a babe more beautiful?' she cooed in her native tongue.

Tessa was shaken by an emotion unlike anything she had anticipated. Even to speak in English was difficult; to hunt for the right words in Spanish quite beyond her.

'Little Amelia,' she whispered. 'Rejoice.' She seemed to hear her grandmother's voice.

Later, when she looked back at Amelia's first year it seemed as if her own life ran on two parallel lines. For Amelia, so tiny and dependent, she felt tenderness she had never previously known; but Giles was her reason for living and marriage to him had done nothing to dim her near worship of him. Physically she loved his appearance, his speaking voice, his well-cared-for hands, his slightly dandy way of dressing. All that and physically, too, she melted at his touch just as she had from the start. She held him on a pedestal above everyone; he knew so much about worldly things, about history, politics, art, literature; she supposed it ought to have made her feel inferior, but instead she looked on him with ever-increasing adoration and pride. She must be the luckiest woman living to share her life with his in this paradise on earth.

So her letters to Naomi – and to Deirdre, too – were a reflection of the perfection of her days. Yet Naomi was less confident. Perhaps her doubts were based on the daily battle of her own life, but was it really necessary for Giles to return to England as frequently as he did? She told Julian something of her unease, relying on him to persuade her she was worrying for nothing.

All Julian said was, 'I fear no one will ever change Giles. If Tessa accepts him as he is and still loves him, as she obviously does, then don't punish yourself worrying about her, my dear.'

He believed he spoke the truth.

Eight

Stubbing out her cigarette in an ashtray bearing evidence of a stressful evening, Naomi leant back in her chair with her eyes closed. Only *she* could know the visions she saw behind those closed lids. *Richard,* she cried silently, *last year was bad but this one is worse. Tomorrow I must take the books to the auditor – there's no way of hiding – after all this time I still make one mistake after another. I've sent lambs to the abattoir which I should have kept for breeding – not just once but over and over I've misjudged what I should have kept and what I should sell. Another few years like this and there'll be nothing left. I've tried, I've worked every hour but what's the use of work when you don't do it right? What am I going to do? Help me to have the strength to do what is right. Show me what is right. I don't know . . . I don't know anything any more. I wanted to keep everything just as you would have; you know I did. Show me what to do. Sometimes I can't even find you.*

Without realizing it she had started to speak her thoughts aloud, but the sudden shrill bell of the front door cut her short. Oh, damn! Who the hell could that be? Before she reached the door her silent question was answered. 'Naomi, it's me,' Julian called. 'Tell me to go away if it's too late for you.'

210

Her spirits lifted before she even opened the door.

'I think a visitor was just what I needed. I'm in the kitchen.' She led the way. 'I've been getting the accounts ready for the auditor.'

'I say!' He sniffed as they reached the doorway of the room where she had got through the evening sustained only by cigarettes. 'You've had a rough evening if my nose isn't mistaken.'

She nodded. 'I've been going over all the figures. They make for depressing reading.'

'But you've done it; it's a hurdle behind you.' How utterly worn out she looked, he thought. His instinct was to reach his hand out to her, to lay it on her shoulder and force some of his own strength and energy into her. But he didn't. Instead he put a bottle of wine on the table. 'You've had a difficult evening and so, my dear, have I. So let us cheer ourselves up with the fruit of the vine. Glasses?'

'In the dining room, in the sideboard cupboard. I'll get—' But as she turned towards the door he put a restraining hand on her arm. 'You sit down, I'll be waiter.'

'We could go in the sitting room.'

'Let's stay here.' He didn't enlarge on why he preferred that they should stay where she had spent the evening, but the truth was that to go into the more comfortable sitting room would distance him from her ordinary day-to-day life. 'Corkscrew?'

'Right-hand drawer of the dresser. Are you hungry? There's a new crusty loaf; we could have some bread and cheese?' she offered.

211

So, five minutes later, they were facing each other across the table, each with a doorstep of bread thickly spread with butter Deirdre had churned, a slab of cheese and a glass of red wine.

'I happened across Geoff Huntley in the village. He said he'd been to see you again.'

Immediately she was suspicious. 'Is that why you're here?'

'No.' But she wasn't satisfied. She knew there was something on his mind and was on her guard. 'No. I'm here because I wanted your company. These days I feel there is no purpose in my life. I came down to Devon thinking it would be a new start for Deirdre and for me. Like a fool I believed that in different surroundings I would be content with days of golf, fishing, useless time-wasters. Everyone needs a purpose – ambition, a shared life, a professional goal whether in art or industry. Had it not been for Deirdre's accident I should have worked all my days. And when it comes to the point I'm no company for the child.'

'She's not a child; she's older than Tessa was when she fell in love with Giles.'

'How can she become an adult when she has no life, no experience, no company? I've failed her and ended up with . . . with . . .'

She reached across the table and took his well-cared-for hand in her work-hardened one.

'How can you say you've failed her? She idolizes you. But, Julian, we must do better for her than letting her come here day after day to work all alone in the dairy. She ought to meet people her own age.'

'What would they want with a girl who couldn't join in their sort of fun? But, Naomi, my dear friend, you realize what you said? "We" must do better for her.' His fingers gripped hers. 'This evening I felt lower than I've ever known. I thought of you, of your courage, your never-changing love for Richard and I . . . I turned to you knowing we have a real and meaningful friendship. We have, haven't we?'

She nodded. 'I don't know how I'd have got through without you.'

'You would have got through. I've been no practical help at all.'

'You've been there for me in my bad moments just as much as in my good ones. So, if you felt low this evening I'm glad you came here.' She took a cigarette then pushed the packet across the table to him.

'I had a letter from Tessa this morning,' she said. 'Apparently Giles is off to London again. Is it really necessary? You read of plenty of writers who live abroad; do they spend their lives hopping back to England?'

'I suspect that for Giles it *is* necessary. Where they live is pretty isolated and Giles likes to hear the heartbeat of life.'

'She deserves better.'

'My guess is that in her sight there could be no better. He is pretty perfect just the way he is. Perhaps later on when Millie is bigger she'll travel with him. You mustn't worry about them. I don't doubt his feelings for her, you know. Over the years he's had plenty of women ready to

213

dance to his tune, but with Tessa he is quite different.'

'But what about *her*? She is an intelligent girl, and a hard worker, too. She's not some dolly bird to be picked up and put down at his convenience.'

His thoughts moved to something Deirdre had suggested: that it was time they took a holiday and couldn't they drive down and see Tessa and Giles – and Millie who was fifteen months old and taking her first steps without their ever having seen her. He had agreed to the idea and only in his secret imagination did he see Naomi joining them. But it seemed she was no nearer giving up the battle of Chagleigh.

As Giles' car drove down the drive and disappeared from view, Tessa felt more desolate than she was prepared to show. Not that there was anyone to see, for Maria was much too engrossed mopping the already clean marble floor of the huge sitting room to waste time looking out of the window. As she worked she sang, as was her habit. Sometimes Tessa wondered whether she was even aware that she did it, yet it wasn't a soft hum of contentment; rather she belted forth as if she were in grand opera – although the songs she sang were traditionally Spanish, melodies she had been brought up with and passed on to her children.

Millie was surrounded by toys in her playpen on the patch of coarse grass. When Giles had picked her up and planted a perfunctory kiss on her forehead, she had struggled to get back to things of more importance. Seeing Tessa coming towards her she beamed with delight and obligingly offered her her favourite rubber doll, a present from Deirdre who always kept her eyes open for small things which might please the child whom she had never seen.

'Let's take her down to see Timus,' Tessa said, swooping the little girl into her arms, complete with doll. 'See, I've got the shawl, so up we go.' She already had a large, brightly coloured shawl around her shoulders and, now, with one deft and experienced movement, she lifted Millie over her head on to her back, where she held her with one hand while with the other she managed to wrap the shawl round them both, gypsy fashion. Then with the child firmly anchored to her back, she tightened the material and tied it securely. 'Off we go.' And, knowing it was a game Millie enjoyed, she put a skip in her step and was rewarded by the baby's chuckles.

As she started down the sloping drive she looked at the almond grove and saw that Timus was there, just as she had hoped.

'I see that Giles has driven away.' He greeted her. 'How long will he not be here?'

'Who can say, Timus,' she answered, forcing a light note.

But Timus was a sensitive soul and recognized that was the way she wanted to play it. So, with a wide smile of welcome, he passed her a rake.

'Then I hope I may be looking forward to two helpers?'

'There's nothing I'd like better, but I can't vouch for Millie. She soon gets bored when she's held so tight to my back. And the ground here is too rough to let her free.'

But Timus had the perfect solution. Since the advent of Tessa at the finca, and especially during Giles' periods away, he had become a frequent visitor to the house. Never was he an invited guest, but he often carried Millie home and stayed a few minutes playing with her or chatting to Tessa or Maria, so he knew exactly how to fold the playpen to carry it down to the almond grove. Waiting for him Tessa looked around her, letting the atmosphere of the place she had come to love come between her and the image of Giles driving mile after mile northward as he moved from the world they shared to one that was alien to her.

'I come with her things.' Timus' voice broke her reverie. 'One rug so that the ground does not hurt her, one pen, one hat and two toys. Maria stopped her song to choose what I bring.' He spoke in imperfect English, with the native good humour of his race.

'Now we're all set. Thanks, Timus.' Tessa answered in Spanish, although there were times when her vocabulary let her down. So, between the two of them, a natural bond had developed, made all the stronger by the challenge of learning. 'Giles never talks about this bit of land. You said he had refused to sell it so I suppose he just enjoys knowing it is *his*. Timus, is it very important to you and your family that you harvest it?' As she talked she held Millie while he set up the pen in the shade of a tree, then she plonked her down on her bottom and gave her her drum and the rubber doll for company.

'For the amount of nuts, no. It is but a small plot. But it is neighbour of our ground and we would not like to see it neglected.'

'Is there a written agreement, what in England we call a lease?' She gave up the struggle and reverted to her natural tongue.

'It was a friend-to-friend arrangement. My father and Giles did a shake of their hands.'

For a few seconds Tessa looked around her, seeing into the future. Then she shared her idea with Timus. As they talked, so their enthusiasm grew. Never before, within a couple of hours of Giles leaving her, had she been filled with such excitement.

That was the first time Giles made the journey by road; usually she had driven him to the railway station. But the journey was tedious, with two changes of train before he reached the ferry. Even more than Tessa had realized, he had craved the sense of freedom. It was more than a week before he crossed the channel, for he had no reason to hurry and preferred to deviate from the main roads, engage in conversation with rural folk and spend two nights in Paris before driving on to Calais and thence to Dover. Once he was back in his London apartment he telephoned Tessa, prepared to hear how worried she had been by his long silence and how empty the place was without him.

'Oh, Giles,' she greeted him as soon as she recognized his voice, 'I've been hoping you'd phone. I'm so excited. There's such a lot to tell you. That silly operator won't keep interrupting, will he?'

217

What could make her sound like that? Oh, God, no! Surely she wasn't pregnant again. Tessa's excited voice soon banished his fear. 'That five-acre plot the Rodriguez boys use – I thought you had leased it to them. But Timus said it was just an agreement that they could look after the trees and add the almonds to their own.'

'Are you telling me they want to give up? Damn. They were only interested because it adjoined their boundary. What a—'

'Stop talking and listen. Giles, I want to use it. Timus says he'll help me and he's already taught me an awful lot about looking after the trees.'

'What the devil would you want with five acres of almonds?'

'I know no one could make a living on a plot that size.' Then with a chuckle that seemed to bring her right into the room with him, 'But I'm not looking to earn my living – I'm a kept woman, remember?'

'When you talk like that, my sweet Tessa, I wish I were there with you. What the hell am I doing in this noisy, smoky city? Right this minute I could make you forget almond trees . . . make you forget everything . . .'

She was sitting at his desk, something she often did when he was away, as if that would hold him closer. Now she closed her eyes as she heard his words. 'Giles,' she whispered, 'I wish that's how it could be – right this minute like you said.' Then, pulling herself back on track, 'But listen, Giles, I was telling you about the trees and what I want to do. Timus said they will be quite happy not to use this year's crop so what I mean to do is write to the really posh shops in London. When we harvest them—'

'We?'

'Timus and me, that's the "we". Giles, my plan is that when we harvest them I shall pack them in red netting bags with, say, three quarters of a pound of nuts in each and with a label attached saying they were grown and packed by me at Finca el Almendros and then the address. It makes them so much more personal for people than just going to a shop and buying any old nuts, not knowing where they've come from or anything about them. I could have a picture of the finca on the label. What do you think?'

'If that's what you want to do, of course you can. You're my wife, so it's your land as much as mine.'

'But I wouldn't dream of doing it – well, that's a lie, I certainly *would* dream of doing it, but I wouldn't actually *do* it if you didn't agree.'

'I give you permission to do anything you like. That label, though – it might be a selling point with those "posh shops" you say you want to write to, if you said the nuts were grown and packed at Finca el Almendros, the Spanish home of Giles Lampton, by his wife Tessa. A name people know carries weight.' He changed the subject. 'Tessa, I shall be in London for perhaps a couple of weeks and then I thought I'd drive down to have a night or so with Julian. I'll look in at the farm, too.'

It was only after she'd put the phone down that she realized that until today on hearing that he was going to see Naomi her first thought would have been that she wished she were to be there too. But on that early summer evening her head was too full of plans. Usually, when Giles was away, she ended her days hating the emptiness of his side of the bed, dreaming of when he was home again and he would draw her towards him; that night her mind was in a whirl, it flitted from red netting bags and whether she could buy them or, if not, where she could get them made, to the wording on the labels, to how many bags could be filled from each tree – and finally to what her replies would be from her introductory letters.

Alone on the stile which divided Lower Meadow from the top field where the sheep seemed to watch her with curiosity, Naomi lit another cigarette (her third since she'd been sitting there). She ought to have been aware of how many she'd had, for she and Richard had always been careful never to throw their stubs down. Each time she came to the end, she lit a new one from the burning tip of the old, carefully crushed the old stub against the wood of the stile then, satisfied it was out, put it into the empty packet she kept in her pocket for the purpose.

On that evening she felt too drained to even contemplate what she had agreed. She had done it! The very thing she had vowed she would never do, and now she had given her word. For thirty-seven years this had been her world . . . no, Richard and what they shared here had been her world. So what had been so different about Geoff Huntley's offer this time? She could have refused out of hand as she had on his two previous visits.

It had been when he'd told her that the local man who had been his manager had left and he had advertised in a weekly farming paper for a replacement. The young fellow who he had found to replace him seemed eminently suitable, was just married and needed accommodation. There wasn't even a tiny cottage empty at Geoff's farm. Losing the chance of filling the post was what had brought Geoff Huntley to Chagleigh, but it had been something quite different which had taken Naomi by surprise as she had been about to refuse. In her mind had been the day she and Richard had found the neglected and run-down farm. Feeling his presence very close, it had been as though he had put the words in her mouth as she'd given her answer.

'Chagleigh will be just right for them. This was our first home too. They couldn't fail to be happy here,' she had said, with an unexpected sense of deep peace. In the two years without him, never had Richard seemed as close.

The business details had been brief; she and Geoff Huntley had shaken hands on the deal and promised to contact their solicitors immediately. She had agreed to leave the basic furniture and to move out as quickly as the sale could be arranged. She had wanted Huntley gone; she had wanted to recall the moment when she had been so certain of Richard's presence.

And hours later as daylight faded it was still what she yearned for. She could remember their years so clearly, but remembering is a far cry from the certainty of his nearness. This morning he had been with her, nearer to her than at any time since his death; by evening he was a memory, a dear and precious memory. Jumping from her high seat on top of the stile, she hurried down Lower Meadow trying to escape her sudden, overwhelming loneliness. Ahead of her was the task of sorting out the home that had been their life, leaving items of furniture they had bought at auction sales, the essentials when they were setting up home, other pieces through the years, all of it woven into the pattern of their lives. Now it was all to belong to another young couple. And for her, what was ahead? She couldn't see ahead; she was frightened to look.

There was a feeling of unreality about what she had done. If only there was someone to tell, but there was no one.

As if to prove her wrong as she crossed the yard she heard footsteps and, with a flood of relief, expected to see Julian. Indeed, one of her visitors was Julian, but the other took her completely by surprise.

'Giles! How nice!' Her natural hospitality came to the fore. 'Tessa told me you were in London when she phoned me while she was at the post office the other day, but I hadn't expected to see you down here.'

'Nor I,' Julian put in. 'He wanted to come and see you to report to Tessa. I hope I'm not intruding.' In that post-war era when so many formalities had been abandoned most people in his circumstances would have said, 'I'm not butting in, am I?' or something similar. But not Julian; it wouldn't have been natural for him.

'I intended to phone you this evening, Julian.'

'Indeed? Nothing wrong, I hope?'

'Geoff Huntley came again today.' And from the way she said it Julian sensed this visit had differed from previous ones. 'I have agreed. We shook hands on it.' Then to Giles, 'You must be wondering what I'm talking about.' In fact he had been doing no such thing, for the events at Chagleigh Farm weren't high priority in his life. But Tessa had told him how supportive Naomi had been and that, if he hadn't been tracked down, she had been willing to make a home for Tessa and his child despite all the holier-than-thou gossip, so he owed her the smile he bestowed on her.

From there on, the evening moved in a direction so unexpected that Naomi felt she was living a dream.

Tessa wrote letters introducing herself to some of the more expensive outlets. She found a producer of the suitably eye-catching red net bags she had envisaged and a printer for the labels, worded as Giles had suggested. Harvesting of the crop wouldn't be for another three months, but never had she been so excited by a challenge. Money had little to do with the venture; for more than a year her grandmother's legacy had been safely in the bank. Add to that the fact that Giles had given her free rein to use the five-acre plot as she liked and to her the sky was the limit. But of course reason told her that that was an exaggeration, for how many pounds of nuts could she hope to export from such a small plot? Reason, ambition and excitement have little in common so she discounted reason, concentrated on ambition and found that excitement followed automatically.

It was her habit to telephone to Chagleigh every two weeks or so, but on that occasion when she phoned the line was dead. Worried that something was wrong, she called Fiddlers' Green and was answered by Deirdre.

'Yes, Auntie is fine,' she was assured. 'I was in the dairy this morning and everything's OK. There was a really big storm last night; I expect the line is down. I'll tell her you tried to get her. You know how busy she is, so I'll pass any news on to her. Now tell me all about Millie.' When the call ended, Deirdre put the receiver back on its stand with a chuckle. At that moment she saw life as an adventure. But, for her, there were still plenty of other moments, times when she was dragged deep into the mire of misery, when her future held no hope and she saw herself as becoming old and withered like Miss Sherwin, only worse, because at least Miss Sherwin was useful, something she could never be. At twenty years old other girls were meeting people, falling in and out of love. But in the last few days she had become involved in plans, plans that she must keep secret. Beyond that she wasn't prepared to think.

'I'm starting back tomorrow,' Giles said. 'Tessa, I want to get home to you. How do you put up with me? When I get home everything is perfect, as if you are the balm my restless soul needs. But how long before I chase after the clamour of life that, right now, I just want to leave behind? I'm sorry, sweet Tessa. You deserve so much better than I give you.'

'Drive fast – but not silly fast. Come home safely. I want you back; I want you to share what I'm planning.'

'Is that all you want me for?'

'I want you for everything; you know that. I want us to talk together, walk together, love together—'

'Is that so far down the list?' She could hear that teasing note she loved.

'No. It seemed a bit pushy to put it right at the top,' she answered in like vein.

'Sweet Tessa, I do love you. I may not be much of a husband, or father either for that matter, but the one true thing is that I love you.' It was something he seldom put into words and she felt her eyes sting with tears of emotion she could hardly bear.

'Giles,' she whispered, not knowing what she wanted to say and frightened of trying to say anything.

'Anyway, my sweet,' he said, moving briskly on. 'I shall start back tomorrow. But it's a long drag—'

'Especially on your own. We could have had such fun if we'd done the trip together.' But in her heart she knew very well that taking her with him would have defeated the purpose of his escape to his old life.

'It wouldn't be the same with a baby in tow. But, anyway, I should be home about five days from now, so get the soil of that almond grove

225

scrubbed off your hands. How's the typing going?'

Another minute and they had both hung up. From the kitchen came the robust sound of Maria singing what Tessa had come to recognize as a Spanish lullaby. There wasn't a sound from Millie, who had a rug in her playpen on the stone floor of the kitchen; Millie's voice usually held her spellbound. Gazing out of the window down the slope to the grove, Tessa felt a sense of peace, of the rightness of where life had brought her. This is where she was born to be, here with Giles, with Millie, with all this – she looked just down the slope but in her mind's eye, as well, she saw the hills behind her rising into the foothills of the mountains. I wish you could see it, Gran, I wish you could know about Giles and Millie. But perhaps you can. I'm still holding you safe in my heart, so you *must* know.

By the time the next five days had passed Tessa's ears were tuned to the slightest sound of a car. Yet when the little convoy turned into the drive she wasn't at home. She had cycled next door – if having the neighbouring house nearly half a mile further along the road can be called 'next door'.

The Rodriguez family finca was much larger than el Almendros. Indeed it needed to be, for the family lived the traditional way. When their eldest son, Phillipe, had married no one had expected that he would leave home. Instead Katrina had become one of the family and now the tribe had increased with the birth of each of

226

their two children. Conversation with them had been difficult for Tessa in the beginning, for their knowledge of English was no better than hers of Spanish. In the two years she had been their neighbour they had improved a little and she had improved a lot – in both cases thanks to Timus who had a natural aptitude for languages. On that afternoon she had cycled to the village to post some photographs to Naomi and had called to see if she could bring them anything. Delivering four skeins of white wool should have taken no time at all, but she hadn't taken into account the fact that Katrina was desperate to share her news. As she held the soft wool against her cheek she was far too excited to school herself into trying to piece together a sentence in English. And even if Tessa couldn't understand each word she was able to follow the gist of what she was being told.

'You must have guessed when you knew I would be knitting in white wool. I expect you had noticed that I am to have another child. It will be born in January. I am going to crochet a carrying shawl; the old one is no longer good enough for a new baby.'

'Gracious! Congratulations. But you're going to be busy, Katrina. Juan will be not quite three, Francesca just as old as Millie is now and then another.'

Señora Rodriguez, the matriarch, answered before her daughter-in-law had a chance. 'Babies today are our future for tomorrow. It is good that Katrina is fertile. A good marriage has the gift of many children. It is hoped that you too will

227

be blessed with a proper family, brothers and sisters, tomorrow's men and women. A home is an empty place without the voices of children. I was sad when our daughter, Sofia, left home to live with her husband and his family. She is far away in Granada. It is her in-laws who are blessed with the sound of the children born of Sofia. Young voices to fill the house, and later, as Marcos and I grow old and our boys take control, we shall be content knowing that there is another generation growing up.' Then with a hearty laugh, 'The almonds will be in good hands.' As she talked she put her not inconsiderable strength into kneading a great mound of dough for the bread she made each day.

As Tessa pedalled home she thought of the family she'd left, the atmosphere of unchanging continuity in the house. Everybody worked hard but, from the youngest in her pram to Señor Rodriguez working amongst the almond trees and teaching his sons all he knew, they were a team. Briefly she envied them their family ties but almost as the thought took shape it vanished, overtaken by what she saw as she started up the steep slope to the finca. Giles was home! That was her first thought and then she recognized the second vehicle – the hybrid.

Standing on her pedals she forced them with all her might, then dropped her bike unceremoniously and ran indoors.

'I'm here, I'm home!' she shouted when she found the living room empty. 'Where are you?'

Coming up quietly behind her, Giles took her by surprise when he pulled her back against him.

'Close your eyes and then turn around,' he said as he might have done to a child.

Tessa did as he said, but with her eyes still closed she drew his head down and found his mouth with hers. Only then did her thoughts go further and she remembered Julian Masters and Deirdre. But when she opened her eyes the first person she saw was Naomi, a Naomi changed and haggard in a way their telephone contact hadn't hinted. The next few minutes were complete bedlam: they needed the noise and excitement. All of them except Giles, who disappeared to return a few minutes later when the initial hullabaloo had abated a little, carrying a tray with glasses and a bottle of cava, Spain's answer to France's champagne.

'The downstairs bedrooms aren't very large, Auntie, but it's best that you and Deirdre use those and the downstairs shower. Mr Masters can have the guest room upstairs.' Then with a shiver of excitement, 'I can't believe it! You don't know the times I've imagined you coming. But who's looking after Chagleigh?'

'I'll tell you all about that in a minute. First and far more important, where is my great-niece? If she's having a nap can't we wake her up?'

'She's in the kitchen with Maria. It's nice for Giles to show the place to you all without having to carry her around. Maria has had children of her own and is an absolute joy with her. Soon I won't be able to dump her in her playpen and leave her there, but when Giles is working he needs the place to be quiet and Maria has been a real blessing. I'll make up the beds for you and

229

Deirdre and then we'll go and tell her that you'll all be here for dinner.'

'We ought to have given you warning, but Giles insisted a surprise would please you more.' Naomi could see from Tessa's expression how pleased she was that Giles had wanted to give her pleasure. 'If there's not enough in the house to suddenly feed so many we could always take you out to dinner.' Naomi had kept house for two for years enough to know how an extra four at the table could create a problem.

'Oh, there'll be food enough. Maria is sheer magic; if we haven't enough of one thing she'll think of another. I don't interfere with the catering, unless there's something Giles and I especially want.'

Naomi suspected that 'Giles and I' really meant just 'Giles'.

'Let's do the beds together. With two of us they won't take long and I'll tell you about Chagleigh at the same time.' Her voice gave no hint of how hard she found it to talk about the last two weeks, but she spoke in a bright, upbeat tone, knowing that if once she let fear even into her thoughts the charade would be over. And so she told Tessa of her decision to accept Geoff Huntley's offer and, in turn, he had given his word that his staff would look after the animals from the hour she moved out, taking the milk to his own dairy. When the contract was ready he would sign and press for a speedy completion. In return, and with unacknowledged thankfulness, she had agreed to leave the house furnished with the exception of personal items, so that Huntley's young manager and his bride could move in as soon as she vacated it, even though contracts hadn't been signed. With her new passport in her handbag and with power of attorney given to her solicitor she had been free to travel. Not to anyone would she describe the moment when she closed the door on the place that had been home to her all her years with Richard. Keeping a smile on her haggard face, she told Tessa simply the bare facts.

Julian's intention was to stay in the Llaibir area long enough to let Naomi realize that she had a life outside Marlhampton. She had spent the single night at Fiddlers' Green between leaving Chagleigh Farm and setting out on their journey, and he had been conscious that she avoided talking about her plans for the future. Even though she told him he was her dearest friend, there was a barrier around her that he couldn't cross.

They were sitting together in deck chairs on that patch of coarse, rough grass, grass so unlike the fine green sward of Fiddlers' Green. In front of them was the empty playpen, for that morning Tessa had pushed Millie down to the almond grove with Deirdre alongside in her electric chair.

'Deirdre won't want to leave all this,' Julian said, lying back in his chair and gazing up at the cloudless blue sky. 'I'm not sure if I shall either.'

Did he imagine it or, for a brief second did he detect a look akin to fright on Naomi's face?

'They've made us very welcome, but there are limits how long visitors should stay,' she answered, making sure her tone was light enough to let him see she hadn't taken his remark seriously. 'You may say you've retired but you still keep a strong hand on the business.'

'I do, but not because I'm necessary to it. It's in perfectly good hands. A monthly report and the occasional visit is all that's necessary – not even as often as Giles finds he needs to go to London.' He was watching her closely as she lay back in her chair, her eyes once again closed as if the conversation had no real importance. 'Naomi, we've not talked about your future. Is that because you have no set plans?'

At his words she sat up, then leant forward with her elbows on her knees and her thin hands gripped tightly together. 'If I knew, then I'd tell you. It's like looking into a thick fog, Julian. I'm frightened to leave Marlhampton and everything that's been part of the years we had there. I must go back. I have money, or I shall have when the sale goes through. I can afford a house or a cottage. In places we've known together I shall feel he's close.'

'My dear, your Richard will always be close. If you moved to the other end of the earth his spirit would be with you.'

'I was frightened to come here, you know.' Then a smile that, at least to Julian, made her thin face radiant.

'And . . .?'

'I think what you say is true. A body dies, but not a spirit.'

'I'm not a churchgoing, religious man, but I do believe that the love he gave to you – and you to him – was surely a meeting of souls, spirits. Nothing can ever change that; it will be with you as long as you live and for all eternity. How can his spirit find peace if he knows you are afraid to live the life that is left to you? For you must live it, you have no choice.'

'I know,' she whispered, 'and I should be grateful for all we had. And for all I still have. I know. I *do* know. It's just so hard, Julian. What would I do without you? I could never talk to anyone else as I do to you.'

'I'm not in the habit of soul searching with friends, but you are no average friend. You are very precious in my life. My dear, tears? What have I said?'

'You must have found a weak spot in my armour.' She sniffed. 'You know what? If we were somewhere away from the house, away from everyone, I'd let myself cry as if it would wash away all the misery.' The words seemed to come before she could stop them and to hear herself talk like that only added to her wretchedness.

'Let's find somewhere away from everyone. Wipe your face and blow your nose. I won't disturb Giles; I'll go and tell Maria we're out for lunch.'

Half an hour later when they were in the foothills of the mountains, away from everyone just as she'd said, she felt exhilarated. He was aware of the change in her, the lessening of tension.

'I found this place when we were here before,' he told her. 'While Tessa was off on her bicycle Deirdre and I didn't shirk, I promise you, and it was a joy to see what it did for the child – no,

233

I forgot, she's not a child. But to me she is; she always will be. Before we go inside the restaurant we'll walk over there. There's a path of a sort through the trees. The view is breathtaking.' Leaving the parked car they started to walk. 'I pushed Deirdre over there.' Then with a laugh, 'She was offended that I insisted she wasn't to switch on the motor. I couldn't have held her back if the chair had got out of control. The sheer drop isn't for the faint-hearted. Are you OK on heights?'

She nodded. 'Julian, it's more than beautiful. Never seen anything so – so strong, grand and yet – it's not threatening.'

He nodded in agreement, keeping his hand firmly on her elbow. 'It makes one feel humble in the great scheme of things.' Then, moving away from the edge, 'Come, my dear,' he said with a change of tone, 'we need food. Last time the restaurant was surprisingly good for such an isolated spot.'

They were the only people eating and yet the food was fresh and the salad, which was brought to the table with new crusty bread and allioli while they studied the menu, was a meal in itself compared with what Naomi had put on the table when she lived on her own.

It was while they were eating the main course that he took her by surprise, his words casting a shadow.

'I'm seriously considering moving out here from Fiddlers' Green. It would be so good for Deirdre. I had my reservations over how easy it would be for Deirdre in her wheelchair when we first came out, but what I didn't tell you earlier – and neither have I mentioned it to her – is that I have already seen a house I think could be suitable. It's not far from here, within walking distance of the village we drove through, Pedrada. That's where the agent is. Naomi, I wish you'd come and see it with me. I felt I could live in it, but you'll see it from a woman's point of view.'

'Of course I'd be interested to see it,' she said in a voice that gave no hint of the aching sense of loss she felt, 'but it's Deirdre's reaction you must listen to.'

'I'm doing this very badly.' Clearly he was annoyed with himself. 'Naomi, I want you to be there; without you it can't be complete. I want you to help in the choice of where we live – and I want that "*we*" to include *you.*'

Naomi looked at him in stunned silence, half frightened and half excited by the unexpected suggestion. But what was he asking of her? Not complete without her? Thoughts of Richard crowded her mind, of the natural growing of the intimacy of their lives. All that part of her life belonged just to him and always would.

'I don't understand.' In her hesitancy Julian heard the answer to the proposal he had wanted to make to her.

More than twenty years ago when he had embarked on that short-lived marriage, he had been driven by physical desire and, if he were honest with himself, by vanity that a beautiful young woman half his age chose him above her other admirers. Now, there was no vanity in his feelings for Naomi; indeed he felt humbled by her honesty, her never-altering love for Richard, the determined way she had striven to keep the farm as he would have. But that was only half of what moved Julian to want to be with her, to share all that he had with her. Sometimes he would look at her, forcing himself to see her as a woman aged beyond her years, worn out by work of which she'd been physically incapable. But none of that lessened his desire for her or his longing to be able to care for her and to love and protect her. How long had he felt like this about her? Perhaps from that first morning when she had called to take Deirdre to the dairy, and as time had passed she had increasingly filled his mind.

But, as they sat facing each other across the table in that empty restaurant, instinct warned him to tread carefully.

'My dear, for all three of us this would be an adventure. You may not see us as we see you – the nearest we have to a family. Think of the home we could make together, all three of us. And surely you and I are better friends than one sees in a good many families. What plans had you for the future?'

She shook her head. 'None. I was too frightened to look ahead.'

'Like it or not, you have a good many years to be lived. Is it such a daunting thought that you might share them with Deirdre and me?'

'I can understand that if you want what Tessa used to call "a carer-oblique-friend" for Deirdre, and you want to live in Spain, then your choice would be for someone of your own nationality.

So much easier, at least until she has learnt the language.'

Despite himself he reached out and gripped her hand that rested on the table. '"Carer-oblique-friend" be damned. You are more than those words could ever encompass. Come, drink up your coffee and we'll go and get the key. Let's see the house first. You may hate it. It's quite unlike Finca el Almendros.'

Twenty minutes later he turned the key in the latch of Casa Landera, a two-storey white house built literally into the craggy hillside. The rooms were large, the floors marble, the windows enormous, the view enough to take her breath away. There were four bedrooms, three very large and one less so, but not small. As they went from room to room her feeling was of light and space, their footsteps seeming to echo through the emptiness.

'I thought I'd make the fourth bedroom a study,' he told her. Then forcing himself to say it, he added, 'There are still three good bedrooms and I doubt if we'd be having any overnight guests so it's plenty large enough. Two bathrooms, so you girls could have one and I'd be able to clutter up the other one as I liked. They both need stripping out and bringing up to date, as does the kitchen. What do you say, Naomi? Surely we could make a good life here.' He came to stand behind her as she gazed out of the window, his hands on her shoulders. 'My dear,' as he heard her stifled sob, 'isn't this what we came for? So that I could give you a shoulder and you could wash away some of that bottled-up misery?'

She let him turn her towards him and draw her into his arms, making no effort to hold back the sobs that shook her thin frame. 'I want to come . . . I want to be here . . . with you and Deirdre . . . but – but it's all so different from anything we shared, Richard and me. At home we knew the countryside, we knew the wind and the weather . . . Oh, Julian, we were like one person. How could I find him where it's so different? If I can't, I can't be complete. I'll have to go back to what we knew.'

There seemed no end to her tears and neither did he try to find words of comfort. 'Sleep on it, my friend,' he said when at last her outburst was over and she mopped herself up with a large handkerchief that must have been Richard's.

'It could be a beautiful house,' she said as he locked the door behind them. 'Even a swimming pool – or it will be, when you have it filled.'

'I wondered about that. Do you think, if I had some sort of lift made to lower her in and to retrieve her, Deirdre could use it?'

'Wouldn't that be wonderful,' she agreed. 'We'd see one of us always went in with her.'

They looked at each other, realizing what she'd said. 'But supposing—'

He knew exactly what she was supposing. 'You're frightening yourself for nothing. As long as you hold Richard in your heart he will always be within your reach. Once upon a time I thought I was in love – I've told you about my brief marriage. I soon knew it wasn't love, not on my part nor on hers either. But it frightened me off ever giving wholehearted affection – except to

Deirdre.' He told himself he was being a fool to say more than that, but the words came just the same. 'Then I met you, you who understood real and wholehearted love that will last as long as you live. If you won't stay here with us it won't change what I feel for you.'

'No, Julian, dear Julian.'

'All right. You don't feel the same about me—'

'But how can I? My heart belongs to Richard. Haven't you just said you understand that?'

'And what do you think Richard would want for you? Life has to be lived. I'm asking you to share the home with Deirdre and me; more than I can say, I want you to share it as my wife. But even if you don't care enough for me to agree to that, then I beg you, Naomi, let us make a new beginning for the three of us.'

'Your wife . . .' she whispered, as if she had heard nothing beyond those words.

'I've bared my soul to you. We could make a good life—'

'But marriage . . . falling in love, the glorious – well, all of it – that's for the young. Look at me, Julian, do I look like a bride?'

'You look like the woman I want to share my life with. But there's something even more important: if you refuse to be my wife, then I beg you, stay with us. You've been the heartbeat of my life for so long.'

She took his hand and raised it so that she caressed the back of it with her cheek.

'I couldn't bear to go home without you,' she told him.

They drove down the hill to Pedrada village

both lost in their own thoughts. He was a fool; he ought to have let them settle happily into the house together before he frightened her with talk of marriage. Naomi's thoughts were on what he had said. She tried to be honest with herself as she imagined living with him as her husband. But Richard was her husband. They had been young together, driven by the same desires, excited as they took the first intimate steps to a shared life, a shared love. But marriage to Julian . . . she imagined the shame she would feel when he first saw her skeleton-like figure, every rib there to be counted, hip bones barely covered with flesh, no high collar to disguise her scraggy neck, arms and legs like sticks. She hadn't always been like that. Sometimes with Richard she had felt ashamed to show her naked-ness, but Richard was Richard, he was her second self. The images moved to Julian desiring her as a woman, wanting to make love to her. He wouldn't need to be ashamed to show his body; despite his age he was still a fine-looking man.

So deep in thought had she been that when he took his hand off the steering wheel and covered hers it took her by surprise.

'Time's not on our side, Naomi, my darling, but a new beginning is just what we need.'

'I know. And Julian, I only hesitate because something in me feels as though I would be breaking faith with Richard.'

'Say no more at the moment. When you're alone with your memories, look to Richard for your answer. This is where we have to return the key; I'll not be a moment. I shall tell them we want the house? Right?'

She nodded, then as he started to close the door of the car she said, 'Julian, you are a truly nice man.'

He smiled, but it was an effort. Was to be a 'truly nice man' such an accolade?

Nine

The news that they were all staying in Spain was received with enthusiasm at Finca el Almendros, where it was assumed that Deirdre's adopted aunt was going with them as 'carer-oblique-friend' – and presumably Julian's 'housekeeper-oblique-friend' too. No matter what the future held for Julian and her, her presence made the arrangement possible. She insisted that he took Deirdre on his own to show her the house, and was rewarded on their return by the sight of the girl looking radiantly happy and with non-stop chatter about the wonders of the place.

Moving house seldom goes as smoothly and quickly as anticipated. And in this case Julian wanted far more work done to Casa Landera than he'd first envisaged. From the large entrance hall he wanted a lift installed to the upper story; the largest bedroom was to be divided to include an en suite bathroom specially adapted for Deirdre. Nothing would give her complete independence, but what he planned took a large step towards it. The seat by the bath would operate electrically, rising to swing above the water then lowering her into the water. It would be luxury such as she had never known. A hoist by the swimming pool would work on the same principle.

All that was only one side of the arrangements. Julian travelled by train and ferry to England

242

where he put Fiddlers' Green on the market and gave a month's notice to the staff, with the exception of Miss Sherwin, who had been with them all Deirdre's life. She was to stay on in the house until it was sold, see the furniture into store if the work hadn't been completed at Casa Landera, and dispose of anything he didn't require. In fact, trusting her implicitly, he arranged power of attorney for her to handle everything on his behalf. When at last the day came for her to catch the bus to Exeter for her onward journey to her bachelor brother in Maidstone, she would have a cheque for a year's salary in her handbag and the knowledge that Julian had arranged for a not ungenerous pension to be paid into her account on the first day of each month.

It had been the last week in July when he had taken Naomi to see Casa Landera, but they knew it would be many months before the work could be completed, the furniture in place and everything ready for them to move in. In the meantime he rented a furnished house in Llaibir.

They knew that Deirdre was suffering mood swings, but none of them looked beneath the surface. It was easier to assume that she was frustrated by the time everything was taking and would be different once they were in their new home. She was probably impatient for the ability to sleep upstairs again and to have her own en suite bathroom. And so the reason for her sulky expression was accounted for and forgiven.

'It hadn't struck me she was gloomy, but I only see her down amongst the workers,' Tessa said when Naomi mentioned how surprised she was that Deirdre was so moody now that a new freedom was on the horizon.

'Doesn't she come up to the house when that nice young Spaniard comes to fetch her?'

'Timus Rodriguez?'

'That's right,' Naomi said. 'He drives over in his van to collect her then brings her with her chair in the hybrid.' It was only then that another possibility struck her. 'You don't think she imagines she's in love with him? Oh, heavens! Whatever we do to try to make her life more normal, in the end it can't alter the basic fact. We ought to have kept our eyes open, Julian and I; perhaps then we could have interested her in something different, away from the Rodriguez family and their almond groves. The only cheerful conversation we get out of her is about that family. I know every other sentence is Timus this or Timus that but I took it that was because it's he who always takes her to the family home she seems so smitten with. His mother sounds a real matriarch, but Deirdre thinks it's all wonderful.'

'Matriarch makes Señora Rodriguez sound bossy and she's never *that*,' Tessa answered. 'More of a mother hen sheltering her brood under her wing. Honestly, Auntie, if she loves being with them there's nothing to worry about. It's such a happy house. Why don't you get Timus to take you to meet his mother?'

'Just at the moment I'm treading carefully. Deirdre is very edgy and I wouldn't want her to think I was muscling into her territory. Do you think she has fallen for Timus? You know him much better than I do. I just don't want her to get hurt. First love can be so overwhelming.'

Had she said the wrong thing? She felt that Tessa had withdrawn into her shell.

'I'd not even considered it. But Deirdre is no different from any other girl: she is sure to fall in love with someone.'

'Now tell me about you.' Naomi changed the subject. 'How's your enterprise going with your almonds?'

'I could have taken orders for more than I have room to grow. Giles was right,' she added, laughing and yet with a ring of pride, 'the selling point was the label and the fact the nuts came from his Spanish home. And I bet they sold for twice the price of those from the Rodriguez groves. It was jolly hard work, but there's something magic about it. It's the continuity, year after year following the same pattern. You must understand; you must have felt the same at the farm, although perhaps it's different if you don't grow things. The Rodriguez boys were great; they helped me so much. After all, it was my first crop and I was really feeling my way. But they both helped and guided me – Phillipe, the elder one, and Timus too. I expect Deirdre told you what fun we had; Timus set her up at a table and she worked as hard as any of us, checking the nuts we gave her and easing them out of their outer, fleshy skins. That and keeping Madam Millie amused.'

'I must be getting back.' Naomi put an end to the subject of Deirdre. 'I'm collecting Julian from Casa Landera. The men were hoping to finish the

245

lift today. They're held up waiting for the bath-room fitments. Sometimes I think we shall be in that house in town forever. When they finish inside, there's all the work to do around the pool and fitting the hoist. I know it'll be months before we shall want to use the pool but Julian wants everything to be finished before we move in.'

'A good thing he has plenty of money,' Tessa said. 'It must be costing him a fortune.'

'One thing I've learnt about Julian: he is a perfectionist. Give my love to Giles; I expect he's tucked away working,' Naomi said, adding with a laugh, 'making sure you have a busy evening typing.' Was Tessa's smile forced, or did she imagine it?

A few minutes later, driving towards the hills and Casa Landera, Naomi's thoughts were still on something about Tessa she couldn't quite fathom. Or was the girl just tired or feeling a bit under the weather? Perhaps there was another baby on the way . . . or could it be something to do with what she'd said about Deirdre and Timus? So clearly she could remember that last evening of Richard's life, his anger at the announcement that inexperienced Tessa had promised to marry worldly Giles Lampton – in his view a man completely unsuitable. With all that had followed the scene, in her mind it had become unimportant. But had he been right? Was it because she had realized her mistake that Tessa seemed to have lost her natural *joie de vivre*? She and Timus probably spent hours together in the five-acre plot she had become so involved with, and there was no doubt he was a very attractive young man. The more Naomi let her thoughts carry her where they would, the more her brow furrowed into a frown of worry. Timus was delightful in his treatment of Deirdre, but then he was a naturally sensitive and kind young man. It had been worry enough to realize the possibility that Deirdre believed she was in love with him, but now Tessa had entered the equation; Tessa with a husband and child.

She felt she carried the cares of the world on her shoulders, but there was a strong, honest streak in Naomi's nature and she admitted to herself that while she worried about the girls she escaped from facing up to the question that was constantly in her mind. She took a left turn on to what was little more than a track and almost immediately caught a glimpse of Casa Landera standing alone on the side of the hill ahead of her. The sight forced on her the real reason for her confusion and fear: Julian would be there waiting for her. She had the strangest sensation: she was alone and yet she didn't feel alone. She slowed the car, and then as if she had no choice she found herself turning off the engine as she slowed to a stop.

'Richard, help me, Richard.' She started to speak her thoughts aloud, but instinct told her she needed silence. With her eyes closed there was comfort in the outpouring of her innermost thoughts. *Suppose I agreed to marry Julian and I lost you. I couldn't bear it. You know all about him – and you know me as well as I know myself. If only you were still here we could all have been good friends . . . but marriage . . . the intimacy*

. . . sex . . . all that belonged to us. The only sort of marriage is a proper one, sex, everything. You know what I'm like, Richard, you know I haven't the sort of body men would get excited about. For us it was different. Not in the beginning; in the beginning I was proud to know I had a good body. So long ago – yet all that we had is vivid in my mind. I miss you so much, so much. You know how I try to bring you close; I ache with longing to be with you, to feel your hands on me, your body and mine as one. What I do by myself is nothing, nothing *like what my body screams out for. But with Julian? I hate God! Yes I do; I hate him for taking you away. Why did he let it happen? No one was happier than we were. I don't know what to do, Richard. Help me. I'm so fond of him, I enjoy being with him, we're good friends – but all those joyous, wonderful things we did, all that belongs just to us. If I told Julian I'd marry him but I want us to have separate rooms, I believe he'd agree – although I know it's not what he wants. But I couldn't do that; it would be dishonest. If I marry him I've got to share my body with him. Then there's another thing: even though I am honestly so fond of him, am I even considering marriage because of how much I need sex? By myself, it leaves me feeling empty and so horribly alone. Can you hear me, Richard?*

Her eyes were closed, her hands clenched making two fists, her expression one of hopelessness. And so she sat for a minute or two, while gradually she relaxed; her hands grew limp, her breathing deeper. She slipped through the barrier

248

of consciousness. For no more than two or three minutes she slept, but they were minutes that changed her life.

She woke to a feeling of peace. In a semi-conscious state she half expected to see Richard, but realizing he had been no more than part of her dream didn't strip her of the calm certainty she was sure had come from those moments with him. For she had no doubt that her spirit had truly been with his. Her problems had been lifted and the way ahead was clear. With a smile playing at the corners of her mouth she started the engine.

As the car turned through the open gateway of Casa Landera, Julian came to meet her. 'I've been waiting for you,' he said as he opened the car door for her. 'Come indoors, I want to show you something.' He ushered her through the open front doorway into the hall.

'This will be its maiden trip – except for being tested by the men who installed it,' he said as he pressed the lift button and as if by magic the door opened. Even in the large department stores of Exeter or Torquay she had never seen one with a door that worked electronically; always there was a lift attendant and the door was an iron latticework which made her feel like she was in a cage. Together they went into the box-like space that was big enough for Deirdre in her wheelchair and one other person.

'We ought to crack open a bottle of champagne,' he said.

'May God bless this lift and all who ride in it,' she added as he pressed a button and the door

249

closed. They felt the motion as they were raised to the first floor. Perhaps it was that in such a confined space there was nothing to look at except each other. Whatever the reason their glances met and locked. For both of them the moment was something extraordinary, as if it had been stage managed for this special purpose.

'Julian,' she whispered.

'Tell me.' Like her he spoke quietly, their voices as small as the space that held them. 'Please God let it be what I want to hear.'

In answer she moved closer to him, simply nodding her head as if she'd lost the power of speech. Then she was held in his arms. They didn't kiss, but clung to each other like drowning men clinging to a lifeline. He reached out and pressed the button, and when the door opened they stepped out on to the gallery that overlooked the huge living room. Suddenly the future had shape. This would be their home, their beautiful home. She looked forward to the future with a certainty she had long forgotten. Soon the year would be over; it would be 1959. When 1958 had been rung in she had stood alone with the back door of Chagleigh open listening to the distant sound of the bells of the church in Marlhampton, gazing at the sleeping farmyard with only memories for company. This year would be so different, different in every respect except one. Day or night, if she closed her eyes she could still see Richard, bringing 'his ladies' down from the Lower Field for milking, tending the sheep, standing in the dairy watching her at work, holding her in a warm embrace, sharing all that they were. He was with her now and he would be with her always.

So the winter passed: a winter of days when the sun warmed the earth and evenings by the log fire. In the last week of January Naomi and Julian were married at the town hall in Llaibir. She was glad the venue was so different from the day she had walked up the aisle to stand with Richard. In Llaibir the town hall would have passed unnoticed, standing somewhere near the middle of a terrace of three-storey buildings on the main road of the small town, sandwiched between a butcher's shop and the local ironmongery store. On the ground floor (fortunately for Deirdre) in a room with uncurtained windows and plain wooden floorboards Naomi became Mrs Julian Masters. On a gold chain around her neck she wore the ring Richard had put on her finger thirty-nine years before, and with it the engagement ring she had worn while she waited and prayed that he would come home safely from what had become known as the Great War.

On that January day they were still living in town with little prospect of the work being completed before spring. It wasn't the fault of the workmen that the alterations had taken so long, but it hadn't been a straightforward job. Decorating, fitting new kitchens and bathrooms they could have done months before, but the equipment needed for Deirdre had to be designed by specialists, hence the delays. It had been arranged that she should stay at Finca el Almendros while the newly married couple spent a few days in Valencia and her air of excitement seemed out of all proportion. She had stayed there for more than two months when they'd first come out from England, but then Naomi had been there to help her.

'This is fun,' Deirdre said. 'Aunt Naomi – or should I call her Mother now? – usually helps me into the water then goes away until I ring a bell she leaves by the bath. Will Giles feel neglected if you sit and talk to me while I bathe?'

'Giles is fine.'

'You could have fooled me,' Deirdre observed, casting a quick glance to see Tessa's reaction. 'He looks fed up. I expect he's bored. When's he off to the bright lights and the scintillating company he looks for in London?'

'Not at this time of year. He's not bored; he's frustrated with his work. Don't they call it writer's block?'

But Deirdre's mind had already moved on. 'We shall be further from here when we live in the house they're so excited about,' she said, her despondent tone telling Tessa more than any words. Of course she imagined herself cut off from all the action of the almond grove and from the Rodriguez family. In her situation it was so hard to break into a new circle.

'I'll collect you sometimes and bring you here for the day. You know there's always plenty to do with the trees – not to mention Millie.'

Deirdre nodded, but her doleful expression didn't lift.

'And the new house will give you so much

252

more independence.' Tessa continued to try to cheer her. Her initial excitement about the house, which Naomi had relayed to Tessa, had clearly evaporated. 'A year ago you would never have imagined what a slot you've made for yourself with your Rodriguez friends; and I bet something like that will happen in the new place.'

From the look on Deirdre's face, her encouraging words had gone unheard.

But whatever her views, the move went ahead and just before Easter they closed the door for the last time on the rented house in Llaibir.

'I'm going to walk down to town to collect any mail,' Giles told Tessa one afternoon the following August when he found her cutting flowers for the house and laying them carefully in her trug: day lilies, delphiniums, African lilies, Pride of Peru and carnations.

'Shall Millie and I come? Or Maria would keep Millie in with her if you like? Wait while I take these flowers in for Maria; she loves arranging them. Perhaps it's because she sings to them that they always look better when she does them.' At the thought of an afternoon with Giles, flower arranging lost its appeal.

Just for a second he hesitated, then, 'No. I'm going to walk on my own. I need to think. There's never a second's peace in that house, if it isn't Maria singing it's Millie shouting. Why can't children speak like normal people?'

'When you're her age, life is exciting, full of adventure that what you call "normal people" have forgotten.'

253

He was surprised by her answer. Had he done that to her? Had he taken away her sense of life being an adventure?

'I don't know how I'm expected to get any work done. There's more chance in the London flat.'

Ignoring the complaining note in his voice, in fact ignoring too the suggestion that London was calling him, she said, 'But it's nearly three miles. If you walk in how will you get back? You can't walk all that way in this heat. Diego Pastor told me yesterday that he had a long job today, taking someone right down to Granada.' And Diego Pastor with his elderly Renault was the nearest the little town of Llaibir had to a taxi service. Childishly, she felt that she had scored a point. 'You can borrow my bike if you want to get away from us by yourself.'

He was watching her, his expression telling her nothing. Sometimes he could be so difficult; he made her feel as though she were some sort of possession he could see little use in keeping. But that was stupid. They were happy, they had a perfect marriage, a dozen times a day she told herself so. She knew he got restless with the restrictions of country living, but that was hardly her fault. The finca had been his choice alone; he had bought it for a retreat almost as soon as he was free to travel after the end of the war. Now his sudden smile banished any shadow of criticism from her mind. She found herself laughing with him as he said, 'Put me on a bike and I'd probably fall off before I got down to the road. Leave Millie with Maria and—'

254

'And come with you? Walking together it wouldn't seem half so far.'

'No. I told you – I want to be by myself. I was going to suggest you leave Millie with Maria and have an afternoon on the bike yourself.' Then with the sudden frown she had come to dread, 'Don't you ever want to get away from everyone for Christ's sake?' Immediately, he could see he had hurt her, but he knew how easy it was to make amends. 'I've gone cold on what I'm doing. I've got to clear my head and think myself back into it. Oh, Tessa' – he held his hand towards her – 'sweet Tessa, I'm no good to you, no companion for you.'

'But you *are*, Giles. We're good companions, we even share your work. I wish I were older, I wish I had a real, proper career behind me so that you could be proud of having me for your wife. But that doesn't stop us being right for each other, loving each other I mean.' When he didn't answer she drew his hand and rubbed it against her cheek. 'I love you so much. I'd do anything to make you content but I know I can't.'

He drew her into his arms holding her tightly and moving his chin against the top of her head.

'It's my fault,' he said softly, 'I don't think I know how to be content. When I come back to this place from London and find you waiting I feel I must be the luckiest man living. I want the feeling to last. But it never does; it never has. We're so cut off here. The world moves on and we're left behind.'

'I think that's why I love it. Look at it, Giles. Look around and see the . . . the . . . industry.'

'Industry? Stuck here amongst people who don't see further than their nut trees, scratching about in the land – this year, last year, next year, like their fathers and grandfathers did before them.'

'That's what is so wonderful. You can rush off to the bright lights, to the bustle of the city that changes with every generation, to your clever intellectual men friends and the flighty ladies who I expect welcome you with open arms and feel sorry for you being stuck in some wilderness with a wife and child. Well, good luck to you. Your values and mine aren't the same.'

He tipped her face up to his. 'And a moment ago you said you loved me.'

'So I do. So I always will. Can't seem to help it. You make me so cross, but being cross doesn't make any difference. Perhaps I don't want you to feel like I do about this place and the people who toil on the land. If you did it would make you a difference person from the one I love.' She pulled away from him, her face lighting into an impish smile. 'Go on, get your walking shoes on. You don't deserve it, but if you like I'll drive into town and pick you up.'

He dropped a light kiss on her forehead. 'Good girl. I was shy of asking.'

'You? Shy?' She laughed when she said it, both of them aware that they had negotiated their way off dangerous ground. 'I'll give you an hour start and pick you up by the bull ring.'

A minute or two later she watched him stride down the slope to the road. She tried to hang on to the lightness of heart they had both made sure

ended their encounter, but there was an underlying feeling she wouldn't let herself consider.
Surely their life together was as idyllic as that
glorious holiday in Shropshire – different of
course because no relationship can remain
unchanged with time and living, but their love
was as wonderful, their shared interest in his
work as great. And parenthood? Didn't that bind
them? She shied away from the question.

Automatically she was drawn to her precious
five acres. Timus had told her that any day now
they could start shaking the branches; most of
the nuts were ready to fall. She half expected to
find him down there, but when she was disappointed she wandered amongst the trees, her
imagination carrying her forward to the day she
would see her second year orders on their way
to London. Could it be as thrilling as last year?
Yes, none of the excitement had faded. If only
she had more ground, more trees. The Rodriguez
had a proper almond farm; hers was little more
than a hobby. And, no doubt, her orders were
due to her using Giles' name on the attractive
card she attached to each net of nuts. Stooping
down she picked up an almond that had already
fallen, its outer coat ripe and split so that the nut
could be lifted out. How many of these would
there be on each tree? How many hundreds –
thousands – would have to be eased from the
soft outer casing, cleaned and laid to dry in the
sun? They had to be perfect, each one ripe but
not dry. Almonds from Finca el Almendros would
earn a reputation of being for the connoisseur.

'Hello!' She was brought out of her dream by

257

the sound of Deirdre calling. And turning she saw her coming at high speed between the rows of trees, the electric chair being bounced as though it would either tip over or take off at any moment. Running behind her was Timus. 'We saw Giles go striding by,' Deirdre said. 'Is something wrong with the car?'

'No. He's gone into town. He wanted the exercise,' Tessa answered, surprised that her remark should make the other two look at each other as if they had a shared secret. Perhaps she imagined it. 'I mustn't be long down here. I said I'd give him an hour start and then drive in to collect him.'

'Good,' Deirdre said.

'Not so sure that it's good,' Tessa answered with a laugh. 'I was looking at the nuts on the ground and thinking I ought to start spreading the nets. What do you think, Timus?'

'To my thinking, they are ready. We have been harvesting all the days this week. And in Deirdre we have a helper of great quality. I did speak with my father and he say it is well for Deirdre and me to work here with you. If we get the nets to the ground this evening, when we come tomorrow the first work will be to stand Deirdre's table – and then' – with a sweeping movement of his arm encompassing the five acres and a voice full of drama – 'el Almendros, we will shake you and you will give us your fruits.'

'Wonderful! Are you sure you can be spared?'

'My father, he wants this land to be of the standard that is high. And we are well in the work of his ground. Tomorrow we will all work, the

258

three of us together – and Millie will have her pen and be happy to be with us. We start at the lower end, so that is where we spread the net this afternoon.'

How could Giles not feel the magic of this never-changing lifestyle? Tessa was determined to persuade him to come and watch the work as his very own trees were shaken to give up their harvest of nuts. The man who wrote with such understanding of the folk of Burghton couldn't fail to fall under the spell of the country work that had been done generation after generation.

Instead of remaining in her wheelchair to be pushed aboard the hybrid for the journey back to Casa Landera, Deirdre put her arms around Timus' neck as he lifted her from the chair and carefully eased her into the passenger seat before stowing the chair aboard. Over recent days this had been the usual way she had travelled. That, and the feeling of being part of the team of workers, had a strange effect on her, although it would have been impossible to put it into words. There in the car with Timus she could almost believe in the pretence of being the same as other young girls; she would feel elated and for the time it took them to reach Llaibir she revelled in an inner excitement. But when he parked in the driveway of the house and brought her wheelchair down the ramp to the narrow pavement, misery would swamp her, misery all the worse because of the illusion that had gone before. No wonder Naomi and Julian found her moody.

On that late afternoon her balloon of happiness

burst sooner than usual, for as they drove towards the little town they recognized Giles' car approaching. Giles was at the wheel with Tessa by his side. The sight of them brought home to Deirdre the hopelessness of her own situation and in that moment she believed – or imagined she believed – she wished she had never met the Rodriguez family. In their house she had been accepted as a welcome visitor, not a person who had to be treated differently because she couldn't leave her chair. Beyond that she was frightened to look. She wished she had never met Timus – no, that was a lie; meeting him had changed her life.

As he drove along the empty road, he sensed a change in her mood. Perhaps she was tired; she had worked as hard as anyone. Her work may have been different from theirs, but it was just as necessary. Two or three times during the afternoon he had come to the table where she sat easing the almonds from their outer casing. She hadn't wasted a minute and it was all work that had to be done so she was as necessary as anyone.

Saying nothing, he slowed the car and then stopped at the edge of the road.

'What's up?' she asked. Feeling as low as she did at that moment nothing would have surprised her.

'Up?' he queried, looking to the sky.

'You stopped. Is something wrong with the car?'

'No. We have stopped because there is something I have to talk about, something I have been trying to say for many weeks of summer.'

She turned her head away, peering out of the window as if she had seen something of importance, but was in fact frightened to let him see her face. Her mouth was dry, her throat seemed closed. The moment she had dreaded had come, just as she had always known it must. He had been kind to her; he had made the months of summer the most wonderful she had known. Even though her days revolved around just *him*, she had always tried not to let it show. He must have guessed and now he was going to tell her – kindly, for he was the kindest person she knew – that she mustn't let herself fall in love with him. Perhaps he had a girlfriend already, a girl who worked in the day and spent the evenings with him, a girl who was pretty and who could dance and run and be like everyone else, a girl who didn't have to be lifted like a sack of potatoes or pushed like something in a handcart. 'Look at me, Deirdre. I need to look at your face as I say this to you. The back of your head will tell me nothing.'

With her chin high, she turned and faced him, schooling her expression not to give her away. 'What is it you have to tell me? Is it some excitement happening in your life?'

'I hope that it may be so. I have never said anything like this to anyone and I do not know the right words. But my heart is so full that I beg you to hear me and – oh but I am saying it wrong. Help me, Deirdre, surely you must understand what it is I am trying to tell you.'

She shook her head, torn between a wild and wonderful hope, an unbearable dread that he

261

knew she was in love with him and didn't want to hurt her, and the anguish of knowing no man would ever see her as anything more than someone to be kind to. Misery overwhelmed her. It took all her courage to speak firmly.

'Is it that you are telling me there is a girl you are in love with?' There! She'd said it! She'd made it easy for him to tell her.

'Yes there is a girl, the most beautiful, precious girl. Deirdre, darling Deirdre, I am speaking this so badly. Do you not see how much I care for you? I did not know I could feel as I do for any girl, even one as lovely as you. But why are there tears? If you cannot feel for me as I want, then it is for me to weep.'

'. . . so happy. Timus, I do love you. I think of you all the time. But how can you love me like men love women – I can't even walk.'

'I have two good legs and two strong arms. Always I will carry you with pride. There is more to living than walking. Say again as you did just now, tell me again that you love me too and that you will take me for husband.'

'I love you more than any words can say.' She made a valiant effort to speak without choking on her words then, feeling in her skirt pocket for her handkerchief she blew her nose and mopped away her tears. 'When we are together I forget that I'm not the *me* I used to be. No, that's not right. I'm *not* the *me* I used to be before the accident. Then, I was just playing at being a proper grown-up person with grown-up emotions. But it's not just me, Timus; what will your family say if you tell them you want to marry a girl who

262

can't run a home or look after children? That's what family life is about; you only have to look at your mother. She is wonderful.'

'And you are wonderful. Children! Just picture it, Deirdre, *our* children. You ask about my family. Yes, they know I want you to be my wife and they are more pleased than I know words. They are most fond of you. They look forward most eagerly to the time you become part of our family. That is the way we live when we take a wife.' Then with the wide smile she loved, 'My parents have a most large house so that their sons and their wives and children are all one family. Will you mind that? Will you think that as a married person you should have a home just for your own?' She shook her head, her mind filled with images of the Rodriguez house, the bustle of activity, the laughter. And seeing her expression he went on, 'If you agree for you and me to become a married two, the thing I want – want more than I know in your language to tell – then they make . . . make . . .' And here he was lost for the right word so he held his hands apart, first one way and then the other, as if he were making a square and then moving them wider while he looked at her helplessly. 'So that we have a place to be. They will give us what you name to be the drawing room – I do not know why, for it is not for drawing – to be our bedroom so that we do not have to go up the stairs each night. Easily I could carry you, but my mother is a wise woman and it was she who say we should stay below so that you could do it for yourself.'

263

A new spirit of confidence flooded over Deirdre. The future had no clouds. She was going to be part of that caring and carefree family; she was going to be Mrs Timus Rodriguez.

'Marry Timus?' Tessa looked at Naomi in astonishment when they met by chance in Llaibir the next morning. 'I know she spends a lot of time with his family, but I never guessed. I'm so pleased for her – and for Timus too. So will Giles be when I tell him.' She made sure there was excitement in the way she spoke; Naomi was perceptive and she mustn't have the chance to suspect the nagging uncertainty that Tessa couldn't escape. Just thinking about it gave her a sick feeling of fear. Was he bored with her, just as he was bored with life at el Almendros? For weeks he had been different – ever since his last trip to London. Sometimes he would sit with the paper in front of him, yet she knew he wasn't reading; his solitary walks were becoming more frequent; he shut himself in his study for hours and yet when evening came there were never many pages to be typed. She pulled her thoughts back on to track and set a smile of interest on her face. She would drive Deirdre in the hybrid to look for clothes. They would share the excitement and fun just like they used to on their outings from Fiddlers' Green – or so she tried to make herself believe. But in those days their joy in the moment had been forced, for in both their minds had been the knowledge that, whatever Deirdre bought to wear, nothing could alter her wheelchair-bound life. Yet now, wheelchair or not, she was the girl

264

handsome, kindly, charming Timus wanted for his wife.

'It's marvellous,' Tessa said, unable to keep her face from smiling. 'All the times I've seen them together and I didn't guess! Imagine all the work that's been done on Landera and now she won't be living there. Or will she? Are they going to move in with you and Julian?' She still felt uncomfortable calling him by his Christian name but Mr Masters was too formal and Uncle seemed ridiculous.

'They will live with his family. The idea seems to appeal to Deirdre. Well, she spends time a'plenty with them. It seems they are to have the largest downstairs room for their bedroom and Mr Rodriguez is having it partitioned to make an en suite bathroom. I can see now why she has been so difficult to live with, moody, ready to find fault. Poor little soul, she must have been frightened even to let herself dream.' For a moment she gazed speculatively at Tessa. 'Tell me to mind my own business, but I ask because I care, not because I'm playing the interfering aunt. Tessa, are things all right with you and Giles? Is he quite well? Tell me it's not my business, but I met him at the post office the other day and he didn't seem himself. He can't still be suffering from writer's block or whatever you called it.' And was it her imagination or did Tessa look scared, trapped? Just for a second before she had control of the situation.

'Poor Giles,' she answered, careful to sound cheerfully casual, 'he really doesn't seem able to settle here for any length of time. Until we married he used to escape here when he'd had enough of the high life, but he'll never make a countryman. He stays because he knows I love it, and he knows too that nowhere would be right for him for too long at a time. The truth is, he is a rolling stone. Sometimes I can feel he's champing at the bit for pastures new. But as for his health, I'm sure he's fine.'

'If that's all it is, that's OK. He just seems to have lost his sparkle.'

'He'll go trotting off again soon I expect and the sparkle will be there for the London crowd. It's like a drug to him. But it soon wears off. It sounds silly, but I'm glad when he goes away because I know how quickly it palls; I know he'll soon be back with all his batteries charged. That's the way he is, Auntie. And I wouldn't change a thing about him.' Was that the truth? She'd been wildly infatuated by him from the first, believing what she'd felt had been love. From that infatuation had become love, love that filled her heart and mind even more fully than had the original hero worship. And now she had her own challenge. Each week she became more deeply immersed in the work. She knew it didn't interest Giles, but surely he must be proud of what she was accomplishing.

With the first day of her second nut harvest ahead of her, Tessa was anxious to get on. 'I promised to pick up the mail,' she told Naomi, 'Are you coming the same way?'

At the post office they parted company and five minutes later Tessa was driving home, her thoughts ahead of her as she envisaged the trees giving up what looked like a splendid crop. There was no post for her, and she had expected none. But there was an envelope for Giles that she recognized as coming from his publisher. It might be important, so she decided to break the rules and take it to his study where she imagined he was dictating what tonight she would type. Instead he was gazing into space, his mind a million miles away and with something in his expression that frightened her.

'Giles! Sorry to burst in on you, but this was in the post. I'm off to start harvesting. Bye.' And with that she closed the door on him and looked in on Maria to collect Millie.

'Leave her with me, Señora. We are happy.'

'Thanks, Maria. If she's a problem bring her down to me.'

'She could never be a problem. I sing as I work; she dances. We are partners.'

Their brief exchange was in Spanish but, speaking English, Tessa told Millie to be good and do as Maria told her. Her instructions were met with a puzzled look. There were moments when Millie wanted nothing more than to help her mother; but there were other times when the atmosphere of the large kitchen, the sound of Maria singing, her ever-ready laugh and words of encouragement, were the only world the child asked. Before Tessa crossed the hall to the front door the singing had started again and from the thuds she heard she knew that Millie was leaping into dancing mode. Tessa smiled, imagining the scene: Maria was cleaning the windows, her movements in time with the music she made and, no doubt, as Millie leaped and thumped she too thought she was in time. No one would ever make a dancer of her, nor yet give her any natural grace. A silent voice suggested to Tessa that it was the lack of it that held Giles away from her, but she wouldn't let herself dwell on the thought. Instead her mind moved back to what Naomi had asked: was anything wrong with Giles? She had been certain there was nothing more than that he was bored and probably resented the happiness she found in the simple life they led. But it hadn't looked like boredom on his expression when she had caught him unawares in his study.

Reaching the five-acre plot where the nets were already spread around the lower trees it was as if she became a different person. Phillipe Rodriguez was already working his way along the bottom row of trees, leaving a shower of nuts on the ground as he moved from one to the next. Taking a large round basket from the shed, she set it on the ground by the first tree and started to gather up the nuts. As she worked she sang softly (not full volume as Maria did) hardly aware that she did it. It was one of life's special moments: the hot sun on her back, the deep blue of the cloudless sky above, the sound of a tractor passing along the seldom-used road, a tractor pulling a trailer taking nuts from some grower further along the empty road to the cooperative depot. Rather than feeling like a novice at the game, she was filled with pride that nuts grown in the grove of Finca el Almendros (home of Giles Lampton, she conceded with a mixture of pride and annoyance) wouldn't be taken to the cooperative but would be weighed and packed by *her* and sent independently to fill her orders.

When she saw Giles hurrying down the sloping drive to the growing area by the road her happiness was complete. Never had he sought her out down there, although she always hoped that he would. One look at his face told her that he had something special to tell her; this was the Giles she had first fallen in love with: vital, interested in life. In his hand he held the letter she had taken in to him.

Ten

Tessa watched Giles packing. Was it only in her imagination that she didn't exist for him? Suddenly his life had colour and purpose, purpose in which she played no part.

'How long do you think you'll be away?' she asked. He seemed not to hear her, his mind taken with selecting which suits to fold carefully for the largest of the three cases he had put out ready. 'An evening suit? I thought this was a working trip?' She tried to tease him into at least noticing she was there.

'That's what I intend it to be. But I'm sure there will be occasions when I need to dress. I don't care how sociable I have to make myself; I'll fight all the way to see my work isn't ruined. Based on books by Giles Lampton, screenplay written by whoever it is, and then they have a free hand to make what he will of my characters.' He sounded bitter, even angry. 'I have to be there. I want a say in who is to be cast. What will they know of the characters in an English village?'

'People may not be so different in America.'

'What?' Clearly he had simply been voicing his thoughts aloud, not talking to her. 'The same? How can they be? We are all as circumstances have made us. We may learn to understand each other, but we're certainly not the same. Ties . . . about eight, I should think . . . Put socks and

270

underwear in the smallest case of the three for me, will you?'

She got off the bed where she had been sitting and went to his chest of drawers. But she still hadn't had an answer to her original question.

'You're packing more than you take when you go to London. Do you expect to be away longer than usual?'

'I've no idea how long I shall be.' Suddenly she had his full attention and something in his expression made her wish she hadn't pressed him for an answer. 'I intend to stay as long as it takes to make sure my work doesn't end up as some fast-moving action-packed ninety minutes of screen entertainment.' He hesitated. She wished he wouldn't look at her like that – as if she were some sort of problem he wasn't sure how to solve. Not a word that he would get home as soon as he could or that he would miss her. 'You know I'm restless, frustrated, cooped up here with just you and the child – and Maria's constant voice.'

His tone took her by surprise.

'Well you needn't hurry on my account,' she retorted, hating herself for wanting to hurt him. 'I have plenty of interests. I shall be too busy to even notice you've gone.'

Packing was forgotten as they held each other's gaze across the bed. What were they doing? Hadn't she told Naomi how she liked him to go away because it helped him see the preciousness of what they shared here? But was it precious to him, or did he come home because he got bored with what he found somewhere else? Ever since his last visit to London he had been different.

271

Most of the time lately he'd wanted no company but his own, and there was even something different in their love-making. It used to be an exciting adventure, rapturously uniting them. But lately she was sure he feigned sleep when he was actually wide awake. Sure that whatever was wrong between them could be put right if they found each other in the ultimate joy of loving, sometimes she tried to arouse him. If his body responded there was none of the former lingering joy of anticipation; instead he would move on to her, unable to restrain his quick movements and almost immediately it was over. It wasn't love, it was simply satisfying his sexual desire so that he could escape into sleep leaving her frustrated and resentful.

As they glared at each other, she holding a pile of underpants and he a small box of studs and cufflinks, all those memories crowded back. So often she tried to push them out of her mind but now she welcomed them – they added to her armoury.

'If you're going to be away a long time perhaps you'll realize how stupid you've been in refusing to have a phone in the house. I suppose, as long as you're comfortable, you won't care if something goes wrong here – Millie ill, or me breaking my leg. It was damn fool pig-headedness. You always think you know best.'

'As invariably I do. However, if I'm leaving you alone here, except for the child, you ought to have a telephone. I'll leave you to arrange it.' She tried to see his capitulation as a sign that he wanted her to feel safe while she and Millie were

272

alone and with no near neighbours. She tried but she didn't succeed. There was no caring warmth in his voice as he added, 'I'll write a letter giving the instruction to have it installed; they may not ask for my authority, but if they do you'll have the letter to give them.'

'How long? You didn't answer.'

He put the stud box into the case and came to her side of the bed. 'I didn't answer because I don't know. Tessa, we need time away from each other. That such an important company has bought the rights to make a film about the people of Burghton is something of a blessing, to you as well as to me. You can't pretend you'll be heartbroken to see the back of me.'

She felt stunned by what he said. But was she being honest? She forced herself to look at him squarely as she answered. 'I hadn't even considered it,' she said, speaking evenly and showing no emotion, for if she let her feelings show she would be lost. 'I can't say you've been much company lately. Even Aunt Naomi and Julian have noticed it. I imagined you were hungering for a fling with some of your lady friends who I'm sure are standing by, ready to oblige.'

'Don't, Tessa! I hate to hear you talking like that.'

'The truth is – seeing that we are being so honest – that you aren't interested in my talking at all. Yesterday I told you that old Señor Cajore is giving up his land over the road from here and I was considering using Gran's money to buy it. And what advice did you give? Not a word. I might not have spoken while you stood there

273

with an empty, bored look on your face. Well, if you're interested, which I doubt, I worked it all out in the night and I have enough money and could still afford to hire help.'

'You don't have to earn a living, for God's sake. You'll never be short of money.'

'It's nothing to do with money. You can't even begin to understand.' As each one spoke, they slipped further down the slippery slope into the mire from which they couldn't climb. She had no idea what went on in his mind, but as she faced him with her chin high and a look of defiance on her face, their glory days were forgotten and all she remembered was his obvious avoidance of her – and indeed of everyone – in recent months and the frantic and demanding love-making that held neither tenderness nor eroticism. 'No, you pay me well for my services just like you'd have to pay any prostitute.'

She felt the sting as he brought his hand across her cheek. Then, before she could get her breath, she was pulled into his arms and crushed against him so that she could hardly breathe.

'God forgive me. What have I done to you?' he muttered.

She drew back from him, clenching her teeth together and barely moving her lips in her battle against the tears that were waiting to gush. 'We're both to blame. Like you say, we need time away from each other.' More sure of her voice, she went on, 'If I'm driving you to Valencia, what time do you need to be there?'

'I've already arranged with Diego Pastor to pick me up. He's due in less than half an hour.

I'll be too late in London to look in to talk to Hector Milward tonight; I'll have to see him tomorrow. I'm getting the morning flight to Los Angeles the next day.'

'I see,' she answered, her tone polite and unemotional. It was an attitude they both needed. She couldn't let him go with hate hanging between them. But was this cool detachment any better? 'Don't forget your passport.'

'I have it in my pocket.'

'You'll write, won't you? I shan't know where you are and I shall want to give you the telephone number when they connect us.'

'Naturally I'll tell you where I am and give you the telephone details. If you think of anything you need me for before I fly, I shall be at the publishers' sometime tomorrow. You'll find their number on the pad on my desk. Just ask to be put through to Hector Milward.' Like strangers lost for last-minute words at a railway station, they didn't quite meet each other's eyes. 'I've a few loose ends to see to in the study – and I won't forget that note about the telephone. I'll see you to say goodbye before I go. I'll take these two larger cases down if you don't mind bringing the small one.'

Wordlessly she picked it up and left the room as he held the door open for her, then, taking the two larger cases, he followed her down the stairs.

He'd been gone more than an hour. By now he must be getting near Valencia. Why had she let them part as they had? If only she could live the time again she would sink every ounce of her pride and beg him to – to what? To love her as he had in the beginning? Was it *her* fault he couldn't find contentment? She'd always tried to understand his need to escape to the city, but since his last trip he had been different. Had he met someone else, someone with a mind like his own, someone cleverer than she was? But no one could love him as she did. Round and round in her mind went all the possibilities for the change in him and his need to get away from her.

Millie didn't seem to notice any change in her as the nightly bath ritual was performed and the story read. Tessa congratulated herself on playing her part well as she kissed the little girl goodnight.

'Didn't say goodnight to Daddy,' Millie announced, as always her voice firm and positive beyond her years. Millie was unlike either of her parents – a clumsy dancer and a straight no-nonsense talker even though she was only three.

'You haven't forgotten already? Daddy's gone away for a little while.'

The child frowned. 'He was here, I saw him 'safternoon.'

Had he forgotten to say goodbye to her? Surely that showed how far from them his thoughts had gone. The wave of misery that swept over Tessa almost destroyed her determination to act normally.

'He went quite suddenly. I expect he couldn't find you,' she said with a bright smile, 'but never mind, he'll soon be home.'

Millie grunted. 'He didn't look for me. Me and Maria were making biscuits.'

'That sounds good. Cuddle down and go to sleep, love.'

Closing the bedroom door behind her, Tessa put an end to the charade. Her footsteps on the marble floor seemed to echo through the emptiness of the house. Going to his study she sat by his desk where he had left the note instructing that the telephone be connected. Even that emphasized the separation that had come between them, a separation far greater than miles.

Uninvited and taking her by surprise she thought of her grandmother. 'Gran,' she whispered as at last the tears gushed. 'What'll I do, Gran? He's all there is, everything. He's fed up with me. Not angry – that wouldn't be so hopeless – but bored, *bored*. His thoughts are miles away. I haven't changed; I'm like I was right from the start. Perhaps he didn't really want to marry me. Wouldn't care if we had to be poor or if I never saw an almond tree; wouldn't care about anything if he'd just want me still.' Her thoughts were tangled: Giles, Amelia, Giles, the almond grove, Giles, the wild excitement of the weeks when she'd first known him, the gradual deepening into what she felt for him now. Probably he'd only wanted her because she'd been a virgin, not like the others he'd had in the past – in the past and since, too, probably. Making herself sit straighter in his chair, rubbing her handkerchief over her tear-blotched face, she consciously forced herself to imagine the future she could make for herself. She'd show him she could manage very well on her own. She'd surprise him with the success she'd make. One day she might even make him proud of her. Tomorrow she'd go and see Señor Cajore and tell him she was prepared to pay his price. The elderly man was keen to sell his land quickly and join his daughter in Granada; he had agreed to leave this year's crop to be harvested. Probably the workers would stay on. Yes, she would do it. She'd advertise in the county magazines in England, an advertisement with a picture of Finca el Almendros, the Spanish home of Giles Lampton and his wife Tessa. She would write a short paragraph to the effect that while Giles Lampton was writing, his wife Tessa tended the almond trees. Under that there would be a second picture, one she had taken of the almond grove last February when it had been a sea of blossom. She had a goal, although at the back of her mind there was the knowledge that in part the challenge was to prove to Giles that she was capable. She would let him see that she was a force to be reckoned with. And so her day ended, her mind set firmly on the success she would make.

The flight to Los Angeles never seemed to end. Giles sipped the champagne the stewardess brought him, but when it was lunchtime he only played with his meal. Thankful to be alone, away from everyone he knew, he let his mind go back some two months to the evening of his arrival in London when he had met Adrian Wilmot at a cocktail party in London.

'Yes, Giles managed to get here in time. Come

278

and meet him,' he'd heard Claudette Malone, one of his numerous acquaintances, say. 'Giles, I have an admirer of yours wanting to meet you. This is Adrian Wilmot, Giles Lampton. I'll leave you to get to know each other; I see Hamish just coming in.' And she'd left them while they'd been at the handshaking stage.

'I feel I know you already,' Adrian had said, his greeting taking Giles straight back to the afternoon he had met Tessa. 'The pictures you paint of that village, Burghton, and the folk there; I tell you, they do what every good book should: you read and get transported. It's as if one knows every bend in the village street, every flower in Mrs Boyce's hat.'

'That's what every writer likes to hear. They've all been part of my own life so long now that they're pretty well family,' Giles had answered, making sure his manner was what his new acquaintance would expect. But Adrian's reply had taken him completely by surprise.

'I boast about you back home. A stretch of the imagination, I guess, to say that we're cousins, but if your mother had brought you over with her when she married my uncle that's how we would have been. Couple of young bucks around the same age.'

'My mother? I've had no communication with her for years. Is she well?'

'Gee man, you didn't get told? She died, oh, I guess it must be about four years ago. And it was a mercy to see her go after the way she had changed. I remember her as a bright and pretty woman when I first knew her.'

Bright? No. Bright wouldn't have been the word Giles would have used when he remembered the years at the rectory, years when even as no more than eight years old he had looked forward to boarding school. Looking back down the years he'd answered with more honesty than tact.

'Children don't see their mothers as pretty, I don't expect. She and I were never close; we didn't like each other.'

'But that's awful, man! To love your mother is just human nature.'

'To me it wasn't. You say she changed, changed from the pretty, bright creature you first remembered, that's what you said.'

'I guess there are many facets to the disease. No one guessed what was wrong when she started getting moods of depression. She had every comfort money could buy and a husband who idolized her. No one could understand the reason for her depression and flashes of temper, not even her doctor. As she got worse she was under a psychiatrist but nothing snapped her out of it. As time went on, her walk got unsteady and her movements sort of uncontrolled. That's when the medic put her on to a specialist.'

'So what was wrong with her?'

'They called it Huntington's disease. I don't know much about it except what it did to her and in the last few years to Pamela, too – your half sister.'

'Is it infectious, then?'

'It can't be. She'd been gone a year or more

280

when Pam started with it,' Adrian had said, passing his cigarette case to Giles. Then, holding his lighter to Giles, after inhaling deeply, he continued, 'But hers is quick – she's going downhill so fast I see a change in her every time I visit. Certainly she gets depressed, but then who wouldn't in her position? No control over her movements, she flings her arms out as if they have a will of their own, her body sort of dips and swoops when she talks to you, and even worse her speech is getting so slurred it's hard to understand. When she walks she never knows where her feet will touch the ground. Poor kid – so far her brain is OK, but that just makes it harder. Can't even cut her own food and feed herself, it's as if her limbs have a life of their own. Her mother got like that, too, but in her case she got dementia, lost track over her mind and her body. My uncle has a nurse living in the house for Pam. Tell you, though, he's turned into a real old man years before his time. Nothing worse than standing by and being helpless. Like I say, he worshipped your mother and now he has to stand by and watch Pamela.'

'But if they know what's the matter, can't they do something for her?' Giles had been impelled to ask the question, but he felt he knew the answer.

'One day they'll come up with a cure, no doubt, but that day hasn't come. Hey, though, man, I've done all the talking. Now it's your turn. Do you have a wife here? Or, like me, do you like to be fancy free?'

'My wife and daughter are in Spain. That's

where we live. I'm only in London for a short stay on business. You're working over here?'

And so the conversation had been steered away from the tragedy of which Giles had been ignorant.

Two days later, much sooner than usual, Giles had returned to the finca. Usually when he came home he wanted nothing more than to be with Tessa, wanting her as a thirsty man might want water. She was pure and innocent; she made no secret of her love for him as a more sophisticated woman might. But after that brief absence his return had been different. From the moment of his arrival she had been aware of a change in him and had felt hurt and rejected.

He had said nothing about his meeting with Adrian Wilmot, nor yet how the next day he had spent hours in the library reading room, determined to read everything printed about the disease that had killed his mother and was well on the way to killing his half-sister. The words jumped out of the page, depression, mood swings, headaches, fits of anger. Onset of the illness happened usually between the ages of thirty-five and forty-five, although there had been cases both older and younger. He'd never been a quick-tempered man, nor yet had he suffered from depression, but didn't the books tell him that there were a variety of symptoms: restlessness was one, the first thing that fitted what he was looking for. Worse than that, though, one thing that was known with certainty was that the disease was passed from parent to child in the genes. His mother had had that gene; she had passed it to Pamela – a case of someone much younger than the norm. Each hour he had become more frightened, more certain of what lay ahead. Between thirty-five and forty-five . . . Sitting in the silent reading room his hands had been clammy. He'd felt sick and shaken with fear as he'd turned the page and read details of what he might expect, what he must watch for. An illness, no matter how serious, which could be helped by surgery didn't hold half the fear of this. No cure . . . nothing but watching as its grip tightened.

The steady drumming of the engine, the gentle snoring of someone seated behind him, the stewardess moving along the aisle between the first-class seats at the front of the plane where he sat with his eyes closed and his mind painfully wide awake. The scene of that last hour with Tessa played again and again in his memory. She would be all right without him . . . she loved Finca el Almendros. Right from his first terrified suspicion of what was wrong with him he had been determined she must never be told. He could almost see her face as he imagined her listening to him telling her how with each passing day he became more and more certain of what his future held. He shied away from the words he knew she would say as she begged him to stay with her and let her care for him as the disease took hold. He couldn't bear to think of it, of what it would do to her life as well as his. How long would it take? Restlessness wasn't new to him, so did that mean that the first stages had been developing for months, even years? After he'd met Adrian Wilmot his life had become a nightmare, the dread of the future never leaving him as he watched himself getting ever more depressed and irritable. It started to become habit for him consciously to note the way he walked and listen to his voice to try and detect a change. He supposed he was a selfish man, for his thoughts had been just of himself. He wanted to be left alone in his misery and fear. A gene passed through the generations, Wilmot had said. So had it been passed to Millie? Hour after hour he'd sat staring into space; instead of seeing the sloping garden and the blue sky he had looked to a future that was beyond contemplation. There had been a morning when, out walking with his thoughts following their same relentless path, he had almost fallen when he'd not seen a deep rut in the parched ground. With his heart pounding he had taken note of the incident – yet more evidence. Night and day there was no escape for him. And then had come the letter about the filming of the people of Burghton and he had seen a way forward and known what he had to do.

After the first two or three days of his absence, Tessa went each morning to Llaibir to collect the mail. Usually there was nothing, one morning an electricity bill, another a notification of which day the telephone would be installed, but never what she wanted. Then halfway through the second week after his departure she was handed an envelope typed and addressed to her personally. Standing outside the little post office she tore it open and read the single-sided sheet. Stunned, frightened she might meet someone she knew and have to talk to and feeling physically sick, she almost ran back to the car. It couldn't be true . . . Finca el Almendros would be made over to her together with a generous allowance. Before leaving for the United States Giles had instructed his solicitor to set in motion the arrangements for a legal separation. 'We need time apart,' she heard the echo of his voice. But this wasn't 'time apart'. A legal separation . . . never-ending time apart. At that moment, though, it wasn't the future she thought about, it was the past: the times they had been happy, the times she had believed he had been as filled with joy as she had herself.

She got into the driver's seat and, acting automatically, drove through the little town and on to the road towards home. She must get away; she wanted to hide from everyone. The solicitor had written from an address in London, so Giles must have left her knowing that he didn't intend to come back. Not come back . . . never be with him again. . . . never feel his hands on her shoulders as he came to stand behind her while she typed the day's dictation . . . never to wake up in the morning filled with subconscious peace at the sight of him sleeping by her side. If he was gone, there was nothing . . . the challenge of making a success of her new venture disappeared now that she had no need to prove herself. The years stretched ahead like a long, straight road through a barren land. But she had Millie, she reminded herself, Millie who had been the reason he married her. For on that morning with the solicitor's letter lying on the passenger seat at her side, she knew without a doubt that without Millie there would have been no wedding.

It took all her courage to tell Naomi and Julian. Their sympathy was harder to bear than their condemnation would have been if she had broken faith with her marriage.

Deirdre was living in a euphoric state of happiness as she had daily reports of the progress of work in readiness for her move to the Rodriguez home. Until the house was ready the wedding had to wait but, as often as Timus had time to take her, she visited. For so long she had felt resentment, believing herself to be of less importance than other people; but now, seeing the work going on and the family's eagerness to make everything right for her, there was no one in the world with whom she would change places.

'So Giles is up to his old tricks again,' she said as she drove her electric chair to where Tessa was working in a shed she had had erected on her five-acre plot. Then, when she didn't get an answer, 'Well, if you ask me, you'll be better off without him. He's been a real pain in the butt recently. Everybody's noticed it. So I suppose you must have been prepared to hear he was chucking you. But Tessa, he's not worth wasting time grieving about if he can't be faithful – and I bet he's been getting all he wanted from some of his flighty birds when he used to keep rushing off to London. Do you reckon he's found someone else? I know what Miss Sherwin always used to say about him. Don't let him make you miserable, Tessa. You've got all of us. Once you've picked yourself up we'll all be fine together, you'll see.'

'Yes, of course,' Tessa made herself say, hoping Deirdre would be content to let the subject drop. Purposely she had gone on weighing and netting nuts while Deirdre had been talking. 'Do you want a job? I could do with a hand tying the labels on. I use this thin gold ribbon; it looks good on the red netting – sort of Christmassy.' Christmas! By the time it came perhaps she would have won the battle and found the courage to make herself look ahead to another year, the first without him. But how could she win the battle when her heart wasn't in the fight? She couldn't even try and tell herself she didn't want him, because she knew it would be a lie. But she pulled her thoughts back into place, realizing that Deirdre was still talking. 'Is that OK? Is that the way you do it?'

'Perfect. Thanks, Deirdre. Have you time to give me a hand for half an hour?'

'As long as you like. I told Timus if I hadn't found him when he was ready to go home for lunch he could pick me up here. You know, Tessa, after Aunt Naomi told me last night about Giles leaving you like that, I lay in bed thinking about it and the more I thought, the more I saw it might be providence. I mean, just look at me! I've *never* – even before I got thrown – had such a wonderful,

287

certain sort of feeling. It's mostly Timus, of course, but it's more, it's something I don't know how to explain. It's the family and knowing I shall be part of it – in fact, I think they see me as part of it already. That's what I want for *you* too, Tessa. And I've got a plan. Timus has a cousin – his family grow oranges mostly, lemons too, at a place down in the valley about seven miles away. He comes over here to the house sometimes and he's really quite handsome – well, they're a good-looking family. I was thinking how good it would be if you and he got together. If you were there with his family, me with Timus' here, then Aunt Naomi and Daddy. It would be lovely for Millie, too, she'd be part of a real sort of community of us instead of being just an only child with no father.'

Tessa started to laugh, but there was no humour in it. Peering at her Deirdre wasn't sure if she was laughing or crying. Perhaps she ought not to have made the suggestion so soon. She'd say no more for the moment, but really there was logic in the plan. Tessa was much too nice to be left here on her own with no one caring about her and what could possibly be more certain, more perfect, than being part of the Rodriguez clan? However, it might be wiser to change the subject.

'I bet folk get really excited when they buy these nuts. There's no difference in these and the ones we grow next door, but I bet these will cost twice as much because they're packed to look so pretty and say where they were grown.'

'It's not just because they have an address of

where they were grown,' Tessa said, 'it's because they come from the home of someone people have heard of – probably someone they feel they know because they have read his books.'

'Huh, seems a bit daft to me. Bet it was *his* idea to use his name.'

'It was a joint idea,' Tessa retorted, loyal despite his having torn her world apart.

Her grief was private. To the world she presented the face she meant even those nearest to her to see; that way she managed to get through the weeks and then the months.

'Is Daddy coming today?' In the beginning that was Millie's question most mornings. Whether or not she hoped he was, it was impossible to tell from her gruff tone. Millie would never win a medal at a charm school, but young as she was there was an honesty about her. She would never cheat, never lie or purposely be unkind; that was probably because her imagination didn't stretch far enough to let her feel fear. If she was angry she let the world know; if she was happy she danced and sang (off key and out of rhythm and yet with joy in every sound and movement).

Deirdre and Timus were married in the last week of January at the registry office in Llaibir's Town Hall just as Julian and Naomi had been the previous year, and Giles and Tessa before that. In Deirdre's case there was a difference for, after the ceremony, the two families went to the church where Father Josef, a close friend of the family for many years, blessed the union and prayed the couple would be granted a full and contented life with the gift of many children. Millie had been left at home with Maria so that morning Tessa's mind was painfully free to wander where it would: she and Giles standing at the table in the registry office – oh, but Millie had certainly been in evidence that day; the certainty that their lives would be full of joy. Watching Deirdre and Timus setting out on that same road she had no doubts about their future. To Timus, Deirdre was the beginning and end, whatever twists and turns life's path held. If only she could have seen into the future in those far away days when her face had worn a permanent scowl! Tessa made sure that her own face wore no expression that would hint at the ghosts that taunted her as she accompanied Julian and Naomi back to Finca el Almendros to collect Millie before they all went on to the Rodriguez house where the family was assembling to celebrate in true Spanish fashion with laughter, music, dancing, more laughter and warm hospitality that threatened to melt the ice around her heart.

When at last they left it was hours beyond Millie's bedtime. As long as she'd been with the other children she had danced (by her own standards) and made merry, but as soon as she was on the back seat of Julian's car, leaning against her mother in an invitation to be cuddled, her eyes closed.

'A day for thanksgiving,' Julian said as he turned the car on to the narrow road for the short drive to Finca el Almendros. 'Since Deirdre's accident a day has never passed without the fear

290

that haunted me. What was to become of the child? Oh, I know, she's no longer a child,' he added, casting a look towards the passenger seat where Naomi sat, 'and I know you would always care for her just as I would myself. But the day will come when we're no longer here.'

'They're a lovely family,' Naomi answered. 'If each of their sons gave them half a dozen grand-children I believe each one would be welcomed as yet another blessing.'

'Children? Deirdre?' That was something he had never considered.

'And why not? She is as normal as the next girl except that she can't walk. Yes, it's a joy to see the way she is accepted, no quarter given because she has a handicap. They're a staunch Catholic family and I bet you anything you like that by this time next year there will be baby number one on the scene. We'll be grandparents, Julian.'

Tessa said nothing, her mind on the joyful atmosphere they had just left and her imagination carrying her to the years ahead for Deirdre. She loved Naomi and Julian dearly; she knew they cared sincerely for her and a cloud would fall across the happiness of their day if she let them guess at her loneliness.

When they drew up at the front door of the finca Julian and Naomi accepted her suggestion that they should come in for a nightcap.

'I'll carry the little one straight up, shall I?' Julian suggested, while Naomi said she would make coffee unless they wanted something stronger. So by the time Tessa came down from undressing the still-sleeping child the coffee was made, and the brandy bottle put unceremoniously on the kitchen table.

'This is nice,' Julian said, stretching his legs in front of him as he sat on the plain wooden chair. 'I've always had a fancy for the warm, lived-in feeling of a kitchen.' Without asking, he poured Tessa's brandy while Naomi poured her coffee. How could she possibly feel so alone and void of hope when they were her family?

Millie was keen to go to school. She was never knowingly lonely, yet she had no companionship from other children and she loved listening to the tales Maria told her of her family and the games they played. Once she started school she would have fun like that and, although the thought didn't form itself into words in her mind, she would be a ringleader. So the following year, even though her fifth birthday wasn't until spring, on the first day of term after Christmas Tessa drove her into town. She was full of self-importance: on her back she wore a satchel, her pencils were sharpened and her lunch packed in a picnic box.

'Better than a picnic, Mum,' she said in her gruff young voice as, having stowed the box in the satchel with her pencil case and a new note-book, she concentrated on doing up the straps of the satchel. Neither of them had a clear picture of life in a Spanish classroom, but Tessa had never been more thankful for the hours the child had spent with Maria, for the outcome was that she spoke Spanish as naturally as English.

Arriving at the school Millie got out of the car and slammed the door shut.

'I'll come in with you and we'll find where you have to go,' Tessa told her, the remark met with a scowl.

'No, Mum. I'm big now. The others haven't got their mums with them. Bye.' With that the not-quite five-year-old marched through the school gate, stepping with a firm tread into the start of her new life.

Watching her go Tessa felt a strange sensation: guilt – not just for not taking her in but for the hundreds of times she had put the almond grove before her needs, leaving her with Maria for companionship. Her little girl . . . Giles' little girl . . . unlike either of them. Where would the years take her? Her own mind slipped back to her own childhood and to Amelia who had been all the family she'd known. Long ago and far away, a house near the cliffs in the Isle of Wight, the never-changing love of Gran. With neither mother nor father she had had all the love a child could need. Both she and Giles had failed Millie. No wonder the little girl marched with a firm tread; life had taught her to stand on her two small feet.

Feeling humiliated, Tessa faced what she couldn't avoid: she had failed as a wife and she had failed as a mother. It was a relief to turn her thought to the jobs that were waiting for her in the almond grove. She kept the same two men working on the additional land on the other side of the road, and spent most of her days in the original five acres. Nowadays not only did Finca el Almendros have a telephone in the house, but there was an extension in the shed she had had built. It was no ordinary shed; it served as a place to pack the nuts and an office, too. Reason told her she ought to use Giles' study, but she hadn't the strength of will to move his things off the desk to make room for her ledgers. Like a shrine it remained as he had used it, typewriter, dictating machine, even his note pad still on the desk, while for her own use in the shed-cum-office she had bought a portable typewriter.

When she arrived back at the house she saw Timus' van waiting. Immediately her mind jumped to Deirdre. 'No sign of the baby yet?' she called as she got out of the car.

'Can you not see me looking different? I am a father most proud. My Deirdre had the pains most terrible at one o'clock this morning. The doctor's telephone did not call; it was silent when I listened. But *Madre*, she has helped with birth times before, so she shut the door on us all. We waited. My poor Deirdre, so hard it must be when she can't move like other women. But she was brave as – as, how you say – a tiger? I stood outside the door and listened. Tessa, I know now the worst sort of helplessness. But at seven o'clock this morning she gave me a daughter.'

'And she's all right?'

'The child is beautiful and Deirdre, she is a goddess amongst women. So much against her but she has such courage.'

'Fate knew what it was doing when it brought her here.'

'You call it Fate; I call it God. And I thank him for her every hour of my life. I must go home.

Madre is now having some sleep; Katrina is there but she has much work to do. I shall not work with the trees this day, oh no. For this is the day I have looked towards. I will care for Deirdre and our daughter. I have spoken by telephone to Señor and Señora Masters but, you and me, we are friends since the day you came, it was important I tell you with my person.' It was proof of Deirdre's determination to speak Spanish right from the start that his English flowed no more naturally now than when Tessa had met him more than five years before.

It was only minutes later, just as Tessa walked through the almond grove, that she heard the shrill ring of the telephone in the hut. 'Finca el Almendros. *Hola, buenas dias.*'

'Tessa, thank God it's you. I thought you might have left, gone back to England, gone away somewhere . . . say something . . .'

She seemed incapable of speech.

Eleven

Leaning against the wooden side of the hut Tessa clutched the telephone receiver, her tight grip on it seeming to be her only hold on reality. Sometimes she had heard his voice in her dream, a dream that would merge with reality as she half woke. But this was morning this was no dream.

'Tessa . . . are you there? Say something.'

She dropped to sit in the wooden chair, the only furniture in the hut except for a bench where she packed the nuts and which doubled as a desk. 'Yes, it's me. Of course I'm here. Where else would I be?' How calm she sounded, cool and distant. He must have phoned to tell her a separation wasn't enough – he wanted a divorce. She schooled herself to be ready for the words she dreaded.

'You sound different. Tell me the truth: is there someone else in your life?'

'You mean you want grounds for a divorce? Then I'm afraid I must disappoint you.'

'Divorce? Christ, no.' It was unlike Giles to sound emotional. 'Tessa, sweet Tessa. Listen. Don't say a word, just hear me out. When I left you it was because I knew that if I told you what I feared – no, I was convinced – you would want to stand by me. I couldn't let that happen. It was as if Fate played into my hands, giving me a chance to come away.'

296

'You lied to me. You said we needed a break from each other, but you knew you wanted it to be forever.'

'You don't understand . . .' And so he told her. Starting from the meeting with Adrian Wilmott to the results of tests that had been carried out at a private clinic. 'I can't believe it, Tessa. I'm in the clear. It's like being freed from a death sentence. It's the middle of the night here and I meant to wait until morning to call you. But I couldn't. You don't know the things your mind can do to you. I had all the symptoms. I had no doubt, and not enough courage to get confirmation. Each week I became less sure of myself. I was irritable, withdrawn, watching the way I walked, listening to the way I spoke, so frightened that I ran away from what I was sure was the truth by doing the craziest thing and not caring if I lived or died.' He paused. 'Tessa, are you still there? Say something?'

'Can't,' she gulped, the one word breaking her reserved.

'You're crying. Please don't cry, Tessa. If it's too late for us, don't cry. I don't deserve—'

'It could never be too late,' her uncontrolled voice blurted out. 'Giles, all I want is for you to come home.' Silence. 'Giles?'

'Sometimes I've come close to ditching my resolution not to spoil your life caring for the crock I would become. But now I'm free. I just want to come home to you.'

'It's like a dream.' She gave up all attempt to hang on to her control as she told him, 'I love you so much, Giles. You're all there is, all there ever could be. I'm so happy.'

That's when she heard him laugh. 'What I hear doesn't sound too happy.' Her tears turned to laughter, too, perhaps with a touch of hysteria mixed in. There was so much to tell him, but neither of them could think beyond themselves and that the nightmare of the last year and a half was over.

He said he was leaving the clinic in the morning and as soon as he had tied up the odd ends of his self-imposed stay in California and arranged a flight home he would phone again and tell her when to expect him.

Almond trees had lost their appeal on that January morning. Instead of working she went back up the slope to the house and collected the car to drive to Casa Landera. She knew that Julian was on his half-yearly trip to England but she wanted to share her thankfulness with Naomi. When there was no answer to her ring on the doorbell she went round to the side of the house where, beyond the swimming pool, the land climbed steeply. Built as it was in the foothill of the mountain, the far end of the garden – for want of a better description for a plot so natural – was higher than the roof of the house, and it was there that she saw Naomi standing on the wooden bridge they had had erected to cross a stream that rushed down from the mountainside.

'A surprise visit. That's nice. Has our young lady gone to school?'

'She's fine,' Tessa said with a laugh, 'she

marched off with determination. By now I expect she's got them all sorted out. But that's not why I came.' And so she told her news.

'Poor Giles. And now that he knows he's in the clear he must wish he'd told you from the start and seen someone in London rather than running away. He must have been going through such hell and no one to share it with him.'

Tessa nodded. 'What are you doing with those twigs in your hand?'

'These?' Naomi chuckled. 'I was being childish. These are my Pooh sticks. Here, you have some. Just see the way they rush under the bridge; the stream moves so fast.'

Like children they threw their twigs on the upstream side of the bridge and then rushed to the other side to see them race with the fast flowing water. One got trapped by a piece of rock, the water battering it until it was sent on its way again.

'Look at that,' Naomi said, 'it's like life, isn't it? Everything runs smoothly, you keep rollicking on, then it's as if you'll never move again, you're stuck, numb. It must have been like that for Giles – but now, thank God, life is moving on again for both of you. Whatever happens, however low you sink, in the end the life wins, just like the force of the water in the mountain stream.'

'Is that how it is with you, Auntie?'

Naomi nodded. 'Higher upstream must be different from down here where the land is gentler. Things change for all of us, but life goes on just like the Pooh sticks. The hideously relentless misery dims.'

'And the memories?' What was there about the isolation of this place that led them to speak with such open honesty?

'Memories never fade, Tessa. In a strange way, love becomes more deeply a part of oneself. Does that sound crazy? It's just the grief that pales.'

'You and Julian always seem so happy.'

'I love Julian dearly. Yes, we are happy. Every age is different. A bit like the stream, I expect. Higher up it rushes, full of hope and energy, but when it gets down to the lower level it ripples gently along. Gosh, hark at me! Come indoors and have a coffee.'

'Lovely. Aren't you cold out here without a jacket on?'

Naomi laughed. 'I'm tough as leather. Anyway, this is Spain. You forget I was used to all weathers on a Devon farm – mud and worse.'

Arm in arm they walked back towards the house.

Julian was due to fly out of Heathrow Airport on the Thursday of that same week so when Giles phoned saying that he was booking a flight to arrive at Heathrow early Thursday morning Tessa half expected they would travel home together. On Wednesday night sleep was impossible. Julian had left his car at the airport, and over and over in her imagination she saw the scene when he would drive up the slope to the finca bringing Giles home. She would rush out to open the door so that when he stepped out she would be there, close to him, held tightly while for both of them the time between would melt away.

Taking Millie to school she didn't attempt to hide her excitement, hoping that some of it would rub off on the little girl. But from her advanced age of almost five, the time when she had been three was distant and only half remembered. Perhaps when he arrived memories would stir, but on that journey to school Millie's thoughts were marching ahead of her and she was anxious to have time in the playground so that she could play with her new friends before lessons started.

The morning went by with neither a phone call from Heathrow telling her what time he expected to land so that she could be at the airport, nor any sign of Julian's car. The day passed, she fetched Millie from school then hurried to take up position by the window again, her ears attuned for the sound of the phone. It had been dark for ages and Millie was eating her supper ready for bed when Tessa saw the beam of headlights from a car approaching the house. In seconds she was outside ready for the moment he stepped out. Yes, it was Julian's car – but when she threw open the door expecting to live those seconds she dreamed of, it was Naomi who got out.

'You've come to welcome Giles! But he hasn't come yet – no message – nothing.'

'We came as soon as we realized.' Realized? Realized what? 'It wasn't until Julian opened his briefcase that he remembered he had bought a copy of the early edition of the evening paper.'

'Evening paper?' Tessa felt the first cold hand of fear. But that was ridiculous; what could the evening paper have to do with Giles' reason for being late?

'You haven't been listening to the wireless,' Julian said while fear tightened its grip on her. 'A plane crash-landed. The morning flight from Heathrow was coming in to land and the wheels wouldn't go down, so the pilot alerted the services he was going to crash-land. Poor chap was killed—'

'Perhaps that's made other planes late, perhaps Giles has been diverted,' she heard herself say. But knew there was neither logic nor hope in what she said.

'The Stop Press of the early edition says the plane burst into flames – only two people were pulled free. One isn't named, the other is the international author Giles Lampton. They were both taken to the local hospital, which is only a couple of miles from the airport. My dear, I am so sorry. But thank God they pulled him free before the machine burst into flames. Get your coat; I'll drive you while Naomi sees to Millie.'

'I know the way. I'll take myself.' How could she speak so calmly when she felt as though she were made of cotton wool and her mouth full of sawdust? 'I've seen the hospital lots of times; I know the way, Julian.' She mustn't panic, she must sound calm. 'He was bound to have been taken in the ambulance; they'd have to check him over. But you said he was pulled free. If he rings, tell him I'm coming to collect him. I'll get my coat.' She forgot to thank Naomi for looking after Millie, just as she even forgot to say good-night to the child.

Although she knew the road well, that night the journey seemed interminably long. But finally she arrived and was directed to the second floor. There she found a nurse and was taken straight to the doctor in charge. Listening to what he told her, she seemed to feel all life and hope drain from her. No, Giles hadn't been burnt, but his injuries were extensive. That much she could understand. But although she could converse in Spanish naturally and easily in her everyday life, she had never encountered the words he used when he described Giles' injuries. The elderly doctor was a kindly man; he hated to see that look of hope die in this pretty young girl's eyes. For even though she couldn't understand the detail, she knew *lesiones internas* could mean only one thing: Giles was injured internally. The gravity of the doctor's voice and the way he shook his head told her what she was frightened to consider.

'May I see him? He'll want me with him.'

'He may not be aware enough to recognize you. He has been in the operating theatre and, although he has come round from the anaesthetic, he is barely awake.'

'Please.' She could trust her voice to say no more.

The doctor took her along the corridor to a room that was no more than a cubicle where Giles was propped on pillows, his eyes half closed. His arm was plastered, his shoulder

303

strapped and his chest bare except for bandages. A cradle held the bed covers away from his body.

The doctor looked at him sorrowfully. Such a lovely young wife to leave behind. There were times when he would have preferred any calling but his own. Turning, he left them, closing the door behind him.

'Giles, darling Giles. Can you hear me?' She leant forward and laid her mouth gently on his. Still he gazed unseeingly into space. 'We'll soon be home again, Finca el Almendros . . . home. Hold my hand, oh, but you feel so cold. Darling Giles, please hear me, please God make him hear me. Make him know I'm here.' Her fingers caressed his, trying to warm him as again she bent forward so that her face was in front of his. His eyes were open, so surely he could see her.

Where his mind was she couldn't know, whether he recognized that she was there or whether he felt he was dreaming.

'Tes . . .' Hardly even a whisper but she sent up a prayer of thankfulness. 'Tessa, my sweet Tessa . . . home . . . loved you . . . always . . .'

Dreaming or aware, either way a sentence was beyond him. But what he whispered wiped away the misery of their time apart.

'Yes darling, as soon as you are well enough we'll go home. We have the rest of our lives. Giles, Giles, hear me, Giles, stay with me, you're all there is . . . love you so much . . .' Talking through the tears she couldn't hold back she laid her face on the pillow close against his.

'Tess . . .' Then, his voice suddenly stronger, he said her name again and, raising her head so that she could see his face, she realized that he was smiling. 'Te . . .' But his strength ebbed as suddenly as it had come. Something was different. She was gripped by fear. Touching his mouth with hers there was no response; and worse, she could feel no breath. Help, she must get help. Frantically she opened the door and looked along the corridor just at the same moment as a nurse appeared, hurrying towards them.

Tessa tried to believe it couldn't be happening; he must have lost his slim hold on consciousness. But in her heart she knew. She watched the nurse feel for his pulse; she saw the expression on her face and even felt sympathy for her that she had to be the one to take away the last strand of hope. Listening to the stark sentence, Tessa nodded.

'Please,' she begged, 'let me just be with him – just one minute more.' Consciously she bit hard on the corners of her mouth and held her chin high. She seemed to be standing on the edge of a black abyss. If she lost control even for a minute she was frightened she would tip over the edge and be lost. She must be strong. Yet did it matter? What did anything matter?

That was the moment when she remembered the drive home from Deremouth Hospital after Richard's death. Hang on to that, remember Naomi's impenetrable calm.

The nurse went out of the room, pulling the door up behind her. Moving to the bed, Tessa sat on the edge and, just as she had before, rested her head on the pillow rubbing her face against his. If only just once more he could say those words that had taken away all the pain of their separation, 'loved you . . . always . . . sweet Tessa'. And that was all she was to have of him; for the rest of her days that had to be enough to give her courage to face a life without him. But he hadn't gone away because he was tired of her; he had gone because he cared about her future more than he cared about himself.

The nurse was back in the room and a second later the kindly elderly doctor and another younger man followed her. 'If you go along to the waiting room, I'll come and speak to you when the doctors have done,' the nurse said quietly.

'Go?' Go and leave him. She heard the door close behind her and walked down the long corridor to a small waiting room. It wasn't visiting time, so she was thankful no one would be there. But she was wrong. There was one man and he stood up as she appeared in the doorway.

'Julian?' The sight of him confused her. She had expected to face whatever had to be faced alone. Instead, as her face crumpled she felt herself taken into his strong embrace. 'He was coming home. Nothing now.' Her courage had deserted her. With Julian there she felt weak and helpless.

'I know, my dear.'

'Told you I was all right, I knew the way. You shouldn't have bothered,' she gulped.

'I'm a stubborn old fool, I dare say, but I wanted to find out for myself how things were. When they told me, I waited. We'll leave your car here tonight; I shall drive you home.'

She didn't argue, and later she didn't remember much of the rest of the evening. There were things to see to at the hospital, but Julian took control. She was like a wind-up toy with a broken spring.

Epilogue

Millie's sixth birthday was on a Saturday and she was having a party. Maria was in her element. The birthday cake was thick with chocolate and bedecked with six candles, there were bunches of balloons hanging from the ceiling and, for the occasion, her brother-in-law had been engaged to come with his concertina to make music so that the children could play the games Tessa had taught her: Musical Chairs, Pass the Parcel, Oranges and Lemons, games played at children's parties in every town and village of England. It was a celebration of the fact that although Millie appeared as Spanish as anyone in her class at school, she had roots in the country of her parents.

While the games were going on in the house, overseen by Maria who was as noisy and excited as any of the children, the grown ups were outside in the sunshine. It was early March but the sun was warm and the sky cloudless.

'The loveliest time of year here,' Naomi said, passing her cup for a refill. 'Blue sky above and a sea of blossom wherever you look. Garden flowers are beautiful, but there is something wonderful about blossom, almonds, olives, oranges, lemons or, back at home, apples, plums,

308

all the things we grew up with. The trees are so full of promise.'

'This year there have been no big winds to blow the flowers from the trees,' Timus said. 'There will be many nuts. Now we are here together, my Deirdre and I have some news for you. You tell it, Deirdre.'

'I bet you've all guessed it after an introduction like that. I'm preggie. You're going to have another grandchild by the beginning of October, Dad.'

'Wonderful.' Julian gazed at her with pride. 'Does that mean you will be looking for a house by yourselves?' That was his one concern, for how would she manage?

'Heavens, no,' Deirdre said, laughing at the thought. 'At home they're thrilled to bits. You've no idea how great it is; extra babies just make it even better somehow.'

No one mentioned her disability. Even though it was at the front of Julian and Naomi's minds, clearly it didn't cast a shadow for either Timus or his happy wife, who was leaning from her chair to pass a rubber dog back into the playpen where fourteen-month-old Nina was standing by the rail ready to throw it out again.

Tessa and Naomi let their glances meet briefly. Thankfulness for the way Deirdre's life had changed was part of it. Certainly at that moment their thoughts were moving on the same line as they remembered those few intimate minutes by the mountain stream. How far Deirdre had come since the days of her resentment and angry misery; the Pooh stick of her life had broken free

309

and gone tumbling on downstream. Looking at Tessa, Naomi wondered whether hers had been washed on its way. Since Giles died they had never talked as they had on the morning by the stream. Tessa worked hard. She gave every impression of finding contentment and satisfaction in her work with the almond trees; certainly she seemed to have an inner happiness which had been missing while Giles was in America. But she was young; she had years of living ahead of her. Would she find love again? Not the same love as the first time . . . and here Naomi's own thoughts strayed into the past and the undying love she and Richard shared.

Tessa's memory, too, was on that morning when they had thrown their twigs from the bridge and watched them flow downstream. That had been the morning she and Giles had talked on the telephone, the morning when her world had come alive again. So where was her twig of life now? Work had had to be her salvation. She had found a sense of peace that stemmed from more than pleasure in her growing success. He had never stopped loving her . . . he had been coming home to her. That year and a half when they had been separated had been joyless and hopeless. Now, even though she would never see him again, that love was always with her; whatever life threw at her, nothing could change that. What was it Naomi had said about memories never fading, and love becoming more deeply part of you? She'd remembered that morning so often over the last year; it had helped her through the anguish of grief and set her on the path to living the years ahead. There was nothing macabre in her keeping his study just as he left it. For her it wasn't a shrine; it was a place to escape to when she was alone downstairs and Millie was asleep. Sitting at the typewriter she could almost feel his hands on her shoulders. When he was in America, in her misery she used to sit there, imagining him standing behind her in just the same way. Then there had been no comfort in the image she created. But now she knew the truth, nothing could take from her the love he had for her; it was like a warm blanket protecting her from the cold winds of life. Rejoice! She smiled at the thought. Rejoice sounded like merrymaking – like the noise of the children singing with Maria's brother-in-law and his concertina. But for her it encompassed something far deeper: it encompassed the joy that he had given back to her when he told her the truth about his going away; it encompassed memories of everything they had shared.